Here's the Thing

Stories

JOHN GORDON SMITH

Here's the Thing
Copyright © 2021 by John Gordon Smith

All rights reserved. No part of this publication may be reproduced, distributed, or transmitted in any form or by any means, including photocopying, recording, or other electronic or mechanical methods, without the prior written permission of the author, except in the case of brief quotations embodied in critical reviews and certain other non-commercial uses permitted by copyright law.

Tellwell Talent
www.tellwell.ca

ISBN
978-0-2288-5669-6 (Hardcover)
978-0-2288-5668-9 (Paperback)
978-0-2288-5670-2 (eBook)

Table of Contents

A Canadian Welcome 1
Buddies 5
Mowing Mondays 15
The Piano Lesson 34
Bennytoo 46
Casual Day 74
My Kid Sister 93
On Your Own 101
Thanks for Coming 115
The Other Side of the Fence 128
The River Cottage 141
Ripple Effect 170
A Guy With A Dog 188
Performance Evaluation 208
Blind Man's Bluff? 220
The Scribe 231
Hummingbird 256

A Canadian Welcome

Steve sounded relieved. "I just heard. They will be arriving at five."

I felt a rush of excitement. It was finally happening. "OK, I'll be there. D'you want me to phone any of the others?"

"No, thanks; Ellie and I have contacted all of them."

Steve and Ellie were the leaders of our church group sponsoring a refugee family from Syria. After months of preparation, the last couple of days had been hectic and confusing. The family had, as far as we knew, got as far as Toronto, but then there had been an unexplained delay, and they had been put into a motel overnight.

For hours Steve hadn't been able to find out when they were to arrive at our town's airport. We had visions of our refugee family arriving, and none of us there to greet them. We had been told it was important to be there for them. They would be tired and nervous, meeting their hosts for the first time. We were the people who would be their supporters, guardians and, hopefully, become their friends, for their first year in Canada.

Big Brenda, who was in charge of Welcoming, had us all organized, with plastic Canadian flags and a sign that said "Welcome to Canada" in Arabic – at least, that was what we hoped it said. So she was particularly and loudly fussed about making sure we were all there.

I arrived at the airport a bit late, and hurried to Arrivals, feeling flustered. It was crowded, noisy and hot; not the best circumstances to welcome our family. Having a large car, I was designated to drive them and our interpreter to the little house one of our parishioners had found for them. A couple of the women would be there to show them everything, but the rest of the team was to be here at the airport.

At first glance, the Arrivals area seemed to be teeming with people I didn't recognize. Finally I spotted our group, huddled around Big Brenda, and wedged near the end of the roped off pathway through the crowd from the sliding doors for deplaning passengers. I began to walk over to join them when I saw a couple nearer the doors leave, so I slipped into the vacant space.

I had seen the family during our Skype talks with them, aided by our interpreter, but I really didn't have much of an idea what they really looked like. All I knew was their names, and that they were a family of four, the children four and two years old. It came to me that, because they were always sitting when we Skyped, I had no idea how tall the parents were, let alone how they would be dressed, and what luggage they had. I knew they would be anxious, and I knew I was.

I was standing at the barrier when I heard some shuffling behind me. I turned to see a tall woman standing there holding the handles of a wheelchair in which sat a shrivelled old man with wispy silver hair and wrapped in a blanket.

"C'mon, squeeze in here." I gestured next to me.

"Thanks," she said with a quick smile.

I moved aside, and the woman, puffing a bit, pushed the wheelchair to the barrier, right under the 'Arrivals' sign. "My son's coming in from university." Her voice was tinged with pride. "And his grandpa wanted to be here." The old man clawed with a wizened hand at the blanket. His eyes darted up at me, then away.

I looked over to the church group. Big Brenda saw me and did a wild beckoning wave, gesticulating for me to come over there to join them. I shook my head and pointed downwards to indicate I was staying where I was. Big Brenda turned away. She didn't take kindly to not having her way.

There was a sudden silence as the doors slid open. Two roll-aboard-toting businessmen came through, texting, and the doors began to close behind them. Then the doors stopped and shuddered back to fully open, and a motley collection of passengers surged through, hurrying by, some looking at the crowd, and then finding and waving at their loved ones.

The doors slid silently shut. I could feel my stomach tightening.

A moment later, they parted again, revealing a biblical tableau.

Framed in the doorway was a gaunt eyed man, the father, carrying his sleeping two-year old son, and pulling an overflowing two wheel fold-up shopping cart. Behind him the mother in shawled exhaustion led her four-year old daughter by the hand, the child pulling, and anxiously looking back at something I could see on the floor in the hallway through the open doors.

"Goddam terrorists!" Startled, I looked down at the old man's virulent face staring at them.

"But they're refugees!" I heard my voice sounding shocked and petulant.

"I fought to save this country from enemy aliens," he quavered, raising his head and glaring at me. "And now we *invite* them to come." It was, it seemed, his mantra.

"Now Dad, don't get het up." The woman patted his shoulder, and glanced apologetically at me.

I looked up to see the family moving forward uncertainly. The doors slid together behind them. The child pulled at her mother, pointing to the doors, and began to wail pitifully.

At that moment Steve and Ellie rounded the end of the barrier and hurried towards them, together with Big Brenda, who was booming "We're from the *Church*," and brandishing her flag. The little boy buried his head deeper into his father's neck, and the girl, weeping, stretched her empty hand toward the closed doors.

3

Suddenly they slid open again and a sloppily dressed teenager came through, dragging a back pack in one hand with something else in the other – I couldn't make out what it was.

"There he is," said the woman beside me, waving.

The youth stopped by the crying girl and, bending down, held out a little rag doll, worn and frayed. The child shrank against her mother. I watched as, in an indelible moment of infinite grace, the young man went down on one knee and proffered the doll. Hesitantly, she reached out and, taking it, clasped it to her, and shyly bestowed on him a grateful smile.

The boy's mother called his name, and he looked up and across. He waved, and, standing, glanced down, it seemed to first ensure that all was well, then, with the guileless beauty of youth, came to the barrier.

"Hi, Mum. Hey, Gramps."

I looked down at the old man's joy-lit face, and found myself putting a hand on his shoulder in benediction, or was it absolution.

Over his head I saw the family, the little girl now enfolded by her mother, taking their first steps together along their new life's pathway.

Then I walked with eyes opened, through the thinning crowd to my group to join them in welcoming the family to our complicated country of Canada.

BUDDIES

Denver guided Belinda onto the trail through the trees into the park. She snuffled around, found a place to pee, did so gratefully, and then sat down.

"That's it?" Denver muttered, looking down at his twelve year old Bernese Mountain Dog, her once glorious coat now looking a little mangy with age. Belinda sighed, and carefully flattened herself in the middle of the trail, signaling that she wasn't going anywhere.

"But this is your favourite walk," Denver said, sounding simultaneously pleading and frustrated. Belinda's response was to remain immobile, save for a shift of her rheumy eyes to look in the direction of his voice.

"Well, you may be going blind, but you can still hear," Denver chuckled.

Squatting beside her, eighty-four year old Denver, still, he liked to think, as strong as a mule, gathered his frail companion in his arms, and, staggering a little as he straightened, carried the old lady back to the car, laid her in her bed on the seat beside him, and drove the five minutes to home.

It was time to call the vet.

Denver was seventy-two when one lady died and another came into his life. For forty years, his wife Dulcie had been his for-ever love. Before meeting each other, they had both blundered through the ecstasies and disillusionments of too-soon first marriages. The resulting children were long ago and far away, leaving them to celebrate the exclusive joy of each other, untrammeled by tedious obligations and reminders of disappointments.

Dulcie had been five years older than Denver. They had taken comfort from the statistics about men's and women's life expectancies, believing that they would grow old together, and that neither would ever leave the other alone.

The C word had, suddenly, it seemed (although it actually had taken six months), changed all that.

The memorial service had been bittersweet. Dulcie's church family, and a long-gone daughter who looked both out-of-place and panicked throughout, had seen to it that she was sent on her way in glory. Denver hadn't been part of Dulcie's church-going – it was pretty well the only thing they didn't do together, other than, of course, Denver's annual fall hunting trip with his next-door buddy Cam. On one of those trips, Denver had vouchsafed to Cam that he figured that the only person in competition with him for Dulcie's love and affection was God, "and I think I have the inside track on Him, so I don't have to check out what they're up to at church." Cam had laughed at that, and told him he was a very lucky man.

Cam was a bachelor – not what you would call a confirmed one, but more of a wistful one. Soon after his retirement from his job as foreman at the warehouse complex down the highway, Cam, encouraged by his workmates at his retirement party, had tried out on-line dating. He had soon abandoned that in favour of television shows and the crossword puzzles in the daily paper. "At least they don't jack you around," he told Denver.

For a couple of weeks after the funeral, Cam watched Denver fold into himself, and decided something had better be done about it. There was no point waiting for the church people to deal with it.

It so happened that Belinda was one of a litter of five that was born on Denver's birthday, April 1. "One fool for another" is what Cam thought. Dulcie had died near the end of April, and the church had been bedecked in May blossoms for the service. Towards the end of May, Cam went to the Mainland to take delivery of what he hoped would be the solution to Denver's doldrums. And he was right. That evening he delivered the squirming nine-week old, together with some puppy food, a sleeping basket (which was abandoned in exchange for Denver's bed as soon as Belinda worked out how to jump), and puppy-pee carpet spray. Belinda took to big Denver in about the time it takes a puppy to eat a treat. The establishment of Denver's devotion for Belinda was only a nano-second behind.

They were inseparable for twelve years. Denver, who had retired from his furniture transportation and delivery business to look after Dulcie in her last months, had landed a part-time job with a food delivery outfit that catered to seniors. After a bit of haggling about whether he could have a dog beside him in the truck when there was food in the sealed compartment in the back, Belinda, to the delight of pretty well all Denver's customers, became an active participant and official greeter-at-the-door.

And then there was Belinda's love affair with Cam, who lived the other side of the wall, in the next-door duplex. Although she wasn't allowed on the guys' annual hunting trip (though she thought she should be), she thought the world of Cam, and perhaps tried to compensate for the lack of a woman in his life. It seems that Belinda somehow figured out that television shows and crossword puzzles were not sufficient daily fare for the brain. Each morning, after her breakfast, Belinda would squirm through the hole in the hedge between the two back yards and scratch insistently on Cam's back door until Cam let her in for a snuggle and a couple of treats. After a while, Belinda would ask to be let out, and she would trot off home, ready to assume her responsibilities in Denver's meal delivery business.

Of course, the bottom of Cam's back door got all scraped, but when Denver apologized and offered to pay for a repaint, Cam declined, saying that the marks were Belinda's signature, and that if they were removed, Belinda might not know how to find him.

When Belinda was ten, Cam, in his seventies, began to have serious difficulties with diabetes. So, Denver and Belinda got Cam involved in their daily walk, figuring that it would help the circulation. There were also weekly visits to the off-leash dog park, where Denver and Cam would sit on a bench while Belinda went socializing. Notwithstanding these efforts, the prospect of amputation began to be discussed, and the annual hunting trip got cancelled, which may have pleased Belinda, but was hardly a good omen.

A year later, in what was described by his doctor as "more as a precautionary measure than anything," two of the toes on Cam's left foot were removed. After a while, Cam got pretty agile with a sturdy walking stick, saying, "at least it's my left foot, so I can still drive." Belinda learned to stay out of his way when he lurched around, but, after a couple of fruitless attempts, joining in the daily walks was out for Cam.

Next, it became Belinda's turn to slow down – after all she was well into old age for a Berner. The daily walks got shorter and slower, meals were greeted with less enthusiasm, and the vet visits became more frequent. Then the day came when she sort of gave up.

By dog years, being seven years for each human year, Belinda, at twelve, was exactly the same age as eighty-four year-old Denver. For the second time in his life, his assumption that his lady would never leave him alone was shattered. Cam drove them to the animal hospital, and sat in the parking lot in his truck. Denver asked him if he'd like to come in, but he said no. With Denver holding her in his arms, Belinda was gently put to sleep by the vet. It was the day after she had lain down on the trail into the park.

It was almost as if Cam's deterioration was planned to prevent Denver from pining too much over his loss of Belinda. He took to watching out for Cam. The disease attacking Cam's body was proving to be relentless, even with all the dietary changes he scrupulously followed. Already, walking any distance, and getting up and down stairs, was a challenge. "It sure puts a spanner in the works," Cam told Denver.

Only a month after Belinda's passing, the decision was made that Cam's left foot had to be amputated. This involved planning for some radical changes to his lifestyle. Denver went with Cam to two consultations, first with the surgeon about how the operation would go, and then with a prosthetist, where they talked prosthesis options, and how long it would take after the amputation before Cam would be ambulatory. Arrangements were made to rent a wheelchair for the period of a temporary prosthesis, *and* the time it would take for the permanent prosthesis to be fitted, *and* for Cam to get used to it. Ultimately, that would be followed by a four wheel walker with a seat. All that took some negotiating with Cam, who wasn't used to all this fussing over him.

Eventually, Denver got Cam to face the issue of where he would live after the amputation. Cam was all for staying where he was. But in a discussion with the doctors, it became obvious that Cam wouldn't be able to manage the stairs in his house anymore, and even the steps up to the front door would be a challenge. "And you don't have a family member to be your caregiver," the doctor pointed out. There had been a short discussion about installing a ramp, and a somewhat scornful chat about those television ads promoting stairlifts.

Finally, common sense prevailed, and Denver and Cam visited a number of care homes. The eventual choice was HarbourView, somewhat ostentatiously called "An Assisted Living Residence" in the big town up the highway. Cam said the name was wildly optimistic – "you need powerful binoculars to see the harbour, such as it is." The decision was partly made because a room was immediately available, rather than going on a waiting list.

While on the subject of waiting lists, Cam discovered that there was considerable demand for his type of home, being an affordable duplex near to a bus route and a shopping centre. So the realtor made her commission quickly and easily. Cam's furnishings were pretty frugal, some of which he was able to take with him to HarbourView. The new owners wanted the dining table and chairs, and the washer and dryer went with the deal. The rest was disposed of, first by a garage sale, which was actually a front yard sale, at which Denver also got rid of some unopened dog food and a 'seldom used' dog bed. The rest of Cam's stuff was taken away by a junk dealer for a ridiculously small amount, paid in cash.

So everything went pretty smoothly, as did the amputation, followed by the fitting of the prothsesis. During his time in the hospital's palliative care unit, Cam first got the hang of the wheelchair, and then, as the move to HarbourView approached, the four-wheeled walker arrived, which, after practice, Cam vanquished.

At HarbourView, Cam's life style changed. He had always said that "aloneness doesn't necessarily mean loneliness", but now he was experiencing new levels of both. The other residents were either older or sicker or both, and "a bit cliquey," Cam told Denver. And, if the truth be told, Cam was missing Belinda as much as Denver was. Denver did consider getting another dog – "Maybe a smaller one," his doctor suggested, but Denver said, "They're yappy."

Then the new owners of Cam's duplex next door added a wooden fence on their side of the hedge, and refinished the scuffed and pockmarked back door, so that somehow put an end to any thought of another dog.

In the first few weeks of Cam's residency in the HarbourView, Denver would call by to say hello quite often after his food delivery run. Cam was in a ground floor room, so Denver could either come in to sit with Cam in the lounge, or they could just chat through the window. Both of them felt vaguely dissatisfied with the way things were going. Often, when Denver came to see him, Cam would, almost reluctantly it seemed, turn off the TV or put away the crossword, to chat. Denver noticed that the puzzles were not the easy crosswords, but the cryptic crosswords.

Denver always checked in with the front desk at HarbourView when he visited Cam, and got to know a couple of the staff, especially Marley, an efficient looking woman with, Denver figured, a heart of gold. One day he said to Marley, "How's Cam doing?"

"Well, he's taking his time to fit in." She looked at him, and seemed to decide to confide a bit. "It's funny how bachelors who come here either have had no life structure at all, or they have self-conformed to rigid schedules. Whichever they are, they find it frustrating to adapt to our routines, which actually are quite flexible."

"And which is Cam?"

Marley laughed. "A bit of each, actually. He's pretty cavalier about meal times, but he's almost obsessive about watching a couple of TV shows, and, of course, setting aside one hour after lunch to do the daily crossword puzzles. One day the paper didn't arrive, and I thought I might have to give him something to calm him down."

Denver thought back to his tough change of lifestyle when Cam had surprised him with Belinda, and figured that, in the end, one good turn deserved another. But, in HarbourView, a dog wasn't the answer, nor even, God forbid, a cat.

It was the middle of the night that the solution came to him. He had been thinking of Dulcie and then he remembered the winter evenings when there wasn't anything good on the TV, and the game they used to play.

The next day, after his food run, Denver drove to the big town up the highway and went to Chapters. He bought the deluxe version of Scrabble, and the 'official' Scrabble dictionary.

Sitting with Cam the following afternoon, Denver said, "I've brought you a present."

"I can see that," grunted Cam, gesturing at the wrapped package.

"I've been watching you do those cryptic crosswords, and figured you like playing word games, so – " He handed over the package.

With a bit of a frown, Cam unwrapped it. "Scrabble! I've heard of it, but I guess there's never been anyone around to play it with – do *guys* play this? I mean, isn't it sort of like Bridge? And don't you need four players?" He looked at Denver doubtfully.

"You bet guys play Scrabble, and although it can be a game for four, it can be played by just two. Why don't you look at it, and the next time I'm here, we'll try it."

Denver felt nervous as he left. Perhaps this wasn't going to work.

After a couple of days, his curiosity drove him to pay Cam a visit.

"I've reserved us a little table in the corner of the lounge. I can wheel my four-wheeler to the table and sit there to play. I told Marley what you brought, and she said I should try it."

So, they played a game of Scrabble. It was slow going, and there were some checks with the rules and a couple of references to the Scrabble dictionary – "How do you spell 'aurora' anyway?" And Cam won, but only because Denver was left with the 'Q' with no 'U' to put with it. A couple of the other residents watched, which Cam quite enjoyed, especially when he put down 'AFFAIR' and one of the old ladies giggled.

Denver and Cam got into the habit of playing one game of Scrabble on Saturday, another one on Sunday, and often a third game during the week. They played a couple of threesomes with a lady, but she moaned and groaned about how one or the other of them had ruined her chance to play "a really good word". They found they were closely matched, and that, as they got more skilled, the scores moved closer to the 250 - 300 range, and sometimes even exceeded 300. They became artful about using the multiple word squares, and blocking the other's opportunities, and making the most of the use of the higher scoring letters.

After a few weeks, they worked out that each of them had won nine games. Then they began to keep track. After a while, Cam was in the lead by five games, but then Denver had a winning streak, so that, after a couple of months, they were pretty well neck and neck, with Cam at eighteen, and Denver at nineteen. So they agreed to play to fifty games, with the loser having the honour of buying the winner a bottle of scotch. The word got around, and a few of the residents started betting on the outcome. Marley kept an eye on all this, but decided that, overall, it was good for morale.

It was a Sunday afternoon when the fiftieth game was to be played. Denver had won twenty-four games, as had Cam, and there had, incredibly, been one tie. The guys placing bets were getting swarmed by little old ladies of both sexes eager to get in the game. The table was moved to the middle of the lounge, and chairs for onlookers were set up. Marley was designated as the score keeper.

Denver and Cam shook hands and sat down, Denver on a chair, and Cam on his walker. Marley made a little speech to the spectators about not interrupting, and not whispering clues. Then they started to play.

After forty-five minutes, all the tiles had been drawn, and the board looked like a maze. Denver played his last tile, and his score was 254 to Cam's 248. Cam looked crestfallen. He had two tiles left, and could see no opening. He looked at Denver.

"I think you've got me, Denver." He stared at the board again and said, "Here's the thing; I've got a Y and a D, and I've looked everywhere." He made to turn his tiles in when Denver muttered, "Look again."

Cam surveyed the board, and then he saw it. Tucked away in the far corner, away from where all the final action had been, there was the little word, 'BUD', with two spaces available after it. Cam leaned over and added his letters to make the word 'BUDDY'. Marley said, "That's 12 points, for a total of 260. I declare Cam the winner."

The room exploded with clapping and cheering, and Cam and Denver hugged each other. Denver walked over to the corner where his bag was, and presented Cam with a bottle of Glenlivet to cheers and whoops.

Later, in Cam's room, each enjoying a small glass of the Glenlivet, Cam said to Denver, "I wouldn't have seen it if you hadn't got me to look again."

Denver raised his glass and said, "Well, isn't that what buddies are for?"

Mowing Mondays

Every Monday during the summer months, Gordon Stillwater mowed the front lawn of the Stillwater family home. It wasn't a ritual, like the family Sunday ritual; it was just something he did. He mowed the lawn on Mondays because the sprinklers went on on Tuesday and Saturday mornings, so by Monday the water had soaked in. He used an old hand mower – the only mower they had. He didn't think he'd be any good at managing a gas-powered mower, or an electric one. If he knew it was going to be a hot day, he would get up early to do it. Otherwise he would aim at getting it done before the morning shade from the trees along the driveway moved away. And if the weather was bad he would leave it until later in the week.

    His Sundays were much more like part of a ritual. He would drive his mother, Prudence Stillwater, to church at 9:45 for the 10 am morning service, taking her to the entrance where there was a ramp for wheelchairs – a ramp she and a couple of other parishioners had been instrumental in getting installed. As he was helping her out of the car and into her wheelchair she would say, "I do wish you would come to church with me, Gordon." And he would say, "Not today, Mother; perhaps another time." Then he would wave over at Bruce, who would be delivering his wife Emily and her mother to the church. Emily's mother, being Prudence's younger sister, was Gordon's Aunt Florence. "See you at coffee," Gordon would call, and Bruce would wave back. Then Gordon would walk over to Clive's Café. For some reason Gordon didn't understand, Bruce would go into the church with Emily and Aunt Florence to get them seated, and then would walk over to Clive's Café a few minutes later. They would meet up with the rest of the gang – a total of seven of them if everyone turned up. They called themselves 'the Agnostics'. They would talk about anything and everything until Gordon or Bruce got the call around 11:30 to "come and pick us up."

Sunday dinner would be promptly at 6:30. It alternated between the family home, when Aunt Florence would come with fruit pie, and with her daughter and son-in-law, Emily and Bruce; and every other Sunday Gordon and his mother would go to Bruce and Emily's home, with apple crumble. It all went like clockwork, and was, Gordon felt, quite ritualistic.

One mid-summer Monday, Prudence Stillwater, still a force to be reckoned with in her eighty-fifth year, sat on the front balcony of the Stillwater family home. Erect in her wheelchair, smoke drifted up from the cigarette jammed between the middle and index fingers of her nicotine stained left hand. She watched with contempt tinged with a sort of grim satisfaction as Gordon made a mess of mowing the oval-shaped lawn. Gordon – Gordie or Gord to everyone but his mother, who had never called him anything other than Gordon – wore a floppy hat to protect his head and the back of his neck. A tall man, now slightly stooped, he stood bare-legged in his gardening shorts, hands on hips, looked at the wavering lines of the cut grass, and shook his head. Somehow he never could get the mower to go straight all the way, and the swaths would waver in width.

"Time for lunch, Gordon," his mother called out in her gravelly voice, stubbing her cigarette out in the ashtray welded onto the left arm of the wheelchair. Then she wheeled around to go in.

"I'll just put the mower away." Gord removed his glasses and wiped ineffectually at them. He pulled his hat off and swept at the sweat on his brow, aware of his receding hair line. Pushing the mower, he disappeared around the side of the house.

The front lawn was an oval of grass stretching across the width of the house to the tree-lined driveway. It was bounded by a bed of rhododendrons on the far side from the house. At one end there was a small ornamental pool with, on a rock in the middle, a statuette of a seated boy reading a book. There was a seating area with a bench and a little table at the other. The lawn was, as people who came to visit said, the feature of the front garden. Prudence expected the mown green-on-green swaths to stretch diagonally, from left to right, and then, the next week, from right to left, across the virid sward, straight and uniform. It irritated her that Gordon never got them either straight or uniform.

Gordon, sixty and never married, and Prudence's eldest son of three, was once again living in the family home, though not in one of the upstairs bedrooms. Stairs being an issue for her, Prudence's bedroom, ensuite bathroom and sitting room were at the back downstairs, an area converted from where a maid's quarters had been back in the day. The whole upstairs of the house was now unused, except for storage. Gordon was living in the self-contained suite in the wing off on the side, attached to the main structure, called the 'Garden Cottage'. It had originally been built for one of his younger brothers, Denis, to accommodate his practice studio and his piano – repetitive scales and arpeggios resounding through the house had aggravated their mother.

"We're a multigenerational household," he joked with his fellow Agnostics over their Sunday morning coffee at Clive's Café. Truth be told, it was just him and his mother, and he was basically her primary caregiver, though there was also Daisy from next door who came in regularly to tidy up his mother's suite and do a bit of cooking. Prudence was still mobile enough to get dressed and look after herself in the bathroom, especially after she had had a walk-in-shower and a shower bench installed, along with handrails. She would brook few assaults on her independence.

Gordon's relationship with the family home was complicated. Although he was the oldest of the three Stillwater sons, there never had been anything done there where he had led the way. He was by nature a follower. There were enough leaders in the family – in fact the rest of them had constantly vied for the position, or a share of it. His father, now long dead from a heart attack self-induced by heavy drinking and smoking had, in his day, been the commander-in-chief, a mantle assumed upon his death by his widow as of right, but with defined exceptions. Other than being exiled to the Garden Cottage, which he didn't mind, Denis had been given unbridled leeway in matters cultural because of his much-vaunted 'artistic temperament'. Philip, the middle son, high school valedictorian and with a degree in Public Administration, had been the apple of his father's eye. When Philip was still a teenager, his father had seen to it that his politics were hewn from the same rock.

Both Philip and Denis had moved from home as soon, and as far away, as possible. Philip went to Ottawa and deftly insinuated himself over time into a permanent position in the upper echelons of the Civil Service, regardless of which party was in power. He now lives in Alta Vista with a wife, the required two-children-and-a-dog, and a mortgage. He sends Christmas letters with adorable family pictures.

And Denis ended up in the music crowd in London "by way of Juilliard" he would like to say, though research would reveal that as an exaggeration – he never was actually a student there, though he had good friends of both sexes who were, so he was often to be seen there. Now he lives in Camden, has had a number of relationships, some overlapping, and is regarded as "a top-class piano teacher as long as he keeps his hands to himself or on the piano".

Here's the Thing

This left Gordon at home, "somewhat bereft of any self-defining characteristics," as his father once said of him. He had trundled through life, first as a company bookkeeper, then as the unlikely acquirer/owner of the town's only independent bookstore, which failed when pummeled by the Amazon juggernaut. During his ill-fated attempt to run the bookstore Gordon had achieved a temporary escape, and had lived over the store for five years. But now, here he was, back in the family home. If asked for his occupation, he would probably respond that he was his mother's primary caregiver.

And, then also, there was the matter of Gordon's relationships with women, or the lack of them. He was, at sixty, technically a virgin he supposed, having never successfully completed an act of intercourse. In his teens his father, probably worried that his son might be that dreadful thing then called queer, and now called gay, had once tried to get him fixed up with a "woman I know in town," which Gordon, appalled by the whole idea, had summarily rejected, thereby further escalating his father's fears.

In his early twenties, near the beginning of his bookkeeping phase, there had been an event after a drunken pre-Christmas company party which had embarrassed him and had made him the butt of smutty office jokes because the woman in question was a blabbermouth. This had left him in a permanent state of trepidation around women.

The Sunday after Gordon's latest failed mowing effort, he diligently drove his mother to church, and went through the usual motions. This time however he saw Bruce ushering three women, not two, through the church door. In addition to Bruce's wife Emily and Gordon's Aunt Florence, an athletically slim, tall and suitably behatted woman was with them.

Bruce arrived at Clive's Café a little later than usual.

"Sorry, guys, I got caught up with introductions and stuff." He bit into his usual chocolate chip muffin.

Gordon glanced over. "Yes, I saw you there – who was that with you?"

"That's Faith Merton. Her mother died a while ago – didn't you know? – and Faith is back to clean things up and list the house for sale. You remember Faith, don't you – I recall you and she were great buddies when we were kids." He wiped muffin crumbs off his lips. "Emily arranged for her to go with her to church."

As Bruce prattled on, Gordon sat rigid. Faith Merton.

Pretty well on time, Bruce's phone rang at 11:30, and he and Gordon walked back to the church parking lot. As they arrived, the women came out of the church door. Prudence in her wheelchair was being pushed by Aunt Florence. Then came Emily and the tall woman who, as she stepped down, said, "Hats are for church," and swept hers off, exposing a blaze of ash-blonde curls, greying a little in places.

Gordon vaguely heard Bruce say, "Gord, you remember Faith?"

And Faith, blue eyes shining, held out her hand, murmuring, "Hello, Gorrie."

The parking lot chit-chat was all a bit of a blur for Gordon, but one outcome was that, when he and his mother went to Bruce and Emily's for supper that evening, Faith was there as well.

In his youth, Gordon's best friend was Faith, the blonde-haired, blue-eyed daughter of the Merton family whose house was a few blocks over. Five years younger than Gordon, she couldn't pronounce his name properly, and from the age of two had always called him 'Gorrie.' When he was eight, three-year old Faith climbed into his red Radio Flyer wagon, and he towed her to the railway station a mile down the hill. A neighbour found him trying to negotiate the purchase of two train tickets with the few dollars he had saved, and drove them home in his truck, the wagon in the back.

Because Mrs. Merton worked at the town doctor's office on Saturdays, and as there was no longer a Mr. Merton as far as

Gordon could tell, Faith was regularly dropped off at the Stillwater home each Saturday morning, and was there until late in the day. During the week she was at preschool and, later, at kindergarten. "It's the least I can do," sighed Prudence Stillwater martyrishly.

When he was ten, Gorrie was into Marvel comics, as well as Charlie Browns. On Saturday mornings he unknowingly taught five-year old Faith how to read. She would watch him reading the comics and would say "What's that word," pressing a stubby finger on the page, and Gorrie would spell it out for her and then pronounce it. When Faith was nine, she taught Gordie a thing or two by showing him how girls were different from boys 'down there', which he found very confusing. In the summers they went to the beach, and blackberry picking, and in the winters they went sledding together. And once, Gordon stole a cigarette from his mother and the two of them tried to smoke it. Faith felt sick, and Gordon *was* sick.

When he was eighteen, he kissed thirteen-year old Faith on the mouth, which Mrs. Merton saw, and told him if he did that again she would tell his father, so he didn't. Gordie wondered if Mrs. Merton did tell anyway as, soon after 'that', he was packed off to Vancouver to stay with a cousin and to take a bookkeeping course at Langara College. He did see Faith during breaks, but it always seemed to be in the company of others – Faith had lots of friends at the time.

When she was herself eighteen, Faith went to Olds Agricultural College in Alberta, and seemingly out of Gordon's life. He heard that Mrs. Merton regularly went to visit with her daughter, but, as far as he knew, for years Faith didn't come back to the family home.

But now, here she was back, it seemed, into his life. Supper that evening was way livelier than usual; Faith was funny and a bit strident, and Gordie was, for him, almost garrulous. Prudence and Florence mostly sat and watched, and Emily and Bruce were busy at the barbecue, which was misbehaving.

"Thirty-five years! That's how long it's been! Where have you been, and what have you done?"

"Well I don't know if I'll tell you all that I've done," Faith said coquettishly, "but I did do some travelling after I got my horticulture degree. I worked as part of the huge staff at Kew Gardens in England for what seemed like years, but I learned a lot. After a while back in Canada with"– she grimaced – "the Ministry of Agriculture, I spent a year in Japan" – she paused for a moment – "and finally settled back in Canada and started my own company in the Niagara Peninsula."

"What's it called?"

"The Faithful Gardener – actually there's a dash in the 'faithful', so it's The Faith dash ful Gardener" – she indicated the dash with a chopping sweep of her hand.

"Wow!" Gordon didn't know what to say.

"I know, it's a bit kitchy, but in a way it says who I am and what I do. After wandering around from job to job, I came to realize that when I take a project on, I want to stay with it, and take it all the way." She stared at Gordon, who glanced away and said, "Please pass the potatoes," and then asked Faith how she was getting on with readying the Merton home for sale.

After supper, as Gordon was helping his mother into the passenger seat, Faith asked if Gordon might drop her off at the Merton home, and he said, "Sure – how did you get here this evening?"

"I walked."

"Oh."

On the way, with Faith in the back seat, Gordon, still energized, said, "If you're a gardener, perhaps you can show me how to make sure the rows are straight when I mow the lawn." He giggled a bit, and Prudence said "Hmph!"

"Sure, all it takes is a couple of pegs and a ball of garden twine."

In the Merton driveway Faith said thank you and goodnight, and, as she walked to the front door, Gordon saw a dusty van parked at the side of the house with *The Faith-ful Gardener* in antique script across the back.

As they drove away, Prudence Stillwater said "Hmph!" again.

The next morning, Gordon mowed the lawn, and the ribbons of grass were still wobbly.

The week that followed was, to Gordon, a whirlwind – afterwards some would say a whirlwind romance – where what one thought would ordinarily take weeks or months only took six days.

That Monday afternoon, after the mowing fiasco, he drove over to the Merton house. Faith was standing at the door as a man went down the steps. Gordon surprised himself as he felt a ripple of – what – envy? He stood at the foot of the steps as Faith smiled down at him.

"Who was that?"

"One of the Real Estate guys – I don't know which company to go with."

Gordon, relieved, said, "Well I'm not much help there, I'm afraid. Actually I'm here because you said something about using string to mow the lawn straight."

"Just a moment." She disappeared for a minute, then returned, carrying a sack. "Have you got a free hour? I told Bruce and Emily I'd have a look at their garden, and there's no time like the present. They have a back lawn that needs cutting."

"Well, I use a hand mower, and I doubt if they – "

"That's fine; I have a hand mower in the van. Jump in."

Gordon, comfortable with the way she took charge, got into the van.

The next hour was spent by Faith showing Gordon how to use a couple of pegs and a length of twine to establish and then replicate straight ribbons of mown grass of equal width. "Your front lawn will be more difficult, because there are no straight edges to line up with – it's shaped a bit like a big fat ostrich egg, but the principle is the same. Just take the time to get the first line right, and move the pegs and the twine line two of your foot lengths for each pass if you feel you need to."

"How do you know what our front yard looks like?"

"Emily drove me by the other day. She told me you were always moaning about how your mother gets pissed off about how you mow the lawn, and my professionalism got piqued."

Goodness, thought Gordon; she's so self-assured. "So, now that you're back, or at least you're here for a little while, perhaps I can show you how this little corner of the world has changed since you've been away." He was mildly surprised by the forwardness of his proposition, and even more surprised by her acceptance of it.

Much of the rest of the week, when Faith wasn't getting the Real Estate Agents organized and Gordon wasn't making sure his mother was fed and watered, they were together. Faith drove the two of them to some gardens she wanted to view, having read about them but hadn't seen. Sitting outside over lunch at Tim Hortons, she was polite about them, but not overly impressed. "You'll find out I have high standards," she grumbled. Gordon liked the bit about 'You'll find out' – it augured well. And Gordon took Faith to a couple of art galleries to show her "the sort of stuff I like – Mother says it's hum-drum, but maybe that fits with me – being hum-drum."

Saturday evening, for the first time in years, Gordon had a dinner date. He took Faith to the restaurant at the Golf Club, a good way out of town. Bruce had recommended it.

"What about your mother's supper?" she asked.

"I got it ready for her before I came to pick you up." He sipped his wine. "So tell me, how come you became a gardener – I thought a degree from Olds University meant you became a farmer."

"It's actually Olds *College*," she corrected him with a smile, "and it has horticultural courses, which is what I took. In England they have wonderful gardens you can go and see, so that's why people like me go there. And going to Japan was, sort of, for the same reason." She sounded hesitant. Then, "After all that I realized that I get the most pleasure out of finding out what people visualize for their garden, and then using my knowledge and skills making it a reality for them; so I started my own company." She smiled at him. "Sorry, it sounds like a commercial, but now you have my life to date in a nutshell."

Gordon hesitated, then, carefully, "You mentioned Japan the other evening, and again just now, but you sounded sort of – I don't know – like you didn't want to think – or talk – about it."

"Well, I went there with someone, but it didn't work out."

"That's it?"

"Yup."

"OK." Then, jokingly, "I wondered if it was because you're tall and blonde, so you would stand out there."

"That too."

Feeling he was sinking into sensitive territory, Gordon took a mouthful of food, then said, "But what I really wonder about is why you disappeared to the college and never came back to visit. Your mother, I remember, used to go to stay with you, but I don't think you ever came here to stay with her."

"I had a baby. That's why." Faith stared at him.

"Oh. Oh, my." Gordon sat dumbfounded. "I didn't know that."

"No-one around here did. Except I have a feeling my mother may have told your mother." She sounded brittle.

"If you don't want to talk about it – "

"No, I want you to know what happened."

Just then, the waiter came to take their plates away. He asked if they would like to see the dessert menu, and Faith said, "Not just now, thanks." She looked Gordon full in the face and muttered to herself, "Here we go," almost as if she was getting ready to make a speech.

"Olds College wasn't exactly mainstream in the seventies, but there were a few of us who knew about cannabis – you know, pot – and were growing it and using it. What the hell, we were a horticulture school, and cannabis was a plant. There were beginning to be pot parties all over the world every April 20 at 4:20. We had an all-nighter – or actually an all-weekender – on that date in my last year at college. I'm not proud of it, but I got pregnant."

Gordon sat rigid. This was way out of his league.

Faith paused and picked up her wine glass, then put it down again. "My baby boy was born on January the first, 1976. My mother was very supportive, and wanted me to come back here, but I just couldn't. I was so embarrassed about being so stupid and doing something which would jeopardize my career – my whole life, that I just couldn't face my friends. So I hid by going to England, where, as I told you the other evening, I worked at Kew Gardens."

"Oh, my goodness! What about the boy's father – did he go with you?"

"I don't know who his father is."

"What! I don't understand."

Faith sighed. "This is the worst part of the story. I was made love to by – had sex with, I might as well say – two men that weekend. I didn't know the name of one of them, and I never tried to find out which was the father."

"Well, there's DNA testing now – "

"I know, but I have completely lost touch with them, including the man whose name I *do* know, and frankly it's not of any interest to me." She paused, then said, "The thing is that I battled for years over my despair about the stupid thing I did that weekend. But I came to realize that you have to move on in the voyage of life. I've come to recognize that what I did resulted in my greatest joy."

Gordon looked at her quizzically.

"You've heard the worst part. The best part is that I fell in love with my little boy, and still love him to bits; he's thirty-four now, and has a lovely partner. He's a promising young lawyer in Toronto. I'm so proud of him." Faith looked away.

"What's his name?"

"Gordon."

"Oh! Was – is there a reason?"

"Gorrie, here's the thing. Of all of the people I was too embarrassed to come back to and face, you were the most important. And, also, I guess, the most I missed. So I called my boy Gordon so that I could have at least your name in my life even if I couldn't have the rest of you. He's my Gordon, and I love him."

Faith leaned across and covered his hand with hers. "Gorrie, this trip back is part of my voyage. You have been my bestest ever friend since I was a little girl. You have no idea how kind and caring you were throughout the first eighteen years of my life. And the best of *that* is the fact that you have no idea how special you are, because being kind and caring is so much a part of you that you don't even know you're doing it. And I'll tell you now that I love you for that."

Gordon sat gaping at her, struck dumb.

Faith watched him for a while, then took her hand away. "So, that's it. And now, let's order dessert."

Gordon threw his head back and guffawed so loudly that a man at a table nearby spilled his drink.

Gordon drove a strangely silent Faith back to her house. She opened the car door, then leaned over and kissed him on the cheek, whispered "G'night", got out and went in. Gordon drove home, once again confused.

The usual Sunday ritual started a little differently, and got progressively more unusual as the day went by. Gordon hoped he would see Faith in the church parking lot, but Bruce arrived with only his wife and Aunt Florence, and without Faith. Instead of his usual walk with them into the church, Bruce came over to Gordon as he was settling his mother into her wheelchair, and said, "I'll walk with you over to Clive's Café."

As they walked together, Bruce said, "I wanted a couple of minutes with you before we join the rest of the guys. It's about Faith – Faith and you." He paused. "Are you OK me talking with you about this?"

Gordon said, "Sure." Though he wasn't, but didn't know what else to say. So Bruce went on.

"Emily had quite a chat on the phone with Faith last night, and, well, the bottom line is she's really – um – *attracted* to you, and always has been, and evidently told you yesterday evening over dinner. But she doesn't know if her feelings about you are reciprocated, because you didn't say anything in return." Bruce paused, then said tentatively, "She said when she told you, you laughed."

"No, no – Oh good heavens, does she really think that? No, I laughed because she told me what she liked about me, then said let's order dessert! It was so odd! I never – oh my goodness, what she must think of me."

"She's been going around with you all week – "

"I know, I know, and – I don't know – I'm just sort of tongue-tied."

"Buddy, she's a wonderful woman."

"I know, and I've got to tell her that I think she is."

"Well, Emily is going to ask your mother if Faith can come with us to supper this evening – it's our turn to come to you – so perhaps –?"

"Oh good. Say, Bruce, thanks for this."

After coffee with the Agnostics, Gordon and Bruce walked back to the church and as they all stood in the parking lot arranging who would do what for supper, Emily said that Faith had already offered that if she was coming, she would make dessert.

Out of the blue, astonishing himself for his moment of ingenuity, Gordon said, "Emily, why don't you tell her to come over to the Garden Cottage early; she can make dessert in my little kitchen."

So Faith drove over in her Faith-ful Gardener van that afternoon with the fixings for dessert, and made it in Gordon's kitchen. It was strawberry cheesecake 'to die for' as she called it. Gordon hunted out a pie dish. "Will this do?" Faith glanced at it and nodded as she frowned at the recipe.

Sitting on a stool watching her, Gordon fiddled with a dishcloth, and then spoke.

"Faith, I'm in trouble with you, aren't I."

"Emily has been talking to you."

"No, Bruce actually."

Faith put down the spoon she was stirring with. "Gorrie, It's just that I don't know where I am with you. I don't know whether you're spending time with me because you think it's your duty or something, or because you like being with me. You never say."

"I know. When I was about eighteen I said to my mother once that I was scared of girls and always would be, and I guess I was at least right about that."

Faith sort of giggled. "Was that before or after you kissed me when I was thirteen and got in trouble for it?"

"After, I think. I'm amazed that you remember that."

"Well, it should tell you something that I haven't forgotten it." She began ladling into the big ornamental dish.

Gordon shifted on the stool. "Well, I will tell you this. During this week It has come to me that I have never felt so relaxed with a woman as I am with you, not that I have much to compare with," he snorted. "And when you said that you – you love me for being kind, I was all confused – as usual – and figured you meant it's a nice characteristic of mine – just a sort of compliment to make me feel good. I thought to say thank you, but before I could, you said we should order dessert, and I was so relieved at being stopped from saying something stupid that I laughed."

"Oh Gorrie. You know, you need to stop analyzing to death everything that you do and that happens to you."

"Well, I have analyzed one thing; and it's this. That I love being with you."

Faith stopped smoothing the top of the dessert with the spoon, pointed it at him, and said, "That's good, because I'm the same – I mean, I love being with you." She walked round the table to Gordon, put her arms around him and kissed him.

Leaning back, she realized she was still holding the spoon. "You've got cheesecake on your ear," she whispered, and licked it off, smacking her lips. Gordon found himself in raw arousal. They grinned at each other.

Gordon said, "You know, my father once said that I was bereft of defining characteristics, but now I find that I have at least two. One is that I'm kind and caring, and the other is that I taste good with cheesecake on my ear."

As Faith enfolded him, he muttered into her hair, "Will you stay after?" To which Faith responded, "Try to stop me."

At supper that evening, Prudence sat in her usual place at the head of the table. Bruce was at the other end, with his wife on his right, alongside Florence. Gordon and Faith sat opposite them. Everybody said supper was lovely, especially Faith's dessert.

Near the end of the meal, the talk turned to regret – what the word meant, and what you do about it. It all started with Aunt Florence, who seldom said much, saying that she regretted not having travelled more after her husband Maurice's death. "He wasn't interested in it, but I would have loved to have seen other parts of the world. Like you, Faith; you lived in England and even Japan. It sounds so exotic when one's lived pretty well all one's life in one place."

"Well," said Bruce, "I've lived here pretty well all my life, and I don't regret that. Anyway, what do you mean by regret? You can't do anything about it."

"I think that's part of the meaning of regret – the fact that you can't do anything about it," Emily said quietly, which made Bruce look at her a bit quizzically.

"I have no regrets," Prudence pronounced, and sat back in her chair.

There was a moment of silence, only interrupted by the clicking of forks.

It was Faith who took up the challenge. "If you don't have regrets, you haven't reached for what you desire."

"What *are* you talking about!" Prudence demanded belligerently.

"I think you get the most out of life if you strive for things. If you succeed, you celebrate, and maybe even get a prize. But if you fail, you regret of course, and then you have to deal with that. That's what I've done."

Gordon looked at her and nodded, as if to say, 'and you know what you're talking about'.

"Well," Bruce cut in, "that may be, but I still say it's over, and you can't do anything about it, so just get on with life."

"Spoken like a man," Emily whispered.

"Huh?" Bruce turned and glared at his wife.

"Nothing."

"Well," Gordon finally spoke, "I certainly have regrets."

"Like what?" Prudence was like a dog with a bone.

"I guess I wish I had done more with my life, and, you know, made a success out of – at least *something*, like my brothers have. So I regret that."

Faith leaned in. "And what *I* say is that you look at a regret, and if you *can* do something about it, like apologize to someone for something you did or didn't do, you go ahead and do that. But if you *can't* do anything about it, like you wish you had travelled," she nodded at Florence, "you can't stop regretting, because it doesn't go away. But you *can* learn from it, and resolve to not let opportunities like that go by again."

Prudence watched as Faith and Gordon turned to gaze at each other. *At last*, she thought.

"It's a bit late in life for me to start that, I would think," Gordon laughed.

"No, it isn't." Faith was passionate. "That's the thing! It's never too late. I read somewhere that you can't rewrite the past, but you can choose to strive to live with your whole heart in the here and now."

Bruce stood up. "Well, talking of too late, it's definitely too late for me for this type of intellectual stuff. C'mon, Emily, lets help with the cleaning up. Faith, do you need a ride? Oh no, you came in your van."

And so the discussion came to an end, unresolved, though Gordon felt – something – he didn't quite know what – jubilation?

Some time in the night, Faith, curled into his grateful body, whispered "Will you now be also my Gordon?" And Gordon, finally not at all confused, said, "I will." It sounded like, and in its way was, a vow.

Prudence awoke to the sound of Gordon pushing the hand mower. It's Monday, she thought. And it's going to be a hot day, which is why he's mowing the lawn so early. She maneuvered herself out of bed, into her wheelchair and into the bathroom, then out and down the hall to the kitchen for her early morning coffee-and-cigarette. As she wheeled out onto the front balcony the sound of mowing stopped. Prudence looked along the balcony to the Garden House and saw Gordon walk from the end of the lawn to stand by its balcony railing. Then she saw with a jolt, still parked by the side of the Garden House, the dusty white van with *The Faith-ful Gardener* scrawled across the side. The sight gave her a little frisson of satisfaction.

Right then, the Garden House door opened. Wearing what Prudence recognized to be an old robe of Gordon's, Faith stepped out, and, her unkempt grey-gold hair haloed by the morning sun, she walked barefoot to the balcony rail.

She looked down at Gordon who, taking his hat off, placed it over his heart and waved at the perfectly striped lawn with his other hand in an oddly comical but theatrical gesture. Prudence could see he was holding something. Then he handed Faith a ball of garden twine, almost, it seemed, as a treasured prize to be shared.

Faith glanced across at the lawn. Then, her blue eyes blazing, she leaned down over the railing and, cupping her hand behind his head, kissed him full on the mouth.

"Perfect," she said.

THE PIANO LESSON

After Miss Starchy died, her house stood empty for a while, and weeds grew in the front yard. No-one in town called her by her real name, which the obituary in the local paper said was Olivia Jones. She was 'Miss Starchy' or 'Old Starchy' because of the starched blouses she wore when giving piano lessons. "She was a sweet lady," was the opinion of those in Ethel Point who knew her, which was pretty well anyone who had a child or had grown up there. She'd had some successes with students at the Kiwanis Festival in the big city, but mostly taught enough to keep the young kids occupied, and herself supplied with sherry, for which she had a fondness.

Shortly after she died, her family arrived with a moving truck and a dumpster and cleared the house out in a weekend.

"Such haste is inconsiderate of the dead," said Pauley over his second beer at the Ethel Point Inn, and Monk, the barman, shook his head in disgust, not having any idea what Pauley meant by that.

The last piece of furniture to leave was the piano. The two-man moving crew managed to get it loaded without dropping it. Mrs. Draper, from down the street, was a bit teary as she watched, along with a small group of old-timers and kids on bikes. "I learned the Chopin Nocturne on that piano – you know, my party piece." Mrs. Draper had one of the few pianos in town, and, of course, there was the one in the corner at the Ethel Point Inn, which no-one had played for years.

In addition to being the town's designated drunk, Pauley was also its self-appointed guru when it came to Ethel Point's history. As far as he was concerned, the loss of the town's piano teacher was Armageddon and the Apocalypse rolled into one. "A town without culture is a town without a future," Pauley intoned, claiming it was a quote from Aristotle, or someone like that. "Where are the kids gonna get their culture?" he demanded. Someone pointed out that the high school had a good drama teacher, but Pauley said that wasn't the same, and that piano lessons keep kids out of trouble, which pretty well put an end to the debate.

After the For Sale sign went up, someone from the Realty Company came to cut the grass and mend the fence where the movers had hit it with the freezer. The neighbours became used to seeing the agent showing the house at weekends. The sign had just about become a fixture, when one day the one word 'Sold!' was plastered diagonally across it. The next day a skinny and bespectacled young man drove up without the agent, walked tautly down the driveway, and let himself in the side door. Mrs. Draper phoned her friend Sandra to see if she could waylay him, but he came out and drove away while they were plotting.

"Looked a bit uptight, I thought," Sandra commented, to which Mrs. Draper replied, "Well, I hope he finds whatever it is he's looking for."

So, when the moving truck arrived a week later, no-one knew anything about the man who had bought the Starchy house. And it was like a religious experience when the neighbours saw the same two guys offloading a piano and trundling it in to the house on its side – not Starchy's old scratched and marked one, but a fine black and gleaming one, partly covered with a rug. "If he'd said he needed a piano he could have had old Starchy's," muttered Mrs. Draper.

Morgan Lynton got settled in, setting up the piano in the back room, which he called the Studio. Then he went to meet the School Principal. "I'm a freelance editor for a self-publishing company, and I also teach piano," he said, showing her his teaching diploma.

The Principal said, "Well, it's nice to have a piano teacher in town again. Since Miss – ah – Jones died, a couple of the girls have talked about going to someone in the big town down the highway, but I don't think they have. I will announce it." She glanced at him, thinking, *he looks a bit fragile – I wonder why he's moved here.* "And good luck."

Morgan paid for an ad in the local weekly paper and had some flyers printed, which he put up around town, including on the Ethel Point Inn notice board. "What's a man doing teaching piano?" scoffed Pauley, "and a single one at that. I wouldn't send my kids to take lessons from him." "Well, you don't have kids," said Monk, which ended *that* discussion.

It was a slow thing, getting students to go for lessons. There were all the excuses Morgan had heard before and then some. The School Principal did announce that there was a new piano teacher in town, but she sandwiched it in between announcements about sports events and earthquake drill, so no-one remembered it. A couple of mothers whose daughters had taken lessons from Old Starchy saw Morgan's flyer on the drug store notice board and talked them into taking lessons. Then little Billy, one of their brothers, started, but he didn't last long. Another one of the families was short of cash, so they paid by having the father look after Morgan's lawn and flowerbeds. So, it was slow going.

One Thursday evening, Morgan turned up at the Ethel Point Inn, borrowed a dishcloth from Monk, dusted off the decrepit old piano in the corner, opened up the lid and began to play. The piano, which had seen a few beer spills, was dreadfully out of tune, and some of the lower notes stuck, but Morgan played some show tune favourites for about twenty minutes, grimacing and laughing at the dreadful sound. As he got up from the bench, they applauded him, and Pauley bought him a beer, which was quite remarkable.

"Ya know," lectured Pauley, wagging a finger at Morgan, "every male piano teacher should have a wife." Morgan looked at Pauley, then at Monk, for help. "Don't bother about him," said Monk scornfully, "he's pie-eyed."

Morgan's piano playing became a regular Thursday evening event, and Monk was heard to say that business on Thursdays was nearly as good as weekends. One humid evening, as Morgan closed the lid, a big guy with greying hair who Morgan recognized as Digger, the town's policeman, walked over and said to Morgan, "Here, let me buy you one." Morgan smiled, and said, "Thanks; it's thirsty work these hot nights." A skinny man wearing a ball cap shouted, "Hey, Digger, what about the rest of us?" Digger looked over and said, "I've got my eye on you, buddy," and everyone laughed. Digger was obviously popular.

While chatting, Morgan found that Digger was the town's last resident policeman. After the police station closed, Digger – his name was actually Digby – became part of the police force located in the big town a fast half hour down the highway. He had been in the constabulary for thirty years.

"The wife and me just didn't see moving there after this station shut soon after the mill closed, so I drive down. It's not far, and I can keep an eye on the highway speedsters as I go to work," he chuckled. Thursday, he explained, was his day off, and he usually came down to the Ethel for a drink with the crowd. His wife Charlotte, whom he called Charlie, had a gin rummy girl's night on Thursdays.

Digger ran a finger round the rim of his beer glass, and then said shyly, "Say, would you be interested in taking me on as a student? I used to play as a kid, and even played for Old Starchy a couple of times way back when our son was taking lessons. And, well, I sort of miss it. But I think I need help getting back into it."

Morgan stared at Digger. "Do you have a piano?"

"Yes; actually it's Charlie's, and she used to play, but she's got a bit of arthritis, so it just sits there. It'll probably need tuning. So what do you think?"

Morgan, realizing he was serious, clapped him on the shoulder. "You're on, pal; when do we start?"

So, Digger became Morgan's first adult student. Pauley claimed he was the first guy not at school taking piano lessons. "Starchy wouldn't have let him do it," he sputtered disgustedly at Monk, gulping down his first pint; "and Digger's not even a *woman*, which might have been understandable in certain circumstances." Monk rolled his eyes and wiped the counter vigorously. "You dunno what ye're talkin about," he muttered.

Although Digger had hardly touched the piano in twenty years, Morgan's teaching skills took over, so that practice techniques became a pleasure rather than a chore. "Besides, you'll find them relaxing."

At their first lesson, Morgan slid effortlessly into teaching mode. "Now, we need to have you sitting upright – you're a big man, so you need to sit well back from the keyboard, not all hunched up over it. I think you'll be better on a chair rather than the piano bench, at least to start with."

So Morgan got Digger sitting comfortably on a chair. They did some simple exercises, and then they discussed his hands. "Big hands don't have to be clumsy." Finally they talked about what sort of music Digger liked; "Positive music."

The hour was over quickly, and they arranged a schedule of practice and lessons which would fit with Digger's shifts. Six in the evening seemed to be a good time. As he was leaving, Digger glanced through to the sparsely furnished front room with windows overlooking the front street.

"Nice place you've made this. It was always a bit crowded when old Starchy lived here."

"Yes, it suits me fine, and it's convenient – I just hope I find some students – some *more* students." They laughed.

It was a pleasure for Morgan to teach Digger, who obviously enjoyed returning to piano playing. The lessons became a time they both looked forward to. Digger told Morgan how, in Grade 7, he was the big kid in class, and everyone told him he was a natural for contact sports. "Because I was a big guy, and reasonably well coordinated, and so on, I just naturally became a football player, and I had already been playing hockey for a few years. Pretty soon, piano playing got crowded out – it was kid stuff anyway. Poor old Starchy didn't have a hope against all those coaches."

Digger mentioned to some friends that he thought Morgan was a pretty good teacher, and two of them sent their sons to him for lessons. Although neither of the boys seemed particularly interested, at least his position as the town's piano teacher was becoming established.

One day, as Digby was leaving after a lesson, he said, "Why don't you put the piano in the front room? The light's good in there."

"What's wrong with where it is?"

"Well, that room's a bit hidden away."

Morgan looked at him. "What are you getting at?"

"Well, you know, people are funny. I just figure people – parents, might be a bit more comfortable if their kids took their lessons in the front room – you being a single man." Digby flushed; he was embarrassed.

"You mean, where they – I mean, *we*, can be seen from the street."

"That's right."

"So it's part of your job to have me under surveillance?" Morgan said half-jokingly.

"Yeah, right; as if I didn't have enough to do. No, I've just heard that some folks would like to send their kids for lessons, but they seem to be cautious. It didn't matter with Starchy; she was a little old lady."

"So Pauley had a point about male piano teachers needing a wife." Morgan sounded irritated.

So, Morgan, with Digger's assistance, rearranged things. They moved the hide-a-bed into the Studio, and rolled the piano into the front room, setting it along the wall by the window.

"It's an outside wall, so it might go out of tune," explained Morgan, "but we'll deal with that if it happens."

From the sidewalk, you could easily see who was playing the piano. Morgan gave most of his lessons late in the day, and the light over the piano shone down on where Morgan sat, as well as on the student; Morgan went out to the street to check that. And he left the curtains open. *It's all pretty ridiculous*, he thought.

For a while it didn't make much difference, but when the big town down the highway announced a music festival as part of its 100th anniversary celebrations, Morgan got some students whose parents wanted to have their kids in the piano competition. So, Morgan's afternoons and evenings became booked, as well as much of the weekends. But he always made time for Thursday evenings at the Ethel Point Inn. He persuaded Monk to have the piano tuned, and get some repairs done. After a while Morgan began interspersing pieces by Scarlatti and even Bach in with the old favourites.

Digger remained as Morgan's only adult pupil. A couple of ladies talked to him about lessons, but, for them, bingo and crib seemed to take precedence. Digger was conscientious, sometimes practising early before going on duty, and pretty regularly walking down to his weekly evening lesson. In addition to the teacher-student relationship, they became good friends, and Thursday evenings would find them together at the Ethel Point Inn. Digger even did a bit of piano playing there, to the amusement of the crowd. Morgan began guiding him towards more challenging music where his big hands with a wide span were an asset. A few early Beethoven sonatas were followed by Grieg and then some Chopin. Digger said one day to Morgan, "I didn't recognise how stressful my job is until I found how different – how relaxed I feel after a lesson, or after practising. Sometimes when I've had what we call a shit shift, I just sit at my piano and play for a while." He paused, then said with a grin, "Charlie says I've stopped being such a bear."

Morgan said. "It's good to have a routine; helps the focus."

One evening at the Ethel Point Inn, Morgan and Digger sat at a corner table, away from the noisy crowd watching the game on the overhead screen. Digger, looking relaxed, started a conversation.

"So, mate, how is it you came to live in this wasting-away place? People usually move out from here, not move in."

"Part of your surveillance, eh?" grinned Morgan, and Digger gestured dismissively. "Well," Morgan looked as if he was settling in to explain a few things; "I basically wanted to find a place to hide for a while; to start over." He looked out at the room, then back at Digger, then seemed to make a decision.

"I came out of the Vancouver Music Conservatory with a performance diploma. I was intent on becoming a concert pianist – so intent that friends and family told me I was missing out on life. I met and moved in with Kirsti, who was stunning everyone with her fabulous coloratura voice. Her teachers were pressing her to get out of Vancouver and go to New York or London. Our lives were completely run – almost *overrun* – by music. We thought we were in love, but, looking back, I realise we never made the time together that it takes to grow a relationship. We were both running around Canada, and into the States, performing, sometimes for a pittance, or for charitable causes, to promote our name. Then," softly, "I had what later I came to identify as a sort of breakdown."

Morgan sat looking at his drink, and Digger waited. Then Morgan went on.

"I was playing one of the Bach concertos with a semi-professional orchestra in a town on the prairies. Rehearsals had been rushed and inadequate, and I felt stressed when I went on stage. Bach can be a problem because sometimes his music builds on repetitive but changing musical figures." Morgan sighed. "About two minutes in, I got lost. I sort of vamped for a moment, but the orchestra ground to a halt and so did I. The conductor whispered to start again, and so we did. I could hear the audience fidgeting. We got to the same place in the music and I got lost again. My brain just fried. I stumbled off the stage. People said why didn't I have the music on the piano stand, but the theory is that if you don't have the music in front of you, you will concentrate on the piece's meaning rather than just playing the notes. Also, it's sort of a vanity thing," he glanced at Digger with a little smile.

Morgan sighed. "Since then I haven't performed in public, other than in here" – he gestured at the room – "which doesn't really count."

"Then my life basically fell apart. First, Kirsti left for the east coast to pursue her career. She's done quite well," he added wistfully. "Then I ran into financial difficulties, trying to survive just on piano teaching. My reputation was damaged by my 'meltdown', they called it. And, frankly there are lots of good piano teachers out there, and not enough students to go round. Then I became forgetful, and lost some students as a result. About a year after the episode on stage, I had just about given up, and was, I suppose, suicidal."

Digger sat watching his friend, his big hands motionless on the table.

Morgan exhaled impatiently. "So, I got some psychiatric help, sold the Vancouver condo, and decided to bury myself in a small town where I could work on rebuilding my self-confidence. I know I have a talent for teaching – I love it, but I also love public performing. I figured that if I struggle here, hidden away, it won't hurt so much. And I do some freelance editing for a publishing outfit to pay for the groceries."

They sat in a silence broken only by the moans of the crowd watching their favourite team losing the game.

Then Digger leaned over the table. "Thanks, buddy. I think you know I've got your back."

"I figured that; that's why I've told you all this."

Digger stood up, briefly put a hand on Morgan's shoulder, and went to the bar to order another round.

The next morning, as if a door had been unlocked within, Morgan went rummaging around for the score of one of his favourite sonatas, Beethoven's challenging 'Hammerklavier'. He sat at the piano and played through the first movement. Although he had the music beside him on the bench, he played it entirely by memory. He felt exultant.

Soon after, on a September day, a year after Morgan moved to Ethel Point, there was trouble in the trailer park development just up the highway. Morgan heard from the mother of his first student, when she came to collect her, that a domestic incident had turned ugly. A woman and, she thought, two young children, were being held hostage by a man, presumably the father. She said Digger had gone there early in the morning and had called for back-up. Morgan remembered having heard sirens earlier.

Morgan walked down to the coffee shop, where everyone was talking about it. While he was there, an ambulance, its siren wailing, went by up on the highway.

During the afternoon Morgan heard a garbled story involving a shooting from one of the mums, who phoned to cancel her kid's lessons. She sounded panicked.

By late that afternoon he had heard pretty well the whole thing. How Digger had gone to the mobile home that morning, and how he had talked through the door with the man for a long time. Then Digger had finally stepped inside, and the mother and the two children had come out, the little girl running. Morgan heard how Digger had gone into the kitchen where the man was sitting with a gun on the table in front of him, and how he had sat and talked with the man for a while. He heard that the man had then picked up the gun, and that Digger had leaned forward and had held out his hand, and how the man had turned away and had put the gun in his mouth and had pulled the trigger.

Just before seven that evening, Morgan's phone rang. It was Digger. His voice was hoarse. Morgan could hardly recognise it.

"Morgan, it's Digby. I guess you heard what happened."

"Yeah, I heard some of it, Digger."

"I'm pretty – shaken, so I won't be able to come to my lesson."

"Are you home?"

"Yes. There's all sorts of stuff going on, but they sent me home."

"So, you could come to your lesson."

"Yes, but – "

"Digby, I think maybe you should."

"Jesus, Morgan." A pause and a sigh. "I'll think about it."

Through the window, Morgan saw Digger shambling down the street shortly after seven, his eyes puffy. Morgan opened the door, and Digger lurched in.

"I'm here, though I don't know why."

"Well, let's just do a little."

Digger heaved onto the piano bench, and put a book of Schumann pieces on the stand.

"No," said Morgan, who replaced the Schumann with Beethoven's Moonlight Sonata. Digger looked at him.

"Let's do the first movement; you've played it before. The secret of this music is, steady all the way."

Digger started, and after a moment Morgan stopped him. Digger's hands were shaking.

"Too fast, Digby, and too loud. Here's the thing; think about it. It's thoughtful and measured; you need to entice and entrance the listeners, make them wait, and steady, steady, steady. Each note counts."

Digby started again, blundering a little, and it sounded mechanical. Then he eased into the piece, gradually getting into the slow, measured ripple of the arpeggios, then adding the mournful, insistent song which rode above them, soft and inevitable.

There were some misplaced notes, but Morgan let Digger play on, his hands now sure, the music almost mesmeric, the quintessence of beauty. Digger played through to the end of the movement. The music faded. Digger sat at the piano, his big hands resting on the keys. The room was quiet. Through the open window, the street, too, was silent.

"Beautiful," breathed Morgan.

Digger got up. "Thanks, Morgan." He walked to the door, Morgan behind him.

Then Digger turned, and the big man clasped Morgan close and almost fiercely, then opened the door and left.

He watched through the window as the policeman strode up the street. In that unexpected hug, Morgan experienced what seemed to be a transference; not just a sharing of anguish, but also some sort of bestowal of – what? – an intimation of resilience.

He sat at the piano, his hands on the keys. Morgan looked at them for a long time, and then softly played Bach's Goldberg Variations theme, delicate, sad, but complete in itself, and full of promise.

Now, he thought.

Now I am ready.

Bennytoo

Benjamin Youngman, who became known to everyone as 'Bennytoo', was just nineteen when his parents, Ben and Joanie, together with his grandfather, David, started looking for a replacement kidney for him.

Bennytoo was a hefty six-foot-two teenager with a shock of black hair and bushy black eyebrows. He had nothing wrong with him except that, after a football injury, he only had one operational kidney left, and that one wasn't doing well.

When word of Benjamin's kidney issue got around college, one of the girls he hung around with started calling him Bennytoo. At first, no-one knew if it was 'Bennytoo' or 'Bennytwo', but then someone got a Get Well Card which all his college friends signed, and it was addressed to 'Bennytoo', so that settled it. They called him Bennytoo to distinguish him from his dad, Ben, who, as a Department Head, was a member of the Faculty of Arts and Social Sciences. Soon, everyone who knew him called him that, including his dad and his mom, and even his grandfather David, though David would often still call him 'Buddy'.

It was some sort of a support team thing for everyone to pitch in and call him Bennytoo. There was quite a dynasty of Youngmans at the College, as Bennytoo's Grandfather, David, now nearing the end of his career, was a long-time part of Finance and Administration. The Youngmans were popular on campus.

Bennytoo's father, Ben, was David and Pamela Youngman's first and only son. Similarly to what Bennytoo had become, Ben was a strapping man, whose mane of black hair, now with tinges of gray, was lasting well, despite the fact that, by 2015, he was in his mid-forties. Before Bennytoo had the football accident, Ben and his teenage son used to wrestle at family barbecues, with everyone cheering them on. Ben's sister, who had come along a bit later for David and Pam, was a slim, slight girl with delicate bone structure, like her parents. With the golden blonde hair she inherited from her mother, she had caught the eye of a wealthy Australian, and, by now, was happily ensconced in Sydney with teenagers of her own.

On a sullen fall day, David left his office at the Administration Building and walked across campus in the late afternoon to chat with his old friend and sometime doctor, Chris, at the School of Medicine, about kidneys. He took along an opened, but hardly touched, bottle of single malt scotch. As they sat and sipped, David got what sounded a bit like part of Chris' lecture to first year medical students.

"Kidneys are a funny thing." Chris leaned back and waved at a diagram on his office wall. "Why we have two of them I don't know – we only have one of most of the internal organs, like the liver, the bladder, the stomach and the small and large intestine – " he jabbed a pencil at each image on the chart as he spoke. "And, of course, only one brain and one heart, though, God knows, some of my students this year seem to have only half a brain. But we have two lungs and two kidneys. Sometimes we thank God that we do have two – kidneys, that is." He sat up. "The text book answer is that renal function is crucial. It's what the kidneys do to maintain the body's chemical balance – what we call homeostasis."

David winced.

"I know, it's another long word, but things like blood pressure, red blood cells and bone strength are affected by poor renal function. Good homeostasis is achieved by excreting waste products and excess fluids – pooping and peeing to you." David raised a hand in thanks for the clarification. "So, mother nature has provided us with a reserve in case one gets diseased or damaged, and now, it seems, to enable us to help someone else by donating the extra one." He looked across at David. "The alternative to a donated kidney is dialysis for life, however long or short that may be, and I wouldn't wish that on any nineteen-year old."

"Tell me about it," David muttered. "Bennytoo is getting pretty agitated about the dialysis trips twice or three times a week. I think he sees them as somehow invading his – I don't know – that he's losing control over his own body."

"Well," Chris said cautiously, "there is, you know, an alternative method of dialysis, where Bennytoo basically looks after it all by himself. Of course he needs to be trained to do it properly."

"Yeah." David sounded uncertain. "What's it called – peritoneal dialysis instead of hemodialysis."

"Well done!" Chris grinned. "It seems you may actually have been listening to me."

"I know, 'unlike half your students.' So, give me the second lecture."

Chris laughed and tipped his glass back. David leaned over to refill it.

"Well, when the kidneys aren't clearing waste by way of your urine, hemodialysis uses a machine to filter and clean your blood outside your body, and you have to go to a clinic several times a week to get it done. Each visit is about four hours – not something a teenager wants to do for ever.

"Peritoneal dialysis filters and cleans waste from your blood internally. You attach a bag of special solution to a catheter which transfers the solution into the abdominal lining. It's in there for a few hours, and you can go about your daily business – not to play football, mind. The fluid absorbs the waste, and then you empty it out and discard it. You do this four or five times a day. An alternative is an automated system which does the job continuously while you are asleep."

"So Bennytoo would look after it himself?"

"That's right, after, mind you, a pretty intensive training session before taking on the responsibility. He'll have to be scrupulous about the way it's attached, and about cleanliness. You don't want him getting peritonitis or infection at the catheter site. That can, frankly, be fatal. There are some potential side effects, but they are manageable."

Chris glanced at David. "Enough of this lecturing, my friend. I also think Bennytoo wants to look after this situation himself, so we should arrange for him to take the training and get on with it."

David raised a hand. "Just before we finish, can you just go over again with me about this Medullary Sponge Kidney Disease that Bennytoo has," David asked.

Chris sat back. "Well, apart from being a mouthful of a name, it's an unusual birth defect in one or both of the kidneys. During the development of the fetus, cysts form on tubes in the inner part of the kidney, called the medulla, which restrict the flow of urine. Normally, symptoms don't become apparent until you are a teenager or later and, of course, the vicious kick Bennytoo experienced in football last year didn't help. In fact he has one basically non-operating kidney and another that is now compromised."

"So, is it genetic, or hereditary?" David sounded a bit plaintive.

Chris glanced at him and waved a dismissive hand. "The jury is out on that one, my friend; some say yes, some no. So don't fuss your head about that. The much more important question is whether someone in the family can donate a kidney. Which brings me to matching. So," – Chris held out his empty glass – "let me tell you about matching."

So, David got Chris' third lecture, being about how to ascertain if someone's kidney was a good match with a patient for a transplant. He shorthanded what Chris told him in a little notebook he had brought along, as he figured it was this bit that he would have to explain to the family.

On his way back to the Administration Building to pick up his car, David, as had become his habit, went in to the College's non-denominational chapel, knelt in his customary pew and prayed for the wisdom and strength he knew he would need to deal with this situation. He was later to discover that it was going to be more challenging than he thought at the time.

Since high school days, David had been in what church people like to call a covenant relationship with God. There had been no 'aha' moment – no blinding flash on his road to Damascus. He didn't even like saying "I believe in God", as that sounded as if he thought there might be some alternative to it. It was a foundational conviction with him, a certainty, rather than a cerebral 'belief', which meant that he found he regularly needed to express his awareness and gratefulness. That was, David believed, his part of the deal – his personal covenant. It wasn't a particularly intellectual position, and he wasn't much good at reading the Bible. His time with God was very private. He seldom prayed *for* anything. One of his favourite hymns was Praise God from whom all blessings flow. That pretty well summed up his role in the relationship. It was all quite simple for David. But the situation with his grandson, Bennytoo, was different. So, recently, during his regular few minutes in the quiet of the campus chapel, he was finding that once again, for he had done this before, he was seeking help. And, this time, there was no escaping it; he asked his God for help. David wasn't looking for a miracle; he was looking for guidance.

David decided that the Youngman family needed to have a sort of family conference about it. Sunday lunch at Ben and Joanie's home was quite a regular event. But this Sunday, David asked Ben and Joanie to come over to his condo for lunch, and to bring Bennytoo, who was still living in the family home, along as well. Family gatherings had to be planned so as not to conflict with David's weekly visits to the care home to sit with his wife Pamela, and now also to fit with taking Bennytoo to the clinic for his dialysis sessions. Sundays usually worked. David thought about arranging for Pam to come; after all, she was Ben's mother and Bennytoo's grandmother. This would have involved going to get her from the care home, and making the arrangements with the staff there. But frankly she had deteriorated so much recently that David didn't think there would be much point, and Ben agreed.

Pam had, for as long as David could remember, suffered from what, in the good times, she had laughingly called "my morning moods". Although, during the early years they had dismissed or downplayed the bad times, David watched with anguish as her sloughs of sadness lengthened and deepened, despite all he did, including praying to his loving Lord to help them through all this. Not long after they arrived in Vancouver as immigrants way back in July, 1969, she started having spells when she would weep uncontrollably. They had only been in Vancouver a couple of weeks when Pam discovered she had become pregnant while on board ship. The day she told David was the same day that the first man landed on the moon – July 20, 1969. He had joked with friends that "Joanie's announcement was a supreme example of upstaging." Although they both tried to laugh off her crying fits as homesickness or a side effect of pregnancy, David later realized that those anguishing times were a precursor to the gradual onset of clinical depression which not only plagued Pamela, but which also, of course, eventually ambushed their marriage and their family.

In June, 1969, newly married David and Pamela, both 24 years old, had sailed on the MS Batory from Southampton to Montreal – one of the last trans-Atlantic sailings of the famous Polish ship, as emigration to Canada had by then become mostly by air. David, with a degree in business administration, had secured employment in the Finance and Administration department at BC's new Simon

Fraser University. In London, David and Pam were assured by people at Canada House in Trafalgar Square, and at British Columbia House on Regent Street, that, with her qualifications, Pam would quickly find a nursing position in Vancouver.

Third Class on the ship was crowded – their cabin had a lower and upper bunk and a shared bathroom down the passageway – but it was cheap, and they were able to take two large trunks which included all their belongings. Also, David, who was somewhat of a history buff, was fascinated to travel on a ship with such a reputation for survival during the Second World War that it had become known as the 'Lucky Ship'. In addition to working as a troop carrier in many convoys, it had participated in several remarkable events, including the evacuation of Dunkirk, and the transportation of the Bank of England's gold to Canada for safe keeping. It also took a ship load of children from England to Australia to avoid the Blitz – a remarkably happy journey, given the times, when the children came to call the Captain 'Hawkeye' and the ship was given yet another soubriquet; 'The Singing Ship'.

There had also been troubling moments later in the ship's history. With mutinous and defecting crews and officers (including the Captain) at the height of the 'Cold War', the Batory couldn't sail into New York, which was just fine for David and Pam, whose ultimate destination was British Columbia, via Montreal and the CP train across the Prairies and through the Rockies.

So, David was delighted to sail on the MS Batory. He spent time with the officer in charge of what was grandly called 'Passenger Recreation', who was a mine of information about the ship's history and Poland's part during and after the war. In addition to talks on Polish arts and culture, there were movies one wouldn't otherwise generally see – almost, David thought, propaganda about the war on the Eastern Front and Poland's relationship with the USSR. David went to see these without Pamela. Pam wasn't particularly interested in all that; she spent wonderful afternoons soaking up the sun on deck. She was slim and slight, "but perky, withal"

David used to say, who took particular delight in Pam's small but definitely perky breasts. Another one of Pam's arresting features was her glossy blonde hair, which attracted lots of attention on the sun deck, made available for third class travellers. Most of the other loungers there were, to be blunt, dowdy by comparison.

For lunch, David had made "Gramp's Famous Quiche", and they had a bottle of Riesling from one of Vancouver Island's developing wineries (Bennytoo said he couldn't have any, though they let him sniff the cork). After a leisurely meal, Joanie helped David stack the dishwasher, while Ben and Bennytoo watched football on TV. Then they all sat back down around the dining table to talk about 'it'.

Bennytoo made a face, and said, "I hate talking about this – I sort of wish someone would just tell me what's to be done, and then just do it!"

"Sweetie, that's what we all wish," Joanie said as she reached a hand across the table to touch his.

"Yeah," Ben said. "If a doctor just could say 'There's only one thing to do and this is it', this thing would be simpler. But, son, there are alternatives, and we need to talk about them."

Bennytoo sighed, and said, "You guys go ahead; I'll just listen," and he sat back. His father shrugged, and looked at David. David pulled out his notebook, and Bennytoo muttered, "Uh oh, here goes the professor." David looked at his grandson over his glasses, and then began.

"What Chris tells me is that there are three hurdles to getting to be a candidate to donate a kidney, involving three blood tests. First, you need a compatible blood type." He looked at his grandson. "As we now know, yours is blood type 'AB', so you are what is called a 'universal recipient', capable of accepting a kidney from people with virtually any blood type. So, there's a good chance we all will jump that one.

"The second hurdle is what's called 'Compatible Tissue Typing' or 'genetic typing'." – David used his fingers to indicate inverted commas. "Everyone has tissue antigens or markers, and evidently" – David referred to his notes – "there are six important ones, some of which need to match to make the transplant successful; three come from one parent, and three from the other. I don't understand this much, but it's connected to chromosomes and DNA which you inherit from your parents.

"So, it seems that you, Ben and Joanie, would be the best first candidates. I, and of course Pamela, could also be candidates, as well as, of course," – he turned to Ben – "your sister in Australia, but let's keep the discussion to those of us here. Pam's informed consent would, I think, be problematic"– the rest nodded – "but I would want to be seen as a candidate."

David saw the impatient look on his son's face, and said, "No, Ben, I'm told that, although the usual upper age for candidacy is 65, I'm only a bit beyond that, and I'm also told that people of my age are considered on a case by case basis, using the criteria of health and clean living." Ben snorted and David laughed, then said, "Well, let's keep my name on the list for the moment."

"Anyway, those who jump the first two hurdles then have a final blood test called cross-matching, and some other tests, like general health tests, to assure the donor's suitability. But they only do that one if the candidate has successfully got through the first two tests.

"So, I think we should all agree that Ben, Joanie and I will be tested for blood type compatibility and compatible tissue typing. Then we will know what we have to work with."

Bennytoo suddenly blurted; "Gramps, do I get a say here?"

"Huh – so much for 'just listening'," David grinned. "Go ahead."

"I just don't think it's such a good idea to sort of inherit an old guy's kidney – won't it be, like worn out?"

"Hey, son," Joanie glowered at him. "Watch it."

"Well, I'm just saying."

David raised a hand. "Actually, I think you also have to consider the other candidates in the room. The expectation is that your mum or your dad would have to live with only one kidney for, what, forty or fifty years, while I, the 'old guy' as you call it, would probably only be living with one kidney for, say, half that time at best, so maybe that's a better option."

Bennytoo shrugged.

David smiled at him and closed his notebook. "I'll take that as a 'yes', so at least let's keep me on the list, and we'll all do the first two blood tests."

As everybody nodded agreement, David glanced at his watch. "I'm going to kick you guys out. I'm on duty for Evensong, and we're back on the fall schedule for four o'clock."

"Why do they call it 'Evensong' when it's not in the evening," muttered Bennytoo belligerently.

Joanie stood up. "Come on, everyone, let's go so that Gramps can do his thing."

As the family got up to leave, and David went to get a sweater, Bennytoo muttered, "Religion is for losers." Ben glared at his son, then glanced back at David, hoping he hadn't heard. At the car, Ben said, "Son, I know you're under a lot of pressure, but I absolutely will not put up with that sort of behaviour. I hope Grandpa didn't hear what you said."

As things turned out, it became apparent that David had heard Bennytoo's comment.

David arranged, through Chris, for the selection process to begin, which included interacting with the Kidney Foundation of Canada. Eventually they all, Ben, Joanie, David, and, of course, Bennytoo, had their first and second blood tests. Everyone qualified as to blood type, which was pretty easy as Bennytoo was a universal recipient.

When the second test results arrived, Chris called David, and said, "Come on over, and maybe bring some of that fine single malt you have hidden away there."

"Uh oh, does that mean bad news?"

"Just come on over, and we'll talk.'

So, David took his last bottle of Glenfiddich 12, and walked over to the Medical School.

He knew something was afoot the moment he walked into Chris' office.

"What's the problem, my friend?" David sat and poured two stiff shots of scotch into the glasses on the table. "You're looking a bit tense – don't any of us qualify?" He waved the bottle, as if it might solve the problem.

"No, it's not that – there are a couple of good matches."

"So, then, what?" David asked as he set the bottle gently down.

"David, I don't know how to say this, other than to give it to you straight. The tissue typing shows that you don't qualify as a kidney donor; and also" – he paused – "that Bennytoo isn't your grandson – biologically, that is."

David gaped at him.

"Bennytoo's chromosome configuration isn't compatible with yours, which means that your DNA doesn't show up in Bennytoo."

David sat stunned. "You mean Ben isn't his dad?"

"No, no. Because we did the blood tests for all of you, I can tell you that Ben is definitely Bennytoo's father, but your DNA doesn't show up in either of them."

"I'm confused," David muttered.

Chris put a hand on his friend's shoulder, and said softly, "It means that you aren't Ben's father."

After a minute, David got up, and muttered, "I think I'll leave now," and he blundered out the door.

Early the next morning, having wrestled with this revelation through the night, David decided the family had experienced enough of mystery. He called the man he knew as his son.

"Are you free for coffee sometime today?"

"Sure; something tells me you must have the results. How about the cafeteria about ten thirty? I can get away from a staff meeting early."

"Actually, why don't you come over to my office instead. I'll make the coffee there."

"Huh. That sounds ominous. I'll pick up some donuts on the way."

In addition to his desk, David's office had a couple of armchairs and a coffee table in the window. They sat balancing donuts for a minute. Then David grunted and spoke.

"Chris told me about the results, and there are matches which mean we can start on the next step."

"That's good," Ben smiled at his father, who, he thought, was looking tired.

"But – " David leaned across and touched his son's arm, an unusual gesture for David, which unnerved Ben; "I need to tell you something else." David got up and stood looking out of the window. "The second blood test checks for compatible chromosomes, and what they tell us is that I'm – I'm not your father – your biological father."

Ben jerked up and stared at David. "Huh? What are you talking about?"

"Just that. Someone else is your father – not me."

Ben stood up, towering over David. "That's ridiculous."

"Well, tell Chris that. He's definite." David looked up at the big man standing before him and suddenly experienced a surge of conviction. *He doesn't sound like me or even look like me.*

"So – am I adopted, and no-one told me?" Ben's voice shook.

"No, no, I promise you it's not that; I'm as much in the dark as you are. But, you know, son, you and Bennytoo both look so different from me, and, for that matter, from your sister, that I have sometimes wondered how that could be. And now, with your mother being stuck in the care home and basically with limited communication ability, perhaps we'll never know what on earth this is all about." David sat down in the chair opposite the man he called his son.

Ben sat slumped over as if he had been punched in the stomach. Then he quietly said, "Dad, I need to go – I need to find something."

David watched with bewilderment as Ben got up and, without another word, left David's office.

Ben went looking for something his mother had given him, the day after he and Joanie told his mum and dad that they were engaged to be married. He figured it must be in the top left hand drawer of the desk in his study at home, along with his degree certification, his high school diploma, his college employment records, a letter – his one and only love letter – from Joanie, and his army discharge papers. He hadn't looked for it for years, but finally located it at the bottom of the pile of documents.

"I want you to keep this safe," his mother had said, handing it to him with both her hands, as if entrusting him with a priceless gift. It was an envelope, on which she had written, in her elegant handwriting;

Ben, as you embark on married life, I need to give you this. You are not to open it until either your father has died, or there is a family situation where you, in your wisdom, believe that our family or a member of it is in a life-threatening or life-challenging situation. I trust you in this, and how you will deal with the letter inside. Your loving mother.

At the time, Ben had thought his mother was being almost ridiculously dramatic, but she had been in one of her moods since he and Joanie had announced their engagement the day before, so he felt it best to go along with the whole thing. "OK, Mum; does Dad know about this?" was all he had asked, and she had simply said, "No". Ben had thought this was frustrating and enigmatic, but he had taken the envelope and had, now for over twenty years, kept his word. But now, he figured, not only did he have a son whose survival depended on a family decision, but also there was a situation which went to the very root of the family's well-being.

It was time.

Ben sat at his desk and opened the envelope. There were two folded pages with writing on both sides. It was dated June, 1994. Ben looked at the calendar on his desk. *That's nearly twenty one years ago.*

His mother's beautiful script stared up at him. He took a breath and started to read.

My dearest Ben;

As I've written on the envelope, I don't want you to read this letter until either my darling David has died (what an awful thought!) or some situation has arisen where the health or welfare of our family or a member of it is in mortal danger. You will know what I mean if and when it happens, and I trust you on this.

As you know, you are so different from your father and also from your sister, not only to look at, but also, I think, from your view of life. As to your looks, you are a big, strong man with striking features, while your dad and your sister are slim and willowy, as, still, am I, I like to think. And you have an 'I'll take life as it comes' approach to life, while all the rest of us in the Youngman family are more questioning – perhaps more introspective.

*The fact of the matter is (*Ben grimaced at this when he read it – it had been one of Mum's favourite phrases), *and I don't know how else to write this; you are not David's son. I have never ever told him or anyone else this. The fact that I have kept it a secret has troubled me almost as much as what happened has been a tribulation for me. I'm going to set out here what happened.*

When David and I were coming to Canada in June, 1969, we came from Southampton on the Polish ship, the Batory which started from Gdansk or Gdynia – I can't remember which – perhaps they are the same. I heard later that it was one of the last Trans-Atlantic trips that ship did, as most English people were by then emigrating to Canada by plane. Anyway, it was cheap, going from Southampton rather than Liverpool, which was convenient for us, and went to Montreal. And we could bring two big trunks of all we owned with us.

One evening, David went to see a movie in the theatre they had. I think the director of passenger entertainment, a very persuasive fellow, had asked us to go, but it was something about the Russians winning the war against the Germans on the eastern front, and I didn't want to go. So, after supper, David went off and I went to the gift shop and got talking to one of the people there, who showed me a beautiful diamond necklace. I think they all thought we were rich, even though we were in one of the cheap 'below the water line' cabins. I had one of my prettiest dresses on; one was expected to 'dress for dinner'.

One of the officers who I had talked to before – I never did get his real name, he said I could call him Ivan, and laughed 'Ivan the Terrible' – anyway he said come and have a drink next door. I said I didn't drink, but he said that's OK, we have that US stuff, coca-cola. I felt it would be rude to say no, so we went into a room by the gift shop which was set up as a sort of sitting room. He poured me a coke, and then closed the door.

I really don't remember much of what happened next, but I do know that when I sort of woke up I was alone and lying on the big chesterfield. I realised that I had been 'molested' is the politest word I can think of. I was terrified and felt desperately alone. I put my clothes right and grabbed my bag and went to the purser's office, feeling very shaky and giddy. I said I wanted to see someone in charge, and suddenly this Ivan man came out and before I could do anything he said that there had been a theft from the gift shop and demanded to see in my bag. When he opened it, there was the diamond necklace. He took it and said to me that if I made any trouble he would report me to the Canadian authorities when we got to Montreal, and we would be deported back to England. Then he walked away. Feeling like I was going to be sick I went to our cabin, washed myself clean and collapsed into the lower bunk. When David came in I pretended to be asleep, and didn't tell him. I never have told David.

I had always taken precautions when sleeping with David, so when we arrived in Vancouver two weeks later and I found I was pregnant I knew it wasn't David. I told him it must have been when we had made love one afternoon and I had forgotten to use my diaphragm. I'm not sure if he has wondered, especially as you have grown to look so different than the rest of us. But he has never questioned me about it. You will probably find that, in life, there are things well left alone, even between married couples. Maybe that's the way marriages work best. It certainly has been, and still is, for us.

If you ever read this, you need to know that I'm telling you because presumably something has happened which makes it essential that you know. I also believe strongly that your father would love you even if he did know. You are his son in every way that's important.

So, Ben, if your dad is still alive when you read this, I leave it entirely to you to decide whether to tell him about all this. I have loved him, and still do love him, too much to tell him myself. I trust you to make the right decision. Perhaps this family has had enough of secrets.

Your loving mother.

Ben sat looking at his mother's elegant signature for a long time before he picked up the phone to do what he had to do.

He called his dad, or the man he had always, until now, known as his dad, and arranged to see him the following afternoon.

David guided Ben toward the comfortable chairs at the window in his office, where they could watch a watery sunset through the clouds.

"Coffee, or something stronger?"

"Coffee will be fine, thanks, Dad."

David went down the hall to get coffee while Ben sat watching the evening shroud the view.

As David handed him his coffee, Ben said, waving a hand at the chairs, "This spot is becoming something like where truth is revealed, or something."

"Like a confessional?"

"Yeah, I guess."

Pulling papers out of his inside pocket, Ben said, "Dad, you need to read this; read what's written on the envelope first."

When David had read it, he looked at Ben. "Should I read the letter?"

"Yes, Dad."

When David had finished, it was nearly dark in the room. David got up and switched the lights on. Then he said, "Well, that pretty well explains everything."

"Dad, I'm sorry – "

"No, let's not be sorry. Instead, let's get on with what needs to be done."

They got up, and, remarkably for both of them, embraced.

The next day, David and Ben got on with the first of the things they knew needed to be done. It was time for David to make his weekly visit to the care home, and Ben agreed to go with him. Ben was surprised to see his mother looking so much frailer than when he had last visited her over a month ago. "She doesn't seem to want to eat these days," the head nurse had told them at the front desk. "We're keeping an eye on the situation."

When they went into her bedroom, Pamela clutched David's hand as he said, "I've brought Ben with me," and Ben leaned down to kiss her cheek, saying, "Hi, Mum." She reached a hand up and stroked his cheek. "Let's go into the solarium; you like it there," said David, cajolingly.

"Yes, that would be nice." Pamela smiled up at her husband.

She got her cane, and they walked through to the solarium, to their customary place overlooking the gardens, and away from a group on the other side of the room chatting about 'the food in this place'.

She settled into a big wingback chair and watched David and Ben as they sat down on either side of her. It was as if she expected an announcement.

Ben sighed, and pulled the papers out of his pocket.

"Mum, do you remember giving me this envelope and letter just after I told you I was going to marry Joanie?"

Pamela sat and looked at him.

"Mum, you know – I've told you before – that little Benny – your grandson, needs a new kidney. We all had tests done to find out if we could donate a kidney. It's called matching."

Ben looked desperately at David, who gestured to him to go on. Ben stared at the floor.

"The results showed that Dad – my dad, can't help because he doesn't match. And that's because – because he's not my dad."

He glanced up at Pamela, who was sitting very still.

Ben wiped his hand over his face, then continued. "So, Mum, I went to find the envelope you gave me – this envelope, and decided I had to open it. I read it a couple of days ago."

Pamela raised her head and looked steadily at her son.

"Mum, I gave it to – to *my Dad*, for him to read."

And David leaned forward. "And, my darling, I have read it."

There was silence in the room. Then Pamela leaned forward and took Ben's hands into her own.

"Thank you," she whispered. Then she started, softly, to cry.

Those were the only words she uttered.

David got up and, kneeling beside her chair, enfolded his wife in his arms as she wept on his shoulder.

The next task David and Ben had was to decide what to do about Bennytoo.

"We could just not tell him – he's got enough to deal with right now," Ben said. Then, seeing the look on David's face, Ben went on: "but then he'd be the only immediate family member not in the picture, and he'll find out sometime anyway."

So, the next day, Ben and his son called in to see David in his office. Bennytoo was taking the training needed to move from hemodialysis to looking after the dialysis himself. They sat in the Confessional, David and Ben with coffee, Bennytoo with water.

"They keep telling me to drink water, as if that'll do anything; anyway, I am." He told them about what was involved in the training. He was excited about it. "I figure I will be ready to start next week."

"That's great, Buddy," David smiled. "Don't rush it."

"Oh, don't worry – they are *really* picky! But at least the nurse is, well – nice."

Bennytoo coloured a bit, and his father laughed.

"Anyway, enough of flirting around – we have another aspect of this saga to discuss."

"Oh?" Bennytoo stared at his Dad.

After David gestured at him, it was, once again, Ben who took on the task.

"Bennytoo, when we all did the blood tests, we found out something unexpected." He paused, then took a breath. "Gramps here is not my father."

Bennytoo's head jerked up. "You gotta be joking!"

David stepped in. "No, Buddy, we aren't. It's come as a shock to us too, but we – there's actually a letter from your GrannyPam that confirms it."

"Ya mean you didn't know? I mean, there's ways to find out, and, well, you know, we sort of *look* different."

"Well, there wasn't such a thing as DNA testing forty years ago."

"So – so what happened?"

David looked over at Ben, who took over.

"Apparently, according to GrannyPam's letter, she was drugged and attacked by a ship's officer on board the ship when she and Gramps were coming to Canada."

"Didn't she report it or something?"

"They said they would charge her with theft from the gift shop and get her sent home if she made a fuss. And, of course, she didn't know then that she was pregnant."

"Gosh." Then, "Poor GrannyPam."

"Yes; she's been living with this all her life in Canada."

"D'ya think that's why she's like, not well?"

"We think it could well have been the start of it all."

"And you didn't know, Gramps?"

"Not until last week."

"Poor you."

"Does Mum know?"

"Yes," said Ben. "I told her this morning."

The three of them sat staring out of the window. Some people were playing croquet on the lawn.

Suddenly, Bennytoo turned to David. "Well, you're still my Gramps as far as I'm concerned." And he got up and hugged him.

Out in the parking lot, Ben asked David if he would come home for supper, so all three got into Ben's car for the drive back to the family home. As he turned out onto the street, Ben glanced across at David in the passenger seat.

"We need to bring Joanie up to speed; I've told her the basics, and she's worried about Bennytoo getting in a state about all this."

From the back seat, came a snort. "Don't worry about me – you're the ones I worry about – coupla strangers pretending to be related." And they all whooped, and David slapped Ben on the shoulder, and Ben nearly drove off the road laughing.

After supper, Bennytoo went to have a rest, and David, Ben and Joanie sat around the dining table. David looked at the other two.

"I don't know where he gets it from – not from me, evidently." They all chuckled. "But that son of yours is amazing. Underneath all that bravado and nonchalance, there's a perceptive and caring young man."

"Yes," said Ben gruffly, and Joanie pulled out a handkerchief to dab her eyes.

And Bennytoo was to show some more of that as the days went by.

Bennytoo transitioned to peritoneal dialysis, first at the clinic, and then, with the 'nice' nurse in attendance, at home. He was scrupulous about the procedure, and graduated to dealing with it all himself. Somehow, however, things began to deteriorate. Bennytoo seemed to be constantly tired, and there were fluctuations of temperature and blood pressure which worried the doctors. There was talk of his immune system being compromised, which galvanised the process for choosing a family member for a replacement kidney into high gear. It was recommended that Bennytoo not be left alone, and the idea of night nurses was discussed and rejected. The family wanted to do this themselves.

So, Ben, Joanie and David took turns doing night shift. They set up a comfortable easy chair by the bed, and a cot by the wall. They were told they didn't have to stay awake all night; once Bennytoo was asleep they could get some sleep themselves, but to be ready to help if he got restless. They had a little buzzer alarm to awaken them when it was time to help with the dialysis.

After Bennytoo's comment about religion and losers, Ben, still unsure whether David had heard it, said to him, "You don't have to do this, you know," but David said, "Nonsense; I enjoy sitting with him."

So, one evening, sitting by Bennytoo, who wasn't feeling sleepy and wanted to talk, David said, "You know Buddy, I did hear what you said about religion only being for losers."

"Sorry," Bennytoo muttered, sounding sort of contrite, but looking a bit belligerent.

"That's O.K; I've heard worse. What did you mean, anyway?"

It took some prying, but in the end Bennytoo said, "Well, you know, if you look at those things – what are they called, the Beatitudes, well, just look at them; they're all about losers. They bless mourners, meek guys, merciful people, persecuted people – I don't remember all of them – 'poor in spirit', whatever that means – "

"And," interrupted David, "those who hunger for righteousness, peacemakers, and the pure in heart."

"That last one I don't get either. But, Gramps, you see what I mean. Why aren't the *happy* blessed, the *contented* blessed – I don't know, the confident, the achievers, leaders, optimists, people who make a difference in the world or in their lives? The only people blessed are guys who mope around mourning and meeking and mercifulling and hungering and getting persecuted. Why can't religion be also for *winners* instead of just for *losers*!"

"Well," David tried not to sound lecturish, "I figure I'm blessed, and I also figure I'm a winner, if by that you mean a happy – a contented person."

"Even with GrannyPam the way she is?"

"Yes, even with that."

Then, carefully, David said, "Do you think you're blessed?"

Bennytoo stared at him. "I dunno."

"Well, I do. I think you are blessed. You left out one of the big ones that I like to add. Blessed are the courageous. You are blessed with courage."

"You're crazy, Gramps. I – I'm *scared shitless.*" His voice quavered.

Although David didn't flinch at the words, Bennytoo breathed, "Sorry about that."

"Courage and being scared aren't mutually incompatible, Buddy. Any front-line soldier will tell you that. There's all sorts of examples of soldiers being scared shitless, as you say, but yet having the courage to stay on task, however terrifying. Think of the firemen in the Twin Towers on 9/11. And that's what you're doing. We're all scared for you, Buddy, but it's you who's showing the courage to face this." David paused, then said gently, "And I, for one, think the courage you have is God's blessing; you are blessed by God with the courage you need to deal with this."

In the days that followed, Bennytoo's health began to spiral down almost out of control. He would unexpectedly throw up, and, although he complained of tiredness, he was having trouble sleeping because of pain. He was becoming so weak that he went from using a cane to needing a wheelchair. Chris started pushing the medical system to speed up the selection process.

Ben and Joanie had already had their third blood tests done, which was for cross-matching, and they both were found to qualify as potential donors. There had then followed several tests for general health, at the end of which Chris told them they would have to decide which of them should be the donor. "Either one of you would be ideal, so it's up to you."

Ben and Joanie sat in the Confessional with David and Bennytoo, now in his wheelchair.

David led off. "So, how do we decide this?"

They all looked at Bennytoo, who blanched.

"C'mon, you guys, I'm not going to choose – you have to."

So, they did it the old traditional way. David held a toonie in his closed fist, and said to Joanie, "Heads or tails?"

She whispered "Heads", and when David opened his fist, it was tails.

"You lose, Joanie, so, Ben, it's your choice."

"I choose me," he said very quietly.

"I'll let Chris know," murmured David. "They'll want to schedule the surgery as soon as possible."

The next evening, it was David's turn for the night shift. They got Bennytoo finished with his dialysis for the evening, and into bed. He was restless.

Then, out of the blue; "So, what's the difference between christening and baptism?" asked Bennytoo, trying to sound diffident.

Hello, where are we going with this, thought David.

"Well, for many Christians, the two words are interchangeable. Some denominations call it christening, while others call it baptism. Technically, I think, *baptism* is the whole process of anointing with water to welcome someone into the Christian family, including naming that person, while *christening* refers just to the naming part, especially when an infant is being baptised. Of course, with an older candidate, who already has a name, the naming, or christening part is, I think, incidental. So, what happens with a mature person is just baptism."

He paused. "Why do you ask?"

"Oh, nothing." There was a long silence. "Actually, I was thinking of asking about getting baptised." Bennytoo sounded as if he didn't believe what he was saying.

"OK," said David cautiously. "I think I can help with that."

Bennnytoo mumbled, "Thanks, Gramps." Then, hesitantly, "Ya know, I sort of got thinking. When you said I can be scared but have courage at the same time, I don't know where the idea of getting baptised came from. I mean, I don't know whether I'm thinking of doing it because I'm scared, or whether it's part of having the courage to – to sort of help me face it all head on."

"You know, Bennytoo, when I get confused about something, like you are, I pray. And I don't pray for an answer, I just unload the whole thing onto God, and leave it for Him to sort it all out. As I think I've said before, I don't pray for a miracle, I pray for guidance."

"Yeah, but I don't have that."

"What don't you have?"

"Trust in this – this thing called God. In fact, that's one of the problems I've got with this baptism thing. It's gonna look like I'm hedging my bets, you know, like, in case there is one, I'd better, you know – "

"Get right with Him," David smiled.

"Yeah."

"Well, Buddy, if there isn't a god, it doesn't matter, and if there is a god, he won't care why you're doing it, so hedging your bets is fine. And don't you fuss about what others may think. This is for you and you alone to decide."

"Well, I think I want to do it."

So David arranged in a hurry for Bennytoo to be baptised, and it was done quickly and quietly by the local Anglican priest in the chapel the next afternoon. Just the priest, David, Ben, Joanie and, of course, Bennytoo in his wheelchair, were there. Each of them put a hand on his shoulders as the priest poured water on his head and welcomed him into the household of God.

Afterwards, when they were in the parking lot, David said to Bennytoo, "You OK, Buddy?"

And Bennytoo said, "I'm good. I feel good."

The next day was Sunday. Early in the morning, to catch David before church, Bennytoo, using his cell phone, called David and asked him if he would be going to the care home to see GrannyPam sometime soon. David told him that he and Joanie were planning to go that afternoon. Bennytoo asked if he could go with him. So, that afternoon, they loaded the wheelchair into David's van, got Bennytoo into the passenger seat and went.

The three of them sat with Pam in the solarium. Pam was so happy to see Bennytoo that he muttered to David that he should have come to see her earlier.

David, Joanie and Pam had tea, and Bennytoo sipped his water.

Pam said, "It's sad to see you in a wheelchair; I'm the one who should be in a wheelchair."

"It's OK; I don't mind much," Bennytoo said softly.

They told Pam that Bennytoo had been baptised, and she said, "About time."

Then Bennytoo said; "You know, my dad told me about this thing about Gramps not actually being my grandfather. You know, I just wanted to say, he's still my Gramps as far as I'm concerned."

And GrannyPam leaned over and patted his arm. "Of course he is."

"And, you know, I think you're sort of amazing."

"Why?"

"Because you kept it to yourself when it mattered – mattered that you did that – kept it to yourself I mean. But now that *doesn't* matter. So what matters *now* is for you to *know* it doesn't matter. That's what I think, anyway," he mumbled.

David watched his grandson smiling at his grandmother, who fumbled for a lace handkerchief, which she held to her eyes, and found himself praying, *"Praise God, from whom all blessings flow."*

Soon after that, Pam was getting tired, so they got up to go. They walked Pam to her door, and Bennytoo hoisted himself up from the wheelchair, all six foot two of him, and hugged his frail little grandmother. "Love you," he grunted.

David had never before heard him say that to his grandmother.

Something was very wrong with Bennytoo. His vital signs were all over the place; the peritoneal dialysis wasn't working well, and the doctors were talking, not just about going back to hemodialysis, but also moving Bennytoo into the hospital where they could monitor what was going on. The kidney donation/transplant project became a top priority. At the beginning of the last week of July, some shifting of surgery times was done so that they were able to book the next Monday, and Ben and Bennytoo were given a final assessment as to suitability and preparedness. The decision was made to move Bennytoo into the hospital immediately.

On the Wednesday, Ben and Joanie, together with David and Chris, were standing in Bennytoo's room talking about the logistics of moving him, when he characteristically said, "Hey, do I get a say here?"

"Sure, Buddy," said David.

"Well, I kinda like it here, and I hate the hospital – it's so – so stuffy in there. Can't I stay here until Friday? The big day isn't until next week. And you guys can have the pleasure of keeping on helping me with my dialysis."

Bennytoo grinned slyly at them. "You're all a bunch of shit disturbers anyway."

Chris hooted with laughter; "Well, it's clear your sense of humour doesn't need a transplant."

So it was arranged that Bennytoo would be transferred to the hospital on the Friday. A couple of days won't make any difference, the doctors said.

Some time in the early morning hours of Friday, July 31, 2015, six days after his baptism, five days after he had said goodbye to his grandmother, and three days before his scheduled kidney transplant surgery, Bennytoo Youngman, aged nineteen years and eight months, died in his sleep. His mother, Joanie, who was on the night shift that night, had fallen asleep in the easy chair, holding her son's hand. When she was awakened by the buzzer for his dialysis, she found his hand still in hers, now inert. His beautiful body was still warm.

Joanie was beside herself about having fallen asleep, but Chris assured her that Bennytoo would have died anyway. He said that Bennytoo's body just gave up.

But David, who was asked to give the eulogy at the memorial service in the campus chapel, had something different to say. The service was attended by all the Youngman family, including Bennytoo's aunt from Australia, and his grandmother, and many supporters of the Youngman family, both on and off campus.

David told them that Bennytoo's death was his glorious moment of grace. He looked out at the mass of expectant faces, then took a deep breath.

"So, here's the thing. In the last few days of his life, this amazing young man went about letting us all off the hook. I think he knew what was coming. Six days before he died, he got baptised, which was not just because he wanted, as he told me, to hedge his bets, which I told him I thought was fine with God. But I am convinced he also did it to comfort me.

"The next day, Bennytoo said goodbye to his grandmother, and told her he was OK with all we have learned in the last few weeks about the burden she has been carrying by herself all these years. And he told her, with a wisdom beyond his age, that she had done the right thing, and that she should feel good about all that has happened. I think she is immensely relieved by that. I saw her cry with relief. He lifted that burden off her shoulders.

"Then, a couple of days before he died, and here I believe we saw this young man act with full knowledge of what he was doing, Bennytoo took charge – took responsibility - for his final days and where he wanted to be and where he wanted to stay, which was with us – with his family, who loved and cherished him, and who he, for all his nonchalance and offhandedness, loved and cherished back. He didn't want to be in, and didn't want to die in, an institutional hospital bed. He knew what was happening, better than we or the doctors did.

"And then, by his death he took the stress of whether we were making the right decisions – the right choices – off *our* shoulders. And, of course, he has taken away the stress and danger of his dad donating a kidney.

"He has set each of us in the Youngman family free from blame, guilt and responsibility. He has absolved us.

"A few days ago, Bennytoo told me he was scared shitless. I told him that being scared and having courage can be two sides of the same coin. And now this lovely young man, who we will miss more than can be imagined, has shown us the grace of courage and selfless compassion, for which we rejoice.

"That's how to remember and honour him. And that's how we *will* remember him, and honour him."

Casual Day

Wednesday, May 24, 9 am
To: Dave Billings, Office Manager
From: Jason Triggs, Managing Partner
   Dave, please have the attached memo circulated to everyone at TW&B, and put up on the Staff Room noticeboard today. Thanks. Jay.

Wednesday, May 24, 1995
To all TW&B partners, associates, paralegals, legal assistants, articling students and staff.
Re: Casual Day
   As you all know, upon the merger earlier this year of Triggs and Bollinger with Wallis & Co. to form TW&B, we agreed to work diligently on integrating the cultures of the two firms. Two popular traditions at Wallis & Co. were Casual Days, and a monthly Newsletter, neither of which existed at T and B.
   As part of this integration commitment, and upon the recommendation of the Staff Relations Committee, we plan to have the last Friday of each month designated as a 'Casual Day'. Therefore, this Friday, May 26, being the last Friday of the month, will be a Casual Day. Smart, casual attire may be worn in the office. Our thanks to Maria Stella, who heads up our new Paralegal Division, for promoting this idea.

As to a Firm Newsletter, please give me your suggestions for an appropriate name. We hope to have this up and running by the end of next month.
David Billings, Office Manager, on behalf of the Management Committee.

Wednesday, May 24, 5 pm
To: David Billings, Office Manager
And To: The Management Committee
Re: 'Casual Day' Memorandum

I was dismayed to discover the above-referenced memorandum on my desk upon my return from court this afternoon. Decisions which reflect upon the public image of Triggs, Wallis and Bollinger should not be made by the Management Committee or the Office Manager, or, indeed, the Staff Relations Committee. Nor am I aware that Maria Stella is on the Staff Relations Committee. The matter should have been put before the partners at a regular monthly Partnership Meeting. I request that this experiment be cancelled, and that the matter be properly reviewed by the Partnership before any attempt to revive it is made.

I do not have time, in the middle of a demanding trial, to set out at any length my reasons for disapproving this idea. However, I plan to immediately verbally communicate my objections to the Managing Partner.
Edmund Bollinger, QC.
cc. Jason Triggs, Managing Partner

Thursday, May 25, 8:30 am
To: Dave Billings, Office Manager
Re: Casual Day
Dave, yesterday evening I was just leaving the office when I was visited by Edmund about the Casual Day thing. Just continue with it. I'll deal with Bolly.
Jay.

Saturday, May 27, 10 am
To: Jason Triggs, Managing Partner
Re: 'Casual Day'

Jason, my assistant and I have come into the office earlier than usual this Saturday in order that I might dictate and deliver this memorandum to your office prior to the arrival of my clients later this morning to prepare them for their cross-examination on Monday.

I was extremely distressed, upon returning to my office from court yesterday (Friday) at noon, to find that my request with respect to 'Casual Day' had been countermanded or perhaps ignored. I saw not only staff members, but also some associates and even partners, dressed in a manner which I cannot accept as reflective of the fine leadership tradition of Triggs and Bollinger, which I understood would be continued by Triggs, Wallis & Bollinger. I had occasion to usher one of our most influential clients to the elevator during the afternoon, and found it intensely discomforting to have to explain to him why both our receptionists were dressed in what I can only describe as 'sporting attire'.

There is a reason for proper dress at a law firm of our standing in the city. We have always represented the highest of standards at the bar in all categories, and in the community. That other professions may have adopted the practice of 'Casual Fridays' is, I believe, of no relevance. Nor is the fact that Wallis & Co. did so. As I said during the merger discussions, we welcome our friend Stuart Wallis and his people into our firm as a move that is mutually beneficial, but that doesn't mean we need to accept every aspect of his firm's modus vivendi. We need to be guided by our own standards, not by how others behave.

There is plenty of time at weekends, in the evenings, and on holidays, when not in the office, for relaxation and informality. However, when in the office, we should live up to the expectations of our clients in every way, including our mode of dress.

How would it be proposed to deal with the situation when a firm member attends a meeting outside the office at another law firm or elsewhere, particularly when clients are present? We cannot have a partner or any member of our professional staff make a spectacle of himself/herself by attending such a meeting inappropriately attired. I also note that the City Men's Club's premises would presumably be out of bounds for a person so dressed.

I must also express my displeasure at the way this idea has been promoted. It was not appropriate for the Management Committee or our Office Manager to have proceeded without Partnership review. They have assumed responsibilities beyond their purview, and, I fear, you appear to have condoned this.

(I also note, in passing, that this matter confirms what I described at our last Partnership Meeting as the idiocy of our new management structure, involving, as it does at present, a Managing Partner, an Office Manager, a Management Committee, a Staff Relations Committee, and some other committees the names of which escape me at present, all of which seem to be vying with each other for their share of responsibility for the management of Triggs, Wallis & Bollinger. We are, I keep reminding you, a Partnership which, pursuant to the Partnership Act, and our Partnership Agreement, is governed by its Partners through decisions made at Partnership Meetings.)

To my mind, some of our staff are already dressing casually on a regular basis. I must particularly mention what Ms. Maria Stella wore yesterday. Surely 'Jeans' are not acceptable, particularly Jeans with decorative designs which accentuate certain physical features. I believe she should be spoken to.

I would hope that common sense will prevail, and that this experiment will, as should most experiments, be discarded.
Edmund Bollinger, QC

Monday, May 29, 6 pm
To: Edmund Bollinger
Re: Casual Day

Edmund, I confirm that you have again spoken with me this afternoon about the above, and, yes, I have indeed read your May 27 memo. This is not exactly at the top of my to-do list, but I will get to dealing with the matter tomorrow.
Jason.

Tuesday, May 30, 8 am
From: Mylo
To: Amina

Hey, Amina, what's up with Bolly? I went to the courthouse with him yesterday, and he was on a tear. I don't know if it's me or something else's up.
As you can see, I'm in super-early; did you work as hard as this over at Wallis?
M.

Tuesday, May 30, 4 pm
From Jason Triggs, Managing Partner
To: Edmund Bollinger
Re: Casual Day

Edmund, confirming that you and I have discussed this. As you have sent me a detailed memo about it, I need to go on record about the decision I have made.

I polled the other partners about this, and each got a copy of your memo. Justin Wallis and the two partners who came with him on the merger are, of course, in favour of a monthly Casual Day. Of the continuing T and B partners, we know where you and I stand, and Merrill, as usual, is on the fence. The other five (including, I might add, Nancy, whose view, as our only lady partner, is pertinent to this matter) are fine about it, so I see no need to have this hashed out at a Partnership Meeting. I'm sorry you feel so strongly about this, but my decision is to stay with a monthly Casual Day.

I have asked Nancy to have a chat with Maria Stella, though I doubt it will achieve what you seek. After all, it was Maria who promoted the idea, and she tends, as we have already found, to want to make a statement, hence the fancy jeans (which I really didn't think were offensive). Don't forget that Maria's paralegal and operational skills were one of the attributes we welcomed as coming with the merger. Nancy will also generally keep a watchful eye on dress code issues.

Lighten up, Ed – it's harmless, and encourages good office relations.
Jason.

May 30, 5 pm
From: Amina
To: Mylo

Sorry – been busy – Bolly's on a roll. Not you, (or me, I don't think) – he didn't like the Casual Day thing, though he was hardly in the office Friday. I wondered if it was my Kikoy, but then I had to help him Sat. am with a memo to the big cheese about CD, and realized he's uptight about all of it.

Yup, the life of an articling student is all work and not much play. A.

5:05
From M
To A
What's a Kikoy? M.

5:07
To M
A sarong, to you. A.

5:10
To A
While on the subject of CD clothing, what about Maria Stella's sparkly jeans? Nifty! M.

5:11
To M
Hands off Maria – she's older than you think, and anyway, I think she's sort of spoken for around here. A.

5:12
To A
Wadjamean, spoken for? M.

5:20
To M
Maybe just girl talk, but from what I hear, she and Bolly go way back. A.

5:30
To A
Oh! Well, she's a fine looking woman, if you like robust Italians. M.

5:31
To M
Obviously you do! A.

Friday, June 1, 1995, 9:00 am
To: Jason Triggs, Managing Partner
From: Dave Billings, Office Manager
Re: Firm Newsletter

Jason, I have received several suggestions for the name of the projected Firm Newsletter. A couple from those two articling students are unprintable (toilet humour), but here's the shortlist.

TWB Tablet
TWB Advocate
Inside TW&B
TW&B Ledger
Let me know how you would like me to go from here.
Dave.

Monday, June 26, 1995, 5:00 pm
From: Edmund Bollinger
To: Jason Triggs, Managing Partner
And to: David Billings, Office Manager
Re: Board Room for Friday, June 30

I have just returned from Court, having completed the last day of evidence in the bridge collapse case. All counsel agreed to making a joint submission to Judge Palmerston whereby the commencement of closing arguments will be deferred to Thursday, July 6, to take into account the Canada Day long weekend and the fact that some of the counsel involved and/or their clients have July 4 commitments in the US.

The real reason for the deferment of closing arguments is that all counsel are determined to investigate whether all the claims and counterclaims in this complex case can be resolved prior to letting Judge Palmerston loose to determine the resolution of these matters.

To that end, I have arranged for all counsel and their clients to convene for a meeting in our Board Room on Friday, June 30 at 9 am. This timing has been arranged in order to accommodate the plans of the CEO of our client, the Insurer, who plans to fly in on Thursday evening in order to attend. As you will appreciate, millions of dollars are involved, not to mention our fees.

We must be completed by 3 pm, as several participants have other weekend commitments out of town. I therefore request that both the Board Room, and the adjoining Staff Room (needed for a catered lunch) be booked for this important meeting.

Mylo Fleming and Amina Abdullali will be with me in the meetings. They have been of considerable assistance throughout this complicated file.

I am aware that it is planned that Friday, June 30, be a Casual Day. I do not have time to express my concerns about the juxtaposition of these two activities.

Edmund Bollinger, QC.

cc. David Billings, Office Manager. David, could you please get the kitchen staff to arrange for a catered lunch for about a dozen in the Staff Room at about noon – simple sandwiches and soft drinks will do. Thank you. E B.

Tuesday, June 27, 1995, 9:00 am
From: Dave Billings, Office Manager
To: All at TW&B
Re: Casual Day

Just a reminder to all at TW&B that this Friday, June 30, will be our second Casual Day. All are welcome to dress appropriately casually. As an added feature, in view of the Canada Day long weekend, we will have an informal drinks get-together up in the Board Room and the adjoining Staff Room starting at 5 pm. Everyone is welcome.

Please also note that on Friday a meeting with respect to the bridge collapse litigation will take place in the Board Room starting at 9 am. Although expected to be finished by 3 pm at the latest, the Board Room and Staff Room will not be available for the setting up of the bar and laying out of refreshments until 4 pm.

Please respect the importance of this meeting.
Dave.

Wednesday, June 28, 9 am
From: Nancy Blainstay
To: Wendy, Amina, Maria, Fernie, Mabelline, Louisa (have I forgotten anyone?)

Confirming supper this evening at the 4th Street Diner at 6:00 – table in my name.
Nancy.

Wednesday, June 28, 10 am
From: Jason Triggs
To: Stuart Wallis

Stuart, Bolly is still fulminating about Casual Day, and we have the next one this Friday. As an old friend of his, are you able to do anything? I wish he would calm down about it, then he might enjoy it.

I know he has this big conference on Friday morning about the bridge collapse case, including the bigwig from the insurers and counsel for everyone involved, including the city, the contractors and the deceased. They are meant to be done by three.

Perhaps Maria.......?
Thanks.
Jay.

Wednesday, June 28, 3 pm
From Stuart
To Jason

Just back from a delightful and long lunch to see your latest about Bolly and CD. Once he gets a bee in his bonnet there's nothing *we* can do, but I suspect Maria has a plan (as usual). Stay tuned.
Stuart

Wednesday, June 28, about 9 pm

She turned and looked down the side-street. The lights at her brother's restaurant – Ristorante Stella – were still on. *I'll just have a look in.* As she walked to the entrance, the outside lights went off. She tried the handle, but the door was locked. She looked at her watch. *Nine o'clock – he turns them off early to stop any more people coming in.* She peered through the side-window. A couple were at the table by the other window, and then she saw him, by himself, at his usual table for two, near the kitchen door. He was reading something, and a small carafe of wine was beside him. She saw Enio, her nephew, coming out of the kitchen, so she rapped on the window. He came across, looked, and, going over to the front door, opened it and motioned her in.

"Thanks, Enio," she blew a kiss at him, and waved at her brother, Dominic, who was looking out from the kitchen, and he grinned at her. She walked quickly over to the table.

Edmund looked up, then with a little smile, stood – that old world charm – his slim figure erect, and said warmly, "Why, hello, Maria."

"Tesoro", she breathed as she touched his cheek with her fingers. As she unbuttoned her coat, she murmured "Mind if I join you?", and then, without waiting, pulled out the other chair, and seated herself opposite him.

Sitting back down, Edmund said, "Can I get you anything" – just then, Enio placed a Campari and soda on the table, and she smiled her thanks.

"So, where have you been this evening – it's past nine."

"Oh, we had a girl's night out, planning for Casual Friday at the end of this week." She sounded almost gleeful.

"Oh my, what are we in for now?"

"Well, you'll just have to wait and see, won't you?"

"So, am I in trouble for my attitude about Casual Day?"

"I wouldn't say that; it's accepted that you are a traditionalist, and we're not to push the envelope. And, well – "

"Well what?"
"We also talked about relationships."
"Uh-oh! Are we both in trouble, then?"
"I think it was agreed that there are exceptions – "
"That prove the rule."
"Something like that."

Then Maria asked softly, as if changing the subject, though it wasn't, really, "How's Molly?"

"She's as well as can be expected; the doctors say she's as strong as a horse." He paused. "She didn't know who I was, the last time I went to see her."

"You poor man."

"Oh, I don't know about that." He reached out and put a hand on hers. "Some people would say I'm very lucky."

They sat easily, smiling at each other, like a long-married couple. The people at the other table were leaving, and Enio was fussing over their coats. After a while, Maria said, "So, you've been busy."

"Yes, it was a lot of preparation, but worth it in the end."

"Are you going to win?"

"We have a settlement conference set for Friday."

"Yes, I heard."

"They've all got a settlement proposal to think about, well before we start closing arguments. I think they'll take it. None of us trusts the judge to get it right, which raises the spectre of appeals, et cetera. Settlements work well in such situations."

"So, you have the night off, even though I see you've got legal papers there." She gestured at the documents at his elbow. He grinned at her and made a show of picking them up and stuffing them in his briefcase down beside the table.

"There, I'm relaxing. And it's good to see you."

She inclined her head in acceptance. Then, "How's your new assistant working out?"

"Amina? She's good – very smart."

"She'd better be – I like her a lot, but she sure needs brains when she has a face like that."

"Now, Maria, don't be cruel – she had smallpox when she was young – she's originally from Somalia – pretty well the last place in the world where smallpox epidemics occurred."

"Another immigrant success story, like us eye-ties."

"You are incorrigible." They grinned at each other, and lifted their drinks as a toast.

Edmund shifted uncomfortably, and glanced at Maria. "Talking of working hard, you've been stirring things up a bit."

Maria took a sip, and glanced over her glass at him. "Yes – and I'm sorry if you were taken aback by it all. I really do think Casual Days are a way to get everyone to loosen up a bit. It worked well at Wallis."

"I don't know how to fit in to it all." He made a face. "It all just makes me feel uncomfortable."

"Well, I know that, and when you get into the office tomorrow, you'll find a little surprise."

"Maria, what have you done –"

She reached over and touched his hand. "Don't worry, Tesoro, you know I would never embarrass you. It's something you might try for the next Casual Day, which, as you know, is on Friday."

"Hmph." Edmund glowered at her.

"And I'm sorry about the jeans – I understand you don't like them."

"It's not that I don't like them, I find them inappropriate, especially with those designs on your – your rear."

"Oh, so you noticed!"

"One could hardly not! Anyway how did you find out I had a problem with them?"

"We-ell, one of your partners came to talk to me about Casual Day generally, and mentioned them particularly."

"Oh, Nancy – I hope she was considerate."

"Oh, yes – Nancy and I understand each other."

Just then, Dominic came out of the kitchen, and Edmund, looking at his watch, said, "Good heavens; Dominic, I'm sorry." Dominic waved a hand. "No problemo." Edmund put some cash on the table, and left his hand there. Maria put a hand on his and said, "You want I come home with you? It's been a while."

"I have my cleaning lady arriving early in the morning."

"Well, I expect she knows all about us."

"Yes, but I don't want anyone to be – embarrassed, you know. And now that you are in my employ, so to speak" – she grimaced – "we will just have to put up with it. So, thank you, but no."

Maria sighed, and, getting up, turned to put her coat on.

As Edmund got up she moved into him, muttering, "What about getting away soon, say, to New York? We need a time-out-of-time together."

"Well, I think your brother needs an update report on that restaurant on Mulberry Street – what is it – Angelo's?"

She giggled softly and swiftly pecked his cheek.

"Can I drive you home?"

No, that's alright". She glanced quickly at her watch. "If I hurry I can catch the last bus."

Friday, June 30, 3:05
From: Edmund Bollinger, QC.
To: Jason Triggs, Managing Partner
And To: Dave Billings, Office Manager
Re: Settlement Conference.

I am delighted to let you both know that the settlement conference is now completed, and the outcome is extremely satisfactory, both for our client and, I may add, for the firm, both from a financial and a reputational point of view. Despite the efforts of counsel for one of the plaintiffs to snatch defeat from the jaws of victory, the spectre of Judge Palmerston presiding over the fate of all participants finally drove everyone to their senses, and the Settlement Agreement was signed and delivered an hour ago. All that is now needed is to advise Judge Palmerston, who undoubtedly will be pleased not to have to try to get his head around it all.

We have saved our client not only a lot of money, but also the cost of appeals and the establishment of a dangerous legal precedent.

I add that Mylo and Amina were of considerable assistance in this matter.

The Board Room and Staff Room are now, as I write, cleared, so that the arrangements for the after-work refreshments can proceed.

Amina is driving the CEO to the airport, and I am going home to change; I plan to be back by five.
Edmund.

Friday, 5 pm
From Mylo
To Amina

Where are you? Are you coming to drinks – I know you're TT, but you can watch the rest of us!

Saw Bolly leave about 3:30 with a grin on his face and a box under his arm. I wonder! M.

5:05
From A
To M

Just back – took his nibs to the airport, and he somehow got me into the first class lounge for a drink – soda water for me, double scotch for him. Bit of a lech. Going up to the Board Room now. A

5:06
M to A See you there.

About 6:30, Saturday morning, July 1
She was awakened by the early morning light. Turning lazily, she nestled into him, and he stirred.

"Good morning, my Tesoro."

He sighed, and sought her hand. "Morning."

After a while, she whispered, "That was nice."

He arose and went to the bathroom. Returning, he slid back within her arms. "It was the jeans that did it."

She chuckled.

Lifting his head, he looked around the room. "Where are they, anyway?"

"I think they got as far as the top of the stairs."

He sighed. "Yes, that *was* nice." A pause. "Do you want anything? Coffee? Breakfast?"

"Maybe later – it's only six thirty."

"Oh."

"You're happy with yesterday."

"Yes." He yawned comfortably. "The settlement conference went well, once we got counsel for the boy that got killed to understand that a bird in the hand is worth two in the bush, especially when you have Judge Palmerston in charge of the bush," he snickered. "These lawyers that work on contingencies find out after a while that 'take the money and run' is as good a plan for themselves as it is for their client. Mind you, it took into the afternoon before we got there. Everyone else was happy with the proposal by lunch time – by the way the lunch was excellent – I must remember to thank – who is it – oh yes, Louisa."

"Well, there's now also Brian who came over from Wallis – he's a sweet boy."

"The gay kid?"

"Yes, he's got aspirations to be a chef."

"Hmff."

"Now, Edmund, don't be like that. He did the sandwiches and everything."

"Oh, I thought they got caterers."

"Well, that shows you how good Brian is at sandwiches."

Silence. Then, "Well, it was Mylo who got the boy's lawyer to look at a couple of relevant cases about punitive damages that finally got us over the hump. Now *there's* a smart young man."

"And I hear Amina did well."

"She undoubtedly did – she had our stuffy CEO from Toronto eating out of her hand. When she smiles that big white-teeth smile of hers, with the dancing eyes, she has you caught."

"Well, she certainly has Mylo caught."

"Does she? I hadn't noticed."

"Edmund, you're sometimes as blind as a bat."

"Well, in any event, I don't approve of in-firm romances."

She jabbed him in the ribs. "Look who's talking!" and sniggered.

Edmund chuckled, then grunted. "I must say, although they were both – what shall I say – informally dressed, they both looked smart, and, actually not out of place, seeing that the CEO from Toronto wasn't wearing a tie."

"Well, there you go." A pause. "And I thought you looked spiffy in your turtleneck."

"Why won't you tell me where you got it?"

"It's so that I can surprise you with more from there, and" – she punched him lightly on the arm – "also so that you can't return it!"

"Conniver!" He tried to kick her under the sheets, then lay back, grinning.

She laid a hand on his chest. "So, what do you plan to do today – it's the long weekend."

"I was" – he felt for her hand – "I was sort of thinking of making this a casual day."

She snuggled into him and whispered into his ear, "I'm not sure that I'm dressed appropriately for that."

An excerpt from the first issue of INSIDE TW&B

No. 1   **INSIDE TW&B**   July 3

Welcome to our first issue of *Inside TW&B*, and thanks to those who sent in suggestions for the name of this monthly Newsletter, even if some of them were unprintable.

And what better way can there be to start this venture off but to share pictures of the informal drinks party at the end of our second Casual Day. Overleaf you will find a potpourri of pictures, including one of our peerless leaders, Jason Triggs, Stuart Wallis and Edmund Bollinger catching the spirit of the day. Yes, that's Jason in the flowery shirt, Stuart in a sports shirt and sweater, and – the winner! – Edmund (Bolly) Bollinger in slacks and a spectacular navy blue turtleneck. When asked how he came by an article of such sartorial splendor, Bolly smiled and evaded the question in true litigation lawyer style. By the way, the woman with her back to the camera, talking to Nifty Nancy, is Maria 'Stella the Stunner', sporting her now famous 'designer' jeans. Nancy, our only woman partner, raised the tone of the place by looking immaculate in something more appropriate for an evening at the opera, but perhaps that's where she was going.

Another picture shows our articling students, Mylo, originating from T and B, and Amina from Wallis, sharing a laugh with Bolly after a successful conclusion of the bridge collapse negotiations, in which, Bolly said, "they were invaluable".

Then there's one of Louisa, our indefatigable kitchen lady, along with budding chef Brian, holding a Brian concoction which we are told was delectable – it was all gone by the time your reporter got there.

Next, there's the obligatory picture of all the Partners – no, wait, where's Merrill? – oh yes, he was taking the picture.

Finally, there's a shot of the Legal Assistants and the Associates, or 'Partners-in-Waiting', as they like to call themselves; They are all there, of course, as, they claim, they seldom otherwise get a free lunch. My goodness, there's a lot of them; in a democracy they could outvote the Partners! But whoever said a Law Partnership has anything to do with democracy? Just kidding.

Thanks to everyone at TW&B for welcoming Casual Day into our Firm's culture.

My Kid Sister

I hadn't been back in town for much more than an hour, and was making my way down 4th Street to get the keys from the lawyers, when I saw Marilyn walking towards me. *Magical Marilyn.* The old phrase came back immediately. Most women her height would wear low-heeled shoes, but hers took her up another two inches to close to six feet.

"Johnny!" The recognition was genuine, and we hugged enthusiastically. There followed the usual "what are you doing in town; I only just got here; you look wonderful; so do you".

And so she did. Her fully curled blonde hair, still in a somewhat old-fashioned cut, framed her lively face, her eyes bright with pleasure, her mouth as invitingly smiling as ever. She was called 'Magical' for good reason.

I felt the old rush, and my mind went into overdrive trying to work out how I might re-organize my day to include some time with her.

"So what are you doing back in town?" she was saying.

"Well, you know, they finally sent Joe to jail" – she nodded – "I guess the years of defending him against the charges must have cost the family a bucket, so Mrs. Lamon has put the Penthouse up for sale. She wants it sold quickly, and the company asked me to take it on. I'm moving in there right now. It's easier to sell that type of place when it's furnished and lived in." I hesitated. "How would you like to come by and see it in a couple of hours?"

"Well, I've never been in *there.*" She said it as if it was the only residential establishment in town she *hadn't* visited. "I'd love to."

"Wonderful. We can have coffee or a drink or something – you know where it is. Just push 'P' for Penthouse and I'll let you in. It will be like old times." I realized I was sounding hopefully eager.

She gave me that level smile with the steady eyes and murmured "Dear Johnny," leaned to press a cheek against mine, and continued on up 4th Street, perfectly aware that I was watching.

I went to the lawyers' office, collected the keys, picked up the basics at the shopping mall – coffee, wine, sushi etc., and drove to the lakefront where the Lamon Penthouse sprawled across the top of the town's most exclusive high-rise.

Joe Lamon, nicknamed Guiseppe Limone by the press after his connections with the underworld had surfaced, had been the town's most colourful society name. He and Betsy Lamon supported charities, raised money for causes and made their Penthouse available for exclusive soirées.

Two thousand five hundred square feet on one floor contained a ballroom- sized reception atrium, with windows overlooking the lake on one side and with a view of the mountains on the other; all together with a lavish kitchen, library, cloakroom and bathroom. A free-standing spiral stairway led to a musician's gallery which went round three sides overlooking the reception atrium. Leading off the gallery were entrances to the sleeping quarters for Joe and Betsy and a two bedroom suite for guests. It was the most sought after venue for social events in town until Joe got hit with a string of ugly charges, starting with fraud, running through bribery of public officials and other corrupt practices, and culminating with a drug trafficking allegation. Suddenly Joe's Penthouse was off the social list. Joe spent four years and a million dollars fighting the charges in court after court and, last month, finally went to jail for a long time.

The first thing Mrs. Lamon then did was to contact my company to list the Penthouse. Carriage Trade Estate Agents only deals with properties that will interest international clientele. In recent years I had become the company's lead agent for Western Canada. I actually take up residence in a subject-for-sale and market it to an exclusive clientele through contacts the company has around the world, enticing them with a tasteful brochure which never mentions the price.

Betsy Lamon wanted no less than $3.9 million for the place, and agreed to pay a 5% commission plus an extra 0.5% bonus for each month short of 6 months that the sale was completed. Furnishings were extra. If I could sell the Penthouse in the first couple of months, I would, even splitting with the office, do very well. Before flying in, I had already had the brochure prepared and sent to a dozen contacts. Now it was time to get on the phone.

Seeing Marilyn again was going to take my mind off the job. I already had a few personal questions which needed answering. When I left town three years ago, moving to the big city to make my fortune, there had been a farewell party, and I had introduced Marilyn to an old college friend of mine, Fuller, who had just arrived in town. Fuller was a match for her, at least in height, and I thought they'd make an impressive couple. Also he was probably wealthy enough to attend to her tastes. It was less than a year later that I received an invitation from my kid sister, Dollie, to return to town for her wedding to, of all people, Fuller! I flew in between assignments and never got the chance (it was hardly appropriate) to ask Fuller about him and Marilyn.

I was still organizing my clothes in one of the guest suite bedrooms when Marilyn arrived, wearing a beautifully cut navy blue pant suit – rather severe, but accentuating the blonde hair and her carefully made up face, exquisite to the last touch of the pencilled eye brows. I gave her a tour, as I would a prospective purchaser. The décor and furniture reflected Mrs. Lamon's fine taste, and highlighted the qualities of the Penthouse, chief among which were the views. Marilyn stood at the windows of the reception area while I poured two glasses of white wine. I joined her to look at the view, and caught the touch of scent that my mind only associated with Marilyn. She had once told me she had been presented by a 'sweet man' with an amphora of *J'adore* by Dior, and, since then, had never used any other perfume. I realized that I was aroused. She smiled at me and we touched glasses.

"It's good to see you again."

Marilyn always spoke as if she meant what she said, and I think she really was. We sat in the library, chatting comfortably, catching up on three years.

"So," I finally said, "how's the old love life?" trying to sound light.

"Full, Johnny, full," she smiled at me.

"Last time we were together I – ah – I introduced you to Fuller." As I said it, it sounded like a play on words, but she ignored it.

"Yes, I like Fuller, but he wanted marriage and children."

"He sure did. He married my sister within a year or so, and now she's pregnant."

"Yes." She was looking down.

"I was quite surprised."

A pause. "Well, they're happy," she said, glancing over at me.

"And you?"

"And I'm happy for both of them." It sounded like a set response. I got up and, bringing the bottle, topped up her glass and then mine.

After a pause, and as if it explained everything, Marilyn said, "Dollie and I are friends."

"That's good. And Fuller, too?"

"Oh, yes," she looked at me. "We've stayed good friends." She spoke as if she was on more familiar ground now.

"Are you his mistress then?" half joking.

"What an old fashioned word." She brushed a hand down the side of her jacket. "We have sex occasionally."

I stared at her. "Your place or his?" I couldn't imagine why I asked, or why she would answer such a gauche question.

"Mine, usually."

"I shouldn't have asked." I waved a hand as if to dismiss my crudeness.

"And I shouldn't have told you, Johnny, but you're an old friend."

We changed the subject, talked about my job for a while, and watched the sun approach the horizon. Whatever I had felt half an hour ago, when we stood at the window, had evaporated. Marilyn sat relaxed, seeming to await the next move.

"Well, I came here to sell this dump, so I'd better get on the phone to those places in the world where folks are still awake."

"Right," said Marilyn. She smiled at me again, put her glass down and got up. At the door she turned.

"Johnny, you're a good friend; I trust you not to spoil things." She gave me a hug, a pat on the arm, and left.

I had, of course, let Dollie know that I was coming to town, and that I would call her when I was settled in. After an hour of business calls I sat back and, sipping the last of the wine, found myself struggling with how to deal with the situation. Here's an old love, Marilyn, and an old friend, Fuller, cheating on my kid sister.

I took the phone off the desk and sat down with it in the big easy-chair.

"Hi there, pretty sister."

"Hey, Johnnie! Howrya doin?"

"Fine. I'm all settled in. Feel like the Sheik of Kuwait or something. I can see why Betsy Lamon will pay a bonus for a quick sale; one could get used to this place."

Dollie laughed. "She's a good judge of character – especially yours." Her voice sounded tired.

"So, how's the coming event?"

"Everything's fine. At eight months you get really awkward, like you feel you might fall over. I'm not sure where my centre of gravity is right now. But it's all going fine."

"And Fuller?" I ventured.

"He's fine too." Her voice brightened. "He's really excited about the baby. Last weekend he wallpapered the third bedroom we've made into the nursery."

"Fuller wallpapering?" I couldn't visualize it.

"Yes," she laughed. "He's pretty proud of it, though he's got the flowers upside down."

I exploded with a laugh. "This I gotta see."

"Well, come round for supper tomorrow, if your busy schedule will allow."

"Sure will."

The next day, I thought about calling Fuller at his office, but then I got busy on the phone. There was a London banker who wanted to fly over later in the week to have a look at the place, which took some arranging. So, that evening I arrived at Dollie and Fuller's house with a bottle of wine, but no new information to tell me how to behave.

Dollie met me at the door, definitely eight months pregnant.

"You'll have to lean over to kiss me," she said.

"Sure it's not twins?"

"Definitely not. I'm sure it's a boy, though. Come on in. You'll have to drink the wine yourself; Fuller just phoned to say he won't be home for supper."

I looked at her. "Why the hell not? He's an old friend of mine, as well as being my sister's husband – and now a father-to-be."

"He's really sorry, and promises to call you for lunch tomorrow."

I felt oddly relieved as I took my jacket off, got introduced to the dog, was given a quick tour of the house, and opened the wine.

Dollie and I had a wonderful evening. We talked about our parents and looked at photographs. The wedding photos were in a smart white book. Dollie and Fuller looked radiant.

"So, Fuller's everything you wanted?"

Staring down at the wedding pictures, she said softly, "No, not everything, but I love him, and he's very sweet to me. He's as excited as any man can be about the baby." Suddenly she looked up. "Oh, I know what Fuller and I wanted to ask you. Would you be the baby's Godfather?"

"Wow – it's not even born yet."

"Johnny, don't say 'it'. Say 'baby' or 'he'."

"OK. Sorry. Sure – I'd be pleased to be. Who will the Godmother be?"

"I was thinking of asking Marilyn. She and I have become such good friends." She looked over at me.

I stared at Dollie, lost for words.

She reached out and put a hand on my arm. "Oh, I know you were sort of in love with her, but that's a while ago now. Don't – don't you think it will be OK?"

"Oh, sure; that's not a problem. Go ahead, ask her – if you and Fuller want it, that's fine with me." I heard myself rattling on.

Fuller hadn't arrived home by nine, and Dollie was getting tired, so I got up to go to the bathroom before leaving. Walking back toward the front door, I paused and peered into the second bedroom. Its rumpled king-sized bed was clearly in use. And then I caught it – a trace of that unmistakable aroma of *J'adore*.

At the front door, I turned to my sister, and blurted, "What's going on here, Dollie?"

She put a hand on my arm and stared at me steadily, without saying a word.

As I blundered through the door, I turned and muttered urgently, "So, here's the thing. I hope Fuller gets home for supper when you have your baby here. I hope he'll be home when you need him, and – and all that stuff." I couldn't look her in the eye.

Dollie reached up and put her arms around my neck. "Hey, big brother, I know I'm your kid sister and you want to look after me, but I'm alright. I know what I'm doing. I trust you not to spoil things."

When I got back to the Penthouse, there was an offer on the fax machine. It seemed some sheep farmer from Australia wanted to buy the place sight unseen – or at least solely on the basis of the brochure. I got the feeling I was going to get the job done very quickly, and that I would soon be gone. And that made me feel good – very good.

ON YOUR OWN

A couple of weeks after Sally's memorial service, Will signed up to deliver the daily newspaper on a local route. After his retirement, he had been kept busy taking care of her. But, after she had gone, he had been looking for something to do, especially in the mornings. He wasn't sleeping too well, and kept waking up early to stare at the ceiling.

He found out that it involved getting up at five a.m., driving down to where the truck dropped off bundles of newspapers, and then sorting and delivering on his designated route, starting no later than six. He walked the circuit one day with Chuck, the fellow who was quitting the job to go away to college. He showed him how to sort the newspapers – about 50 copies, into different piles to fit with his delivery schedule. The houses and duplexes he was to deliver to were ranged over six blocks, with non-subscribers between. He could park his car in the supermarket parking lot and walk up one side of the street with the big canvas bag, and back down the other side; then go back to the car to pick up another pile to cover the next section; and finally drive to the other end of the route and walk the final section. None of the driveways were long, and the front doors were easily accessible. The bigger houses with longer driveways were at the end of the route. Chuck told him he had it down to just over an hour unless the weather was bad.

"You have to be done by seven, or the guy in number 3315 complains, and then you get shit from head office."

Will figured he knew about that sort of thing. When he was a teenager, he had earned his first money delivering newspapers before going off to school. He had needed the independence his own money brought him.

Now, Will didn't really require the extra money; the car was paid off, and he had a reasonable pension from his career at the bank. Nevertheless, he figured that it would be nice to make enough money to cover the taxes and utilities. Although the house seemed big and sort of hollow with Sally gone, he didn't want to move – at least not yet.

Sally hadn't actually been her name; it was Selina. But she was known to everyone as Sally. Will remembered being confused when he first met her at the bank, where he had started as a junior teller. He had been helping her to open an account and she told him her name was 'Sally Glover', but her ID showed her name as 'Selina'.

"How are you going to sign cheques?"

"Sally Glover". She said it as if that was obvious.

"Well, what name shall we print on the cheques?"

"How about just 'S. Glover'?" She smiled winningly at him, which was the beginning of his downfall.

'Will' wasn't actually *his* name either. He had been named 'Wilbur' by his parents, but who gets safely through school with *that* name? So, he called himself 'Will", and was stuck with it throughout his life.

Will decided he could do the paper route easily despite the fact that he had reached his seventies. He was a walker from way back. Until she got sick, Sally and he had owned a succession of rescue dogs which demanded exercise. Also he was an early riser, or at least an early *waker*. In the glory days of their marriage, their favourite time for lovemaking had been in the early morning hours – delicious and leisurely lovemaking. It was in those times that

Will would murmur her real name, "Selina", drawing the second syllable out as he gently stroked her awake.

It was when she started to reject him, batting his hand away in the pre-dawn dusk, that Will began to accept how ill she was. Her malignant brain tumour had been giving her excruciating headaches, and, due to its position, was inoperable. It would, in time, kill her. Will was shown how to do injections of Toradol solution to ease the pain, so that they didn't have to keep calling a nurse in.

Sally's memorial service wasn't held until a couple of months after she died. Will found he measured his time alone from the date of the service, rather than from the time of her death, even though he had certainly been alone and very lonely during that confusing time. He had kept hoping against hope that she would be found alive. The other problem was that even when she was found, her exact date of death was not known. She had disappeared from home on July 10th, but her remains weren't found until over a month later. A logger slogging through the woods beyond the hills to the north of the town had come across her, or what was left of her, while doing a survey in preparation for clearcutting.

It appeared that Sally had deliberately taken steps to make herself difficult to find. She had parked her little old Volkswagen in the parking lot near the coast trail, so that volunteer searchers concentrated on that area, and combed every inch of the trail and the beach it connected to. But it seemed she had then gone, presumably by bus, to the ski hill north of the town, and had then trekked miles into the forest, where she buried herself under fallen branches and undergrowth. It was not possible, from the state of her remains, to tell if she had been assaulted in any way, other than by animals and insects. They also found, next to her remains, an empty pill bottle with the label torn off.

Some months before 'all that', as Will found himself calling it to himself, he had been going through old phone bills before chucking them, and noticed that, in one month, there had been a flurry of long distance charges he didn't recognize. He asked Sally about them and, after first denying any knowledge of them, she confessed that she had been in touch with The Right to Die Network of Canada. They had been cautious about it, but, in the end, they gave her the contact information for Evelyn Martens, the woman some called a 'Death Zealot'. Sally admitted that she had been in contact with the Network and Ms. Martens a number of times.

Sally didn't want to talk about it, but Will had then done a bit of research online, and found that Martens lived on Vancouver Island, as did Will and Sally, but down near Victoria. A couple of years before, in 2004, she had been charged with assisting some people with their suicide. That, of course, was illegal – actually, he learned, it was still a crime. There had been an earlier case about a Victoria woman named Sue Rodriguez where the courts had failed to find the criminal laws about assisted suicide unconstitutional. Evidently Martens had since then been working for the Right to Die Network for years. Nevertheless, a sympathetic jury found Martens not guilty.

Will had confronted Sally about this.

"How could you have done this behind my back? You know how much I love you, and would do anything to help you."

Sally sighed. "Will, I just didn't want to get you involved in something criminal. Anyway, it doesn't matter now. Ms. Martens told me the trial had exhausted her, and that when she found how she had been investigated by a police undercover operation, it had upset her. She told me she didn't have anything more to do with the Right to Die Network. She basically told me I was on my own, and wished me luck."

After her body was found, it came to Will like a thunderclap that Sally had deliberately made it difficult for him, or anyone for that matter, to find her when she disappeared, so that no-one could be accused of assisting her. She was, as Evelyn Martens said, 'on her own', and had to be.

So, with his paper route job, when he awakened in the shifting glint of early dawn, instead of lying absorbed in grief, Will could walk the streets as he used to when he was a schoolboy, lobbing the paper so that it would land just by the door, or cramming it into a box if there was one. He didn't generally meet anyone that early, and didn't expect to, except, occasionally, a couple of really early dog-walkers. He figured that both the walkers and the dogs were doing their duty before the owner went off to work.

It was during his second week on the job that Will met Judy, though he didn't know her name at first.

It was 6:45 a.m., and Will was very nearly at the end of his route, where the houses were a bit more upscale, and the driveways a bit longer. Just as he was about to underarm the paper towards a red-painted door, it opened. A little woman in a dressing gown and a mess of white hair stood in the doorway holding a marmalade cat.

"Oops!" she said, grinning at him; "I was just putting the cat out." She bent and dropped the cat, which sat and stared at Will.

Will walked to the door and handed her the paper. "Just in time for this."

"And personal delivery, I see." She looked at him. "You're new, I think."

"Yes, Chuck ran off to college, so we old guys have to take up the slack." She chuckled, and the cat delicately began to wash its face with an elegant paw.

"What's the cat's name?"

"Magnificat, or Maggie for short."

"She's beautiful."

"Actually he's a *he.*"

"But I thought you said her – *its* – name is Maggie."

"Yes, but that's short for Magnificat." She spoke as if that explained everything.

Will looked bewildered at this logic.

Then came a sound from inside the house – a strangled sort of moan; "Juuudie."

"Coming," called the woman. "I have to go," she said as she started to close the door. "Good to meet you."

Will raised his hand and did a little salute. "And I must be on my way before one of your neighbours files a late delivery complaint."

So that was it. Or so Will thought at the time.

A week later, Will was hobnobbing with a couple of old friends at the branch where he used to work, and telling them about his new job. It was mid-afternoon, and the bank wasn't busy. He could have used the ATM machine to deposit his paper route cheque, but he liked 'fraternizing', as the new guy in the corner office (Will's old office) called it. So he would go to the counter if he recognized who was on duty. He was just saying goodbye when someone pushed the automatic door opener from outside, and through it, sitting erect in a wheelchair, came a gaunt man with fraying hair and blazing blue eyes. It was being pushed by a little woman wearing a red hat which was trying unsuccessfully to control her abundant white hair. The wheelchair wheels caught on the lip of the door, and Will went to help, but the woman yanked at the handles and, puffing, got the wheelchair through.

She pushed it to the counter, where the teller leaned over and said, "Good afternoon, Mr. and Mrs. Benjamin."

As Will stepped away, the woman looked across at him and said, "Why, there's the paper boy!" and Will and the teller laughed. She turned to the seated man and said, "Darling, this is our new newspaper deliverer that I told you about."

"Preezed tu mee yu," the man monotoned. "Mi namz Barri."

Will looked at the woman. "He says he's pleased to meet you, and that his name is Barrie." She was completely calm and straightforward about having to help with the introduction. "And my name's Judy." She held out her hand, and Will shook it.

"I'm Will."

"Hello, Will; don't go for a moment – we won't be long."

My goodness, thought Will; *she certainly is in control of everything.*

Will stepped back to near the door, and watched as the two dealt with some simple bank transactions that they could have done at the ATM, depositing some cheques and withdrawing some money – quite a lot of money, Will noticed. He watched as the teller came round the counter with two pieces of paper and a pen. Judy unclipped a table from the wheelchair's armrest and folded it down; the teller put the papers and the pen on the little table, and Barrie maneuvered the pen into his hand and scrawled a shaky signature on the papers.

The bank clerk looked at the signatures and said, "Barrimore Benjamin – that looks fine, sir. Thanks for coming in."

Will thought; *there isn't a single person I can think of right now who uses his or her actual name: Selina was Sally; I, Wilbur, am Will; Magnificat is Maggie; Barrimore is Barrie, and I wonder who Judy really is.*

Then there were thanks all round, and Judy turned the wheelchair to head for Will. "Barrie likes to do his own banking," she said with fondness. "He still has the use of his right arm and hand."

They exited the bank, Will helping with the door, and stood on the sidewalk in the sun.

"Can I help you – where are you going – home?"

"Oh, thanks, we're fine; we have a fabulous van with a lift, and everything's mechanized. Barrie works the buttons." Will could see that she was proud of him.

"Espain" muttered Barrie.

"Barrie wants me to explain to you that he has ALS – you know, the same that Stephen Hawking has."

"We-ere chintreth sphirihs."

Will leaned in. "I think I got it – we are kindred spirits?"

"Yes! Amazing! You are amazing!"

Will saw Barrie nodding and contorting his face with what Will took to be a smile.

"But what I really wanted to say is that Barrie is so grateful that you are such a punctual newspaper deliverer. The paper is really for him. He doesn't sleep very well, you see, so we have developed the habit of me reading parts of the newspaper to him at seven each morning while he drinks his breakfast. The previous young man – Chuck, wasn't it? – was not very prompt, I'm afraid, and sometimes missed us out altogether. I wondered if, being at the end of the route meant that sometimes he ran out of papers!"

"Well, thank you. Judy, I'm happy to help."

"Well, we must be on our way; the van is just round the corner. We're off to the supermarket to do our weekly shopping. I'm glad we bumped into you."

"Me, too." Will leaned down to say goodbye to Barrie, then suddenly straightened, and looked over Barrie's head at Judy.

"You know, why – why don't I read the paper to Barrie? I can be at your place before seven, and I don't have anything else to do – my wife died a few months ago you see. And it would give you a bit of respite." He was rambling.

Judy gazed at him. "What a wonderful idea. Let's try it for a while."

Barrie smiled his crooked smile and waved his good arm, and Will did his little salute. *I think I'm going to enjoy getting to know this guy*, Will thought.

So, Will took on the responsibility of reading the newspaper to Barrie. He got up at five so that he could finish his round by about 6:45, and was usually able to get to the Benjamin home before 7 am.

On his second visit to the house, Judy showed him round the downstairs; "We don't use the upstairs bedroom now. We could have installed one of those chair lifts up the stairs – you see ads about them on TV – but there was already a downstairs bathroom, and it was easy to change part of the downstairs into a bedroom. It used to be my studio for my painting." Will though she sounded a bit wistful about that.

Fortified by Judy with a cup of coffee and one of her scrumptious muffins – the cranberry ones became his favourite – Will would unfold the paper and settle into a deep armchair by 'Benjie', his special nickname he came to call him ("a privilege not accorded to many", Judy told him). He would quickly scan the front section while biting into the muffin. "Yur machin mi djool", Barrie would mutter, he being now restricted to liquids due to his inability to swallow any solids. Will would start with the day's political shenanigans, followed by the editorials, op-eds, and letters to the editor. Then he would scour around for the more lurid bits; *Couple accused of kidnapping teenager*, and *Protesters bare all to illustrate their point*, so that it wasn't all doom and gloom.

Will soon caught on to how Barrie would signal approbation or condemnation, and what it was that interested him (anything political or scientific) and what bored him (sports and horoscopes). They developed a sort of shorthand understood by just the two of them, which so bonded them that they became, and called each other, 'best buddies'.

Will would leave the house at nine, when the in-home care people arrived to give Barrie a "wash and brush up" they cheerfully called it. They had installed a hoist to help them get Barrie in and out of bed, and to get him bathed, dressed and into his wheelchair.

Barrie was a bit fixated on Stephen Hawking, so Will scoured not only the daily news but also the internet for articles and stories about him, and would read them to Barrie. Barrie said, more than once that he wished he had available to him "orl zhat teshnoroghy Orchin has," – "all that technology Hawking has," Judy translated.

Inevitably, Barrie's illness inexorably progressed. Will watched as, almost weekly, his friend's ability to use his right arm was declining, so that it came to the point that he could no longer use the button board he relied on to manage his equipment. His speech relentlessly deteriorated, so Will and Judy were resorting to wild guesses about what he was trying to say, which frustrated them and irritated Barrie. Clearly, Barrie's brain was still firing on all cylinders, which made the progressive collapse of his physical abilities all the more infuriating for him. It was also becoming exhausting for Judy, and Will found himself helping more and more around the house. Judy had to increase the in-home care yet again. Wonderful as the caregivers were, there was still lots left to be looked after by Judy, and the strain was taking its toll.

Will began dropping by in the afternoons to keep an eye on Barrie while Judy had an afternoon nap on the couch. He would read Barrie internet stuff about the fractious state of world politics. After a while, Judy would rouse herself and make tea, which she and Will drank sitting in the kitchen. Barrie would be propped up in his wheelchair, Magnificat curled on his lap, in front of the television in the next room. He had taken to watching some of the more ridiculous daytime soaps, and could be heard snorting with disgust or amusement — they both sounded the same. Will had become comfortable enough with Judy to tell her about his final months with Sally, and Judy confided to Will some of her difficulties with Barrie.

Their outings by van were becoming more complicated to organize, and tiring for them both. Barrie had not only had to give up doing his banking, as he had lost his ability to sign, but also motoring around the supermarket in his wheelchair. Even getting through the French doors into the garden was a challenge. Barrie was becoming virtually housebound, which depressed him.

The three of them discussed, more than once, getting Barrie moved to a full-care facility, but these discussions agitated him. "We ca affor i – ge mor hel". "Yes, darling we can afford it, and we can get more help, but," – she put a hand on his arm, — "even more help isn't going to work for long."

When he thought about it in retrospect, Will realized that he probably should have seen it coming. One morning, the three of them were together, Judy feeding Barrie his liquid breakfast, when

Judy said, trying to make it sound casual, "Will, do you have any experience with injecting people?"

"As a matter of fact, I do. When Sally was going through lots of pain, I was shown how to give her pain-killer injections. I did them regularly for a while." He sat quietly, thinking about his Selina.

Then he heard Judy almost whisper; "Barrie and I've been talking about it – an injection to, you know, bring all this to an end."

Will looked at Barrie, who he saw was watching him. Barrie twisted his face into that comical grin of his. Will knew, from that smile, that Barrie was telling him he was OK with this conversation.

"But I would need help," he heard Judy say. "I don't know how to do it safely – or properly, I think I mean. And I can't go somewhere and learn how to do it. People would ask why."

"You know it's illegal – criminal, actually. People have been charged and sent to jail for doing what you're talking about."

"Yes, we know that," Judy breathed, and Barrie grunted an acknowledgement. She swallowed and continued.

"The last time we went to see Doctor Joe – you know him?" Will nodded; everyone in town knew Doctor Joe. "We talked to him about it, and, you know, he's a sweet man, but he said he couldn't help. He said it wasn't only illegal but also completely against his professional ethics, and that he shouldn't even be talking to us about it because he could be said to be counselling us about it."

"So, you see, we're on our own."

Will stared at her. "That sounds familiar."

They sat for a while, then Judy said; "So, we will understand if you don't want to do this – get involved, I mean."

Will got up. "Let me think about it." He laid a hand on his dear friend Benjie's shoulder, and left.

As he was driving home he suddenly remembered. "You're on your own." That woman – what was her name – Martin or Martins or something like that – had said that to Sally, and look what it made her do – made her creep away from him, hide her tracks and bury herself in the forest with a pill bottle so that he wouldn't – *couldn't* help her. He had been prevented by the law from being with Sally – his own wife, for goodness' sake, when she needed him more than any time in their life together. It was barbaric. He wasn't going to let it happen to again, if he had anything to do with it.

He thought about trying to contact that MP Svend Robinson who he had heard was trying to get the law changed. But then he remembered that Robinson was no longer an MP, and he didn't know how to do that anyway.

So, the next day, he told Judy, "Whenever you guys are ready."

He worried about the fact, not so much that it was technically a crime, but more that he, and, he supposed, Judy, could be charged and found guilty and sent to prison. He remembered that some anonymous doctor had helped Sue Rodriguez to die, and got away with it, or perhaps the police just didn't have the heart to chase him or her down.

Will never knew, and never asked, how or when Judy got the necessary drugs, which he understood to be a mixture of a barbiturate and a paralytic. But he did know how she got the necessary paraphernalia – the injection equipment. It was he, Will, who had rooted around in his bathroom cupboard at home, and found what he had used when helping Sally with her pain. He handed it to Judy and instructed her about how to use the syringe to draw the drug from the vial. One day Judy had muttered something about being able to find anything you want online, even how much to administer, but he didn't know when, or how, or where the drugs came from.

All he knew was that, one day, when Will had finished reading the newspaper to Barrie, and Judy was feeding him his breakfast, she said to Barrie, with infinite kindness in her voice, "Ready when you are, my love." Barrie gave her his maniacal grin of acknowledgement – pretty well the only communication tool left to him.

So, one morning soon after that, Will finished reading the newspaper to his buddy as he lay unblinking in his bed, and, glancing up, saw Barrie staring at him with his cockeyed grin. He looked over at Judy and saw that she was standing there with the equipment.

Will was totally calm about it, and Judy helped. It was all over in a few minutes. Will took the paraphernalia and the left over medication, put it in a bag and took it to his car. "I'll deal with these," he told Judy.

Judy made a phone call and Doctor Joe came. He saw that there had been an injection. He stared at the two of them for a while, then rummaged in his bag and pulled out some papers. He sat at Judy's desk and filled out the form, certifying the cause of death as ALS, dated and signed it, and left without a word spoken.

Will helped Judy with the funeral arrangements; he knew a bit about that sort of thing.

He watched her during those following days. She was, as usual, competent and composed, but also, it seemed to him, quietly happy. She was, she said, weary, but relieved. She told him that the most difficult part of the last few months had been that Barrie had become to her just a patient that it was her job to look after, rather than a husband to cherish. She said she had felt a bit guilty feeling that way, "but now I don't have to feel that any more, now that I'm on my own."

After the funeral, Will just stopped going to their – now *her* – home after his paper delivery route was done. And, of course, he had no reason to go round for afternoon tea any more.

He cautiously thought about whether Judy wanted to see more of him, and found that he didn't know what he would do about it if she did. Then, one day, the issue got cleared up for him. As he was walking towards Judy's front door with her paper, the door opened – she must have been waiting for him, he afterwards realized – and there she was, still in her dressing gown, wild white hair, cat and all.

She put the cat down. "Hello, Will; how are you?"

"Fine. How are *you* doing?"

"Oh, I'm doing fine, thanks. Will, here's the thing. I've decided I don't want the paper delivered anymore; can you tell me how I stop it?"

"No worries; I'll look after that for you." He stepped forward and handed her the newspaper. "There's the last one for you."

"Thanks, Will." She smiled at him. "And Will, thanks for everything – you were a true friend for Barrie, and a comfort for me. I will never forget your kindness."

"Thanks, Judy." He looked up at the second floor. "What do you figure you're going to do? It's a big house."

"Oh, I think I've decided to stay here. I've moved back upstairs to our old bedroom. It was a part of the good times with Barrie," she added softly. Then, more firmly, "And I'm getting the downstairs room changed so that I'll have a studio again. Now that I'm on my own I'd like to get back to painting. I will relish that."

Like me with the paper route, thought Will. They smiled at each other, then Will did his little salute; "Look after yourself, Judy, won't you."

A few days later, Will notified the newspaper delivery people that he was quitting. He arranged with a realtor he knew, who lived round the corner, to list his home.

Once again, he was on his own, and it was time to move on.

Thanks for Coming

This is going to be the hard part, Gillian thought, as her younger son guided her wheelchair across the gravelled parking lot toward the church hall. She figured that the Memorial Service was what everyone had wanted – lots of nice things said about dear Jerry. The head of the History Department wasn't as unctuous as she thought he'd be, and Winifed looked imperial in purple.

"Well, Mum, what did you think?" Charlie was reversing the chair to ease her backwards over the one step up into the hall, careful but adroit.

"They got what they came for, I suppose."

"I really liked Aunt Winnie's story about Dad's early efforts at trying to date girls, and how he got all tongue-tied – I could just see him!"

Gillian chuckled. "Yes, he wasn't much better courting me."

The traditional service had been, even with eulogies by Winifred and the head of Bernie's Department, somehow impersonal, but Gillian had wept a little for the futility of her husband's death. The Celebration of Life reception, with an open mike, was something she was more nervous about, with all those muttered 'Condolences for your bereavement' - why not use good old English 'Sorry for your loss'?

And there was the issue of whether Chas would come. Gillian had looked for him as Charlie wheeled her out of the church, but everyone was standing, so she couldn't see past them. He had sent her such a sweet note, having read about the accident in the newspaper, and, nearly a month later, she had replied and told him about the plans for the Memorial Service, leaving it to him to make the decision whether or not to come.

"Where do you want to be, Mum – first in line or at the end?"

"People will want to stand and talk, so I'd better not be at the beginning, or the line-up will be out the door. Let's go over there" she gestured.

Charlie, blond hair flopping, wheeled his mother to under the window furthest from the door. Gillian sat watching the family sidle in, uncomfortable in the unfamiliarity of a church hall; her other son, Charlie's older brother Vince, and his wife; then Uncle Eddie, darling Jerry's younger brother, looking dreadful, and his priggish wife Eunice – she hadn't really needed to come; and finally Jerry's older sister Winifred, the unmarried family matriarch, grandly dressed in purple, but graciously taking second place to Gillian for this occasion. *Not many of us,* thought Gillian, *and now with Jerry gone there's one less.* And it was sort of miraculous that she hadn't been killed too.

The crash on the highway, over a month ago now, had been gruesome. After sideswiping the truck behind them, the car that killed Jerry ricocheted off the median barrier and slammed into the driver's side of their car, killing him instantly, they later assured her. Their car toppled onto its side and, despite seatbelts and airbags, Gillian's lower spine was brutally compressed as the killer car landed on top of theirs and Jerry was thrown on top of her. It took over an hour to extricate her from under her dead husband and from their demolished car.

Amazingly, her only injury was a spinal compression fracture, which the experts finally decided would not need surgery, but with a requirement that she undertake a rigorous regime of remedial exercises. Other than experimental trips to the stores, to the church office about the service, and then to the hairdresser just before the service, this was her first public outing after the crash. She was rigid in a back brace, but determined to tough it out. "I'm alive," she said to her sons, "That needs to be celebrated too."

Brave words, she thought. Losing her dearest Jerry so needlessly was proving to be so hard that she had almost welcomed the distraction of planning virtually every daily action. After two interminable weeks in the hospital she had insisted on moving back home. Jerry had been starting the first signs of knee problems, so a couple of years ago they had moved into a single-storey house, with no stairs and not even a step up to the front door. There, she was being looked after by home visit nurses and the amazing people at the Rebalance Clinic, who were achieving wonders with what they called Functional Restoration Exercises. So, things had already progressed from only being able to put food in her mouth to, thank goodness, being able to attend to most of her bodily functions. She was using a walker in the house and a wheelchair for trips. She wasn't yet driving, and dressing and showers were was still challenges.

The guests were drifting in; University colleagues of Jerry's, even the Chancellor for goodness' sake – *takes a lurid car crash to get his attention* – and, as if trying to balance the representation from the Department of History, a whole pile of people from her discipline of political science. And, of course, the neighbours, and most of that odd little group, the "Dozen Diners", who gathered once a month at someone's home to eat a gourmet meal and drink too much wine. *Talking of wine, Uncle Eddie is going to need some before the speeches begin.*

The church ladies had prepared a mountain of food, and wine was available at a table in the corner, as Uncle Eddie soon found out. The guests came over in ones and twos to chat with Gillian. She was finding it awkward to talk with them from her wheelchair, constantly having to tip her head back and smile at all the right moments.

Charlie, who had, without being asked, taken on the job of looking after her, brought a plate of assorted appetizers over and a glass of white wine.

"Thanks, sweetie – that looks good. But I don't think I'll have any wine right now – anyway, I might spill it."

Then Winifred, the designated emcee, started the open mike rolling, and Gillian, relieved that she could leave the talking to others, settled back to listen.

It wasn't until the procession of speakers was well into the "I remember when" reminiscences that Gillian turned to look toward the door, and saw him, leaning – *almost loafing,* shot through her mind – against the wall just inside the room, watching the speaker. Tall and slim, in a light pearl-gray suit, his hair, she was startled to see, now speckled with silver, and, for goodness' sake, glasses; light, gold rimmed glasses, she saw with satisfaction, not heavy owlish ones.

There was a sudden burst of laughter, and Gillian realized that she had missed a witticism of some sort. She saw Charlie was watching her, and she smiled at him.

By the time it was over, Gillian was feeling not just tired, but wiped out. She had found the comments about Jerry, some funny, some laudatory, made her feel more wistful than she had been prepared for, and she had resorted to using her handkerchief – a lace one, one of a pair so uncharacteristically given to her by Jerry for her most recent birthday, her fiftieth. She was looking for Charlie to help her home when the man by the door swiveled and walked across to her. She tipped her head to greet him with her intense blue eyes, aware that her still glorious blonde hair framed her face. "Thanks for coming, Chas," she murmured. Silently, he took her hand and, bending down, brushed his lips across her fingers. His touch was electric. He released her hand, smiled his generous smile, and walked away, out through the door. He hadn't said a word to her, and yet she felt as if she'd had a full conversation with him.

Then Gillian experienced the oddest sensation. She sensed a presence in the room, and looking away from the door where Chas had just gone out, she thought to see Jerry. Although she couldn't see him anywhere in the crowd, she was intensely aware of him, and felt that he was smiling at her with that shy smile of his.

"Are you alright, Mum?" Charlie was leaning down in front of her, looking worried.

"Yes, yes, I'm fine – just tired, that's all."

Charlie drove her home and helped her in. He made to come in, but she said, "Sweetie, I can manage from here, and I'm so tired I think I'll go straight to bed. Go and spend some time with your brother. I'll see you tomorrow. And, thanks so much for coming up from College."

The next day was Saturday, and Charlie, who was staying the weekend with his brother, was there, bright and early, to help Gillian with breakfast.

"Aren't there things you should be doing back at Law School? You're probably missing out on some campus activity."

"I'll drive back down tomorrow evening. The guys can do without me for a coupla days."

"But not the girls, I bet."

"Prying will get you nowhere, Mum."

They chatted about Law School, which he was enjoying, and about beginning to look for a summer job at a law firm in town.

"So, Mum," Charlie raised his coffee cup and waved it at her, "Who is Dapper Dan the Gentleman?"

"Who do you mean?" Gillian asked archly.

"Oh, come on, Mum; actually, I think I know him, but I can't place how or where."

"Well, if you must, he's Chas Weatherly".

"Aha! The QC!"

"That's right; how do *you* know him?" deflecting the enquiry.

"He came to give one of those 'Keynoters', last year, a series of special lectures by practitioners not on Faculty. He was amazing.

He had just won a big tort case in the Supreme Court of Canada – they say they just had to make him a QC after that. He just propped himself against the table and launched into the whole issue of vicarious liability" – Gillian rolled her eyes – "sorry, Mum, it's about – well, it doesn't matter." Charlie was animated. "The point is he made it sound exciting, instead of technical, like some of the Profs do. He was mesmerising."

"Yes, he would have been," Gillian said softly.

"And he did it without notes or anything!"

Gillian poured herself another cup of tea.

"Well, anyway, Mum, you obviously know each other, so, what's the story?"

"You *are* impertinent, aren't you."

Charlie grinned at his mother.

"Well, have you got an hour?"

"Tell me," he said, sitting back.

So, Gillian told her son about how, when she was in her third year at College, she had signed up once again to sing in the College's Festival Chorus, and met Jerry and Chas at a 'meet and greet' at the beginning of the season. Gillian, an outgoing – some called her 'brash' – blonde, and now in her third year with the Chorus, was part of the organizing team for the event. She described Jerry as a nervous tenor, just new to the campus, while Chas was a confident bass who had already graduated and was about to qualify as a lawyer and join one of the prestigious law firms in the city. Gillian found herself attracted to both of them, for divergent reasons.

And both of them were clearly smitten by her, so she found herself spending time, not only on rehearsal nights, but also at other events, with one or the other of them. The choir had taken on a big challenge, with a performance of Mozart's Requiem, so there were extra rehearsals, some followed by trips to the pub, and, after the concert, a big pot-luck party.

"They were so different, as I found out during the year. Chas had a sort of old world chivalry about him; he was courteous, even solicitous, and was able to carry off courtesies, like giving me little presents, or flowers, without awkwardness. He treated me so – so *considerately*. And of course, he was wickedly good-looking. But, you know, I was never sure if he was showing me the real him, or whether it was all a sort of an act with him."

"But Jerry, on the other hand, was awkward, even *gauche*, if you know what I mean. He was such a *young* twenty-one, with not much in the way of social graces. But there was a sort of fundamental honesty about him which I found irresistible. I found we could talk without ever feeling I had to watch what I said, or how I said it. He accepted me totally, and I was captivated by that – by him, actually. I always had the feeling he needed protection."

"How young were you all?" Charlie asked.

"Well, I was, let me see, just twenty four. Chas was, I think, twenty six, and Bernie, bless him, was just twenty one."

"Even younger than I am now," muttered Charlie.

Gillian patted his hand, then went on.

"Anyway, there was a formal event just before Christmas, something called the Chancellor's Ball, and both Jerry and Chas invited me to go with them. I told Chas that I was sorry, and that I had already agreed to go with someone else, and I accepted Jerry. I figured Chas could easily find someone else to take to the Ball, while Jerry couldn't. It had, he told me, later, taken all his courage to ask me. Later, when we got engaged, it was me who proposed, not him," she chuckled.

"Years after that, I came to realize how momentous a decision it was when I agreed to go to the Ball with Jerry. It was like the road less taken, full of uncertainties and delicious surprises. Chas would have been more predictable."

Gillian looked down at her hands in her lap, and twisted her wedding ring.

"Just a few days ago I was clearing out stuff, and I came across my diary for that year."

Charlie looked doubtful, and rolled his eyes.

"Yes, sweetie, I used to keep a diary, just like most girls did, back then. Anyway, I was surprised at how – well, *wise* I was; confused but wise. I had written about how difficult it was to distinguish between needing and wanting. I really *wanted* Chas – sorry, Charlie, I'm making you blush, but you asked for this. But – " she hesitated, then plunged on. "So, here's the thing. I realized that not only did Jerry need *me*, but, in a way, I needed *him*. Under the façade of that brash young woman that I was, I was still hunting for some level of self-confidence to, sort of, round me out. In a strange way, I needed him because he made me feel needed, which was a great comfort for me."

Gillian looked at her son. "So, there you have it. And, I always felt I made the right choice. Your father was a lovely man, and, although, as you know he wasn't demonstrative, we adored each other. And I have no idea where or what happened to Chas."

"Well," said Charlie, "I googled him after he gave the Keynoter. He's never married. He lived with a lawyer, Jessica Stanworth, until she became a judge. The story seems to be that they both felt it would have caused difficulties if he had a case where she was the judge, so he moved out. So, it sounds as if it was sort of a convenience liaison rather than a love match."

"You are quite the sleuth, aren't you."

"Well, you can find out stuff if you know where to look," Charlie said a bit smugly. "Anyway, so, Mum, he's single and unattached."

"Now you're beginning to sound like a dating service."

"Just observing, Mum," he grinned.

Gillian looked at Charlie. "You're too young for this, you know."

"Aw, c'mon, Mum, I'm fine."

"Well anyway, Chas was a fine gentleman about the whole thing, and sent us a lovely gift for our wedding, that crystal dessert bowl, you know the one" – Charlie nodded – "which made me think of him every time we used it."

She sat quietly. "And then, before you ask any more impertinent questions, he disappeared out of my life."

"So, Dad won?"

Gillian bridled. "Well, I wouldn't say I was *won*."

"No, I don't mean that; I mean he won the competition."

"And I was the prize," tartly.

"Aw, c'mon, Mum, you know what I mean."

"No, as I said, it's more that I realized that he needed me more than Chas ever would. I think I worried about becoming sort of a possession of his. But, with Jerry, I suppose it was a bit of the maternal instinct, or something like that. And I was right; he did need me, which was a wonderful part of being married to him. His need was fulfilled and, I suppose, satisfied, and I had the joy and comfort of being the provider, if you like, of that, and" – softly – "knowing I had made the right choice."

She sat looking out at the garden for a minute.

Charlie said carefully, "Was he the reason I'm called Charlie?"

"I think so; it was your dad who wanted it. I think he knew that it hadn't been an easy choice for me, and somehow he wanted to honour that – the difficult choice I made."

Gillian winced as she sat up, her hand going to her back. "Good heavens, what nonsense we're talking!"

"And now?" Charlie grinned at his mother as he got up to clear the dishes.

"Who knows, Charlie, who knows."

It was a month later when Gillian received the hand-written invitation on the elegant stationery of the law firm of Breston and Weatherly. By then, she was walking well, only using a walking stick when going to a place where she was uncertain about what the pathways were like, or if she didn't know how far she would have to walk; more of a back-up than a necessity. And she was driving comfortably, though she did find the head-rest useful.

But she was still having trouble sleeping through the night, awaking at odd hours in the early morning to the sound of silence instead of Jerry's steady breathing, and then not being able to get back to sleep properly.

Dear Gillian; I wonder if you might be free next Friday evening to be my guest at a symphony concert at the Philharmonic Hall. It will include a performance of Mozart's Requiem by a massed choir including the Festival Chorus. You may remember participating in a performance of it when we were all in the Chorus together. I have happy memories of the singing we did that year, and of that particular event.

My Law Firm is a co-sponsor of the concert, and it will be followed by a reception hosted by us. I would be honoured if you will be able to accompany me. Dress is 'formal'.

By the way, I recently interviewed your son, Charles, for a summer position with my firm; he seems a personable young man.

Please let me know if you are able to come. If you are, the concert starts at 7:30 pm, and I suggest we meet at the main door to the Hall at 7:15.

Chas.

Gillian saw that his phone number and email were shown at the bottom of the page. She sat for a long time looking out at her garden, Chas' note in her hand. Then she smiled. *That son of mine has got to have some involvement with this. I wouldn't put it past the two of them to have hatched something here. If I accept the invitation, Charlie gets the job? What chicanery! But, what have I got to lose?*

So, Gillian sent Chas an email accepting the invitation, but not mentioning her son. Then she went out and bought a lovely, shimmering gown, and got her hair done.

Gillian admitted to herself, as she got ready for the concert, that she was a little nervous. *I hope he recognizes me when I get there.* She decided she was managing well enough to dispense with the walking stick, but gave herself the luxury of ordering a taxi, which took her right to the entrance to the Hall, so that she didn't have to walk too far. Sure enough, there was Chas, watching out for her; he smiled broadly when he saw her in her new finery. *I did the right thing*, she thought.

"You look wonderful," he said as he tucked her arm in his to walk her through the door.

"Well, so do you – the years are looking good on you."

Gillian was relieved to find that there were no steps to get to their seats – the best in the house – just an inclined aisle, with Chas helping firmly. Chas introduced Gillian to his partner, Jackson Breston, and to Jackson's wife, as 'an old friend', and the four of them were comfortably seated well before the start of the concert. Gillian saw from the program that the first half would be one of the Beethoven Symphonies, with the Mozart Requiem in the second half. Comfortable that she didn't need to do any reading up, she and Chas chatted easily about college days and how much he was enjoying working with his colleagues at the firm.

"I understand you saw my son recently," Gillian ventured.

"Yes, and I expect to see lots more of him."

"Oh?"

"He has one more year of Law School, but we have taken him on for the summer," he glanced at her.

"Well, that's lovely; he hasn't yet told me."

"Well, we think he has what it takes to make a good advocate," Chas grinned.

Just then the conductor came on to the stage to applause, and Gillian was left to puzzle whether there was more to that comment than the obvious. Then she became enthralled by Beethoven.

At the intermission, Chas was solicitous about whether she wanted to go into the foyer or remain seated, and Gillian told him she was happy to stay where she was. He told her he and Jackson had to go out to check on the arrangements for the post-concert reception, so she chatted pleasantly with Jackson's wife, whose name she couldn't remember, but it wasn't a problem; she was an animated chatterbox.

The second half of the concert took her back to that final year at College, and how hard they had all worked at their music. She had a sudden recollection, long since forgotten, of sitting with Jerry at a piano to coach him with a difficult part. She found herself tearing up, and, feeling for a handkerchief. *This is ridiculous.* Chas either didn't notice, or stayed quietly by her side, leaving her to deal with it.

After the clapping and cheering, the concert was over and Chas escorted Gillian to the reception, held in a room off the main foyer. She watched how he was treated by others, both colleagues and clients, with cordial deference, and also how he was, it seemed, genuinely liked by them.

She found herself caught in a corner by a small, round man and his wife, she an unlikely foot taller than him. She was intent on telling her how Chas saved her husband from what she appeared to think was a fate worse than death, but which Gillian thought was a simple case of breach of contract. As the story was entering Act Three, Chas appeared at her side and, with grace and diplomacy, steered her away to meet some of the younger members of the firm, including a couple of young women who, Chas said, will be taking Charlie under their wing. *The firm seems to think they have my son well-organized*, she thought. *That'll be a challenge!*

Gillian was finding the standing to be tiring when Chas turned to her and murmured, "It's nearly over; permit me to drive you home."

"That would be nice."

"I just need to make sure all is well with the caterers, and then we'll be off. Why don't you have a seat." He guided her to an armchair, and she sat down gratefully.

As Chas turned away, Gillian experienced that same uncanny feeling that Jerry was in the room. It was more a movement than a presence. Her hand went to her throat as her mind's eye caught the impression of Jerry walking away from her, waving – what? – waving goodbye.

Chas was by her side. "Are you feeling alright?"

Gillian smiled up at him. "Yes, just a little tired."

"We'll go right now. My car is in the parking lot under here." He walked her to the elevators.

On the way to her home, Gillian settled comfortably in the passenger seat, Chas said, "Thanks for coming, Gillian; your being there meant a lot to me."

"Well, I enjoyed it."

"Perhaps we can do things together that aren't so formal."

"I'd like that."

The conversation was guarded.

"I know it's not long since – "

"Chas, dear, don't fuss about that."

Chas pulled into the driveway, and turned off the engine. Gillian leaned across and touched his arm. "Chas, I don't know how to describe this, but I know that Jerry has let me go. Somehow I know that he knows about you and – and me, and he's happy. So that's a good thing."

Chas got out, walked around and, opening her door, helped her out. "Might I ask if you would have lunch with me tomorrow – just the two of us?"

Gillian leaned into him and, putting her arms around his neck, whispered, "That would be lovely," and she kissed him on the cheek.

As Gillian let herself into her home, she thought; *Thanks, sweet Jerry, and thanks Charlie, whatever you did.*

Gillian lay in bed that night, musing happily. *All that stuff about 'needing' and 'wanting' was very complicated. This is so much easier. Loving Chas will be a given. But this courtship thing is an added gift – and I'm loving it!*

Gillian snuggled down, and slept soundly.

THE OTHER SIDE OF THE FENCE

It didn't mean much, if anything, to him. Or, at least, it didn't at the time. And it all worked like clockwork, at least for a while.

Regularly on Fridays, Vincent's wife, Pauline, Polly to her friends, would grab a quick breakfast, and then leave shortly before 8 a.m. to make the one hour drive to the family's satellite hardware store in the new development up-Island known as the Village. She would spend the day doing the books, inventory, payroll, and ordering. They had an in-office acronym for it – BIPO. And there were usually some staffing issues to sort out. Around four in the afternoon she would phone Vince at their home store, and say "I'm on my way", and he would say, "See you soon."

So, recently, on Friday mornings, Vincent would walk Lefty-the-dog at 7:15, going past the old Cartwright house to check if the side-door light was on, and getting home in time to kiss Polly goodbye. Then he would feed the dog, and put her in her doggy-bed in the bedroom with her water bowl and one of her favourite squeaky toys. Soon after 8 a.m., he would walk down through the back garden, and squeeze through the gap in the back fence that divided their property from Bevvie's. He would walk through her already unlocked side door and discard his clothing, so that he was sliding between the sheets of her sumptuous king sized bed to join Bevvie's sleek and lithesome body by 8:10.

Afterwards, it was a rush to get home, take a quick shower, grab some toast or a muffin, and jump in the truck, along with Lefty-the-dog, to make the 10 minute trip to the main store. But Johnnie knew not to expect Vincent at the store on Friday mornings until 9:30.

It had all started at the Treadwell's traditional 'post-party-time party'. Everyone was so busy with family get-togethers before and during Christmas, followed by New Year's bashes at the end of the year, that no-one had any time to squeeze in a neighbourhood party. So, for several years, the Treadwells had hosted an open house on the first Saturday in January, held in their big house on a double lot at the corner. Vince and Polly always went. It was the only time they connected with some of the people living around them, what with everyone leading such busy lives. Others they knew better.

Gloria Treadwell, boomy and buxom, greeted them at the door with a "Happy New Year" for both of them, "Hello, Polly, is it snowing out there?" for Pauline, and "Hi, tall, dark and handsome" for Vincent. She gave them each a huggy sort of kiss, and took their coats as they struggled with their boots, Pauline puffing a bit as she bent heavily down. There had been some slushy snow, and shoes and boots already cluttered the floor off to one side. Vince brushed back his greying hair as he looked through to the Great Room where people were gathered.

Gloria said, "Turn around," and deftly stuck a sticky note on their backs. "This year, it's a Christmas carol or a Christmas song – you know the rules."

Vince groaned; he knew how much Polly hated this stupid game. "O.K., Gloria, just this once." He always said that.

"Just one yes or no question to each person, mind," warned Gloria, handing them each a glass of punch, "and you move on round the room until you guess what song or carol you are." This meant you had to keep wandering around the room, talking to pretty well everyone. Polly, as usual, soon gave up, and went to join her walking group friends by the fireplace. But Vince, to please Gloria, decided to keep going round the room. *At least they've given up not letting you have a drink until you got it,* thought Vince, sipping his punch. That hadn't worked at all well.

So, Vince started trying to find out if he was Silent Night or Jingle Bells, or whatever, saying hello to people he sometimes only encountered fleetingly, and to others he saw more regularly when walking Lefty-the-dog.

Little Herb, an erstwhile drinking buddy, who lived on the next street over, slapped him on the back. "Vince the Prince, how are ya, my friend? Haven't seen you much at the Castle lately."

"Well, I've been told by my doctor to keep the weight down, so I've been going to the gym instead of the pub."

Herb looked up at big Vince; "You look pretty fit to me."

"Well, you wouldn't want to see me naked."

"Spare me the details," Herb sniggered.

"Although I've got to tell you, owning a dog certainly helps; the walking routine seems to keep things trimmer."

"Dog owners are a secret terrorist organization, meeting only early in the morning or late at night," Herb muttered, as he turned to the punch bowl.

Vince had it down to something like Drummer Boy or Chestnuts Roasting, when Gloria appeared at his side, saying, "Vincent, have you met our new neighbour, Beverly? She's just moved into the house behind you."

Vincent turned to look down at a diminutive woman in a sparkling sheath dress, smiling up at him, her smooth oval face ornamented by black eyebrows, and encircled by graying curls. He heard her say, "No, we haven't met, but I see you walking the dog past my house." Vincent awkwardly shifted his punch glass to the other hand, and shook hands with her – her elegant, dainty hand, enclosed within his, was warm and firm. Vincent, suddenly intensely aware of his burgeoning paunch, sucked in.

"Good to meet you, Beverly – I heard about you moving in, what, a coupla weeks before Christmas." She nodded, still smiling up at him. "Welcome to the neighbourhood."

"Well, thank you. I understand there's only a fence between us." The comment sounded curiously flirtatious.

"Yes, and one that needs some looking after – there's a place where a dog, or even a slender person like you, can get through. So," – he looked around the room – "Is there a Mr. Beverly somewhere around?"

"No, there's just me, now." Vince felt a warning bell go off; *widowed or divorced? Leave that one alone.*

"That makes you even more of an empty nester than we are." Vince gestured toward the fireplace. "That's my wife, Pauline, in blue." Beverly looked appraisingly over at Pauline, comfortable in a flowered blue gown. "We are just the two of us, now that both our children have gone out on their own."

He looked at his glass and then at the one she was holding. *No ring on that hand.* "Beverly," – he said her name so that he would remember it – "can I get you another glass of punch?"

"That would be nice; and please call me Bevvie – everyone does."

So Vince got himself and Bevvie some more punch, and then led her over to join their host who, with Herb and another man, was standing by the food sideboard. Vince completely forgot that he was meant to find out whether he was Rudolph or King Wenceslas.

When they were leaving, Vincent gave Bevvie his business card.

"We have the only hardware store in town. There might be things to be done in your new home. The Cartwrights were getting old, and maybe didn't look after things much. And we have a list of handymen we can recommend."

"Why, thank you, Vince. That's very thoughtful of you." She smiled up at him, and he just stopped himself from ducking down to kiss her.

Walking home in slushy rain, Polly said, "So, who was that little elf you were talking to?"

"Oh, sorry, that's Bevvie – uh, Beverly, who's moved into the Cartwright house behind us. Nice lady."

"I'm told she's a good deal older than she looks – probably pushing sixty."

"Really! I wouldn't have put her at any older than me. Maybe mid-fifties, but no more. Anyway," he clumsily put an arm round her, "I prefer younger women, and," – he tried some gallantry – "someone I can hold on to."

"Pshaw! Just help me get home through this muck."

It was the next Friday that Beverly first came into the hardware store. Vincent saw her talking to Johnnie about paint. Such a slim slip of a thing, she looked oddly out of place in his store. He waited until she was at the till, with a can of paint and a bag with a paint tray, a brush and a mixing stick, then walked over to her, Lefty-the-dog getting up from her bed behind the till to sniff hello.

"Well, hello, Bevvie. Starting on house renovation projects?"

"Oh, hi, Vince. Yes, as you said, some things need touching up, so I'm having to learn about paint."

"Well, you've got the right man in Johnnie. He's been at it longer than I have, and knows everything there is to know about everything, don't ya, Johnnie," he turned and called.

Johnnie, stocky and grizzled, his short sleeved store shirt showing off his bulging biceps, circled a hand in the air as he walked away.

"As for me, I know where stuff is in here, and how to screw in a light bulb, but, if you need a handyman, Johnnie's your man."

Bevvie smiled at him as he stood by her. She paid for the paint, and then said, "Gloria Treadwell told me your wife works here as well as you."

"Yes, we're a real family business here. But today she's at what we call the satellite store, up in the Village. She does the books and inventory and stuff there every Friday."

"I saw you walking the dog by, early this morning."

"Yeah, well Polly leaves really early. I didn't see any lights on at your place when I went by."

"So, next Friday morning, if you see the side-door light on, you'll know I'm ready for visitors."

Vince stared down at her, and she locked eyes with him.

"Well," she picked up the paint, still looking at him, "I need to get going. Thanks, Johnnie," she called out, and Johnnie, down at the back of the store called out, "Welcome." Bevvie walked by Vince and out onto the street, Vince watching her all the way.

The next Friday, Vince walked Lefty-the-dog past the Cartwright house shortly after seven in the morning. The light by the side door was shining. After he got home and kissed Polly goodbye, and she had left, and he had fed and watered and bedded the dog, he slipped out the back door. He crept, feeling his heart thudding, down the back yard, and squeezed through the gap in the fence, catching his sweater as he went. He swore softly and pulled it clear. He tiptoed to the side door where the light shone, and tried the handle. It turned. Breathless, he pushed the door open and stepped into the dimlit hallway. A slim figure whispered "Hello there." She took him by the hand, and he could feel she was naked. She led him to a room, the closed-draped darkness of which was etched by the soft wavering light of a tall, scented candle on a dresser by her enormous bed. It struck him, *why would such a tiny little creature have such a huge bed?* He soon found out that it wasn't so much a bed as a playground.

By the third or fourth Friday, Vincent was beginning to figure things out. The 'dalliance', as he liked to think of it, was going so smoothly, with no hitch in the timing and the arrangements, that it was like clockwork, everything ticking along perfectly, with the clock chiming just once a week, each Friday morning. It wasn't interrupting anything else. Each evening, Vince and Polly stayed comfortably in their routine of watching the 10 o'clock news, then retiring to their conjugal bed where they would, if they both felt so inclined, indulge in some gentle lovemaking. If anything, Vince found his appetite enhanced, and Polly seemed delighted with that.

But there were things to think through.

First off, Bevvie was so unlike Pauline that he didn't even consider his involvement with her as a threat to his marriage to, or, indeed, his love for, Pauline. It was as if his sessions with Bevvie were taking place on another planet to that which he and Pauline occupied.

For one thing, the word that came to him when he surveyed Bevvie's body was *'uncomplicated'*, while Pauline's was complex, with hills and dales to appraise, negotiate and relish. Their topography was so different that there was no comparison, and so, no contest. With Bevvie, there were hardly any swelling breasts to ponder, or surging buttocks or spreading thighs or a rounded tummy to contemplate, or, for that matter, to negotiate or relish. Nor were there any curves or crevasses, or blemishes for that matter – just simple, flat and straight lines, surfaced by flawless skin. For Vincent, it was a delight of a different kind, exhilarating, but also, somehow, sanctioned.

And, when it comes to uncomplicated topography, one could also say that of Bevvie's needs. There was nothing that went on in bed with Bevvie which came within Vince's conception of lovemaking. He knew, from years with Pauline, what lovemaking was; it involved care and compliance and mutuality and consideration and reciprocity and gratefulness. Their consummations were complex, subtle and nuanced. What was happening every Friday morning in Bevvie's bed was none of those things instead, there was raw demand, almost greed, urgency, strenuousness, and lusty tumult. There was little in the way of mutuality, and certainly no complexities, subtleties or nuances.

In some way, Vincent began to feel that he was being used. It was a sort of uninhibited transactional sex, but with Vince feeling a bit short-changed.

Furthermore, to Vince's consternation, he discovered that Bevvie liked to talk dirty, or *'whisper dirty'*, as he thought of it. It excited her, she said. She encouraged him to try it, but he never got beyond the 'f' word. She laughed at him about that, and said he should try it with his wife sometime. The very thought of that appalled Vince.

But, most significantly, Vincent quickly came to realize that it had absolutely nothing to do with love. Yes, there was exhilaration, but it was all physical. And initially it didn't even seem to him to have anything to do with the word 'infidelity' or that ugly word 'adultery'. Vince felt that what was going on was almost with someone who wasn't even the same sex as Polly – Bevvie belonged to some other branch of womanhood, or even of personhood, who wasn't a challenge to Polly or a threat to Vince's relationship with Polly. But then, later, in the weeks that followed, Vince thought that, if that were the case, why wasn't he able to tell Polly about it, apart from the obvious reason that she'd probably kick him out of the house, and then who would look after Lefty-the-dog?

Vincent and Bevvie didn't talk about their sessions much, if at all, any more than Vince and Polly would talk about their lovemaking; it just happened, is all, every Friday morning, for weeks. Once, after a particularly arduous rough and tumble, remarkable for people their age, Vince mumbled, as he was struggling into his clothes, that he hoped she had enjoyed 'that'. Bevvie's response, that he was quite a bit more satisfying than a dildo, dumbstruck him. He wondered how much 'quite a bit' was. At least she hadn't said "marginally', or some such word. Anyway, it shut him up for good.

Easter came early that year, so the last Friday in March was Good Friday, and the hardware store – both the main store and the satellite store – was closed. So, for the first Friday for weeks,

Pauline didn't go out of town, and Vince didn't go through the fence to Bevvie's. Vince and Polly spent quite a bit of the morning reading in bed.

It came to Vince that weekend that perhaps he should discuss putting an end to the dalliance. After all, the habit had been broken by the Good Friday lay-off, and, as far as he could determine, by walking Lefty-the-dog past the Cartwright home (as he still thought of it), Bevvie was home and well, so no harm had come of it.

An opportunity presented itself the next Tuesday, as Bevvie came into the store to discuss floor tiles with Johnnie. Johnnie had told Vince that Bevvie wanted to hire him as a handyman, and Vince had told him, "Go ahead, I don't mind you making some money on the side as long as it doesn't interfere with your store work." Vince had seen Johnnie's truck in Bevvie's driveway a couple of evenings, and on the weekend. Vince understood from Johnnie that Bevvie had, with his help, undertaken a few little projects around the house, but now she was, Vince heard her telling Johnnie, ready for them to move on to bigger things together.

Johnnie gave her some sheets with sample colours, and she was heading out the door, Vince called out, "Hi, Bevvie," and walked to the door with her.

"Hallo, Vince – I hope you don't mind if I ask Johnnie to do some work for me; I've found he really is so good at a lot of different things." She smiled sort of coquettishly at him.

"No, no – that's fine." He looked over his shoulder at the people at the till. "Say, I might not be free this Friday, and – "

"You'd better be."

Vincent stared at her.

"Be there, Vincent, or face consequences." Bevvie walked away.

It came to Vincent with a thudding feeling, as he stood there watching her cross the street in her high heels, that she held all the cards, and that his marriage was on the table.

Vincent was on time that Friday, and, as things turned out, he seemed to have been forgiven.

In mid-April, a series of rapidly cascading events over two days didn't just turn the page; it closed the book.

First off, on a Thursday afternoon, Polly hung up the back office phone, and went to find Vince. She told him that she might not need to make the trip to the satellite store on Fridays any more, as Enrico, one of the young staff in the satellite store in the Village, had just approached her with the suggestion that he take on overseeing the books, including the Friday BIPO work. Vincent looked confused. "You know, the books, etcetera." "Yes, yes," said Vincent, distracted.

"So, here's the thing. He's just passed his preliminary accounting exams, and wants to get hands on experience, with me keeping an eye on it. Each Friday, after he's finished, he would drive down here with the books and stuff, for me to check it and integrate the results with the main store books."

"Well, let's think about that." Vincent felt he was going to be sick.

"He can start next week, so I'll still go up tomorrow. His mother lives here, and she isn't well, so he'd appreciate the opportunity to visit with her once a week."

"I said let's think about it," Vincent snapped.

Polly stared at her husband. "Well, I'd like to make the arrangements when I'm up there tomorrow. It's not all that difficult a decision."

Vincent felt trapped. "O.K., O.K., if you say so." He turned on his heel and walked away, Polly staring at his rigid back.

Vincent had never been one to pray, but he did, right then and there, pray for a way out of this.

That evening, he realized he had never spoken like that to Pauline before, and apologized to her over supper, saying he hadn't felt well.

"You've been looking tired lately, darling." Polly put a hand on his. "That's one of the reasons why I'm looking forward to being here on Fridays."

The next astonishing event in the series happened only a few hours later. It was Friday morning, and, despite a troubled night, Vince arrived, on time as ever, at Bevvie's bedside, dutifully naked. Wordlessly, Bevvie pushed him, and he landed on his back in the middle of the huge bed. Then, straddling him in candlelight, she pleasured him, first with her hands, then with her tongue, and then with her lips. Vincent had never experienced anything like it.

Afterwards, she nuzzled his ear, and whispered, "Just something for you to remember me by."

The final incident was even more astounding.

An hour later, when Vince arrived at the store promptly at 9:30, Johnnie came into the back office, looking a bit bashful for a change.

"Just to let you know, boss, I'm going to be moving in with Bevvie; we've – we've sort of hit it off." Vince stared at him as if he was an angel from heaven.

"Oh – oh, that's so good, Johnnie; she's – from what I know of her, she's a fine woman. When do you plan on moving in?"

"Tomorrow, I think. There's lots to be done in the house, but I don't want it to interfere with my work at the store, and Bevvie wants me to get started over the weekend." Johnnie looked a little awkward. "She's talking of getting a dog, so one of my first jobs, if you're OK with it, will be fixing the hole in the fence between your place and hers – she tells me you wouldn't mind."

"No, no, not at all."

"Anyway," Johnnie said, "about my work here at the store – "

"Don't worry about that, Johnnie – get settled in, and get back to work at your convenience." Vince tried not to sound too elated.

That evening, he told Polly. "Oh, by the way, apparently Johnnie is moving in with Beverly – you know, the woman who lives back of us." He tried to sound nonchalant. Polly told him that yes, she had heard. Vince wondered a little nervously what else she might have heard, but nothing could dispel his relief.

On Sunday morning, Vince stood at the kitchen window watching Johnnie working on the fence, eliminating the gap, which had grown somewhat bigger from constant use over the past weeks. He didn't know if Johnnie saw him watching, but when he had finished hammering the final piece in place, and was walking back to the house, Johnnie did that little wave over his head, and Vince muttered "Welcome".

The next Friday went like the clockwork of a new timepiece. Vince walked Lefty-the-dog past the old Cartwright house a little later than usual for a Friday morning. He saw that Johnnie's truck was in the driveway, and that the side entrance light was not on, and he felt a surge of elation. Johnnie was late for work, as he had been most of that week, and Polly, for the first time in ages, didn't drive up to the satellite store. Enrico arrived in mid-afternoon with the books and the results of his BIPO work, and Polly was delighted. Enrico had devised a simpler recording system for inventory and ordering, and Polly told him he had already proved this was the right decision.

Soon after, Vince and Polly closed the store and went home happy. That evening, when Vince took Lefty-the-dog for his evening pee-walk, he noticed that Johnny's truck was in Bevvie's driveway, and that all the house lights were out. Then he saw the flicker of candlelight through the bedroom window, which made Vince feel slightly envious, but mostly an intense relief which bordered on euphoria.

Just before the ten o'clock news, Polly took her man by the hand, and said, "The news can wait until tomorrow; let's go to bed."

Later, much later, Vince, spooned with his wife, dipped a toe into what might be icy water, and mumbled, "I hope Johnnie knows what he's getting into."

To which Polly made a reply so enigmatic that he wondered about it for days.

She whispered, "I should think he's more her type."

Vince lay enfolded with his Polly for quite a while. Then, hearing her steady breathing in sleep, he shifted and, drifting off himself, he slept long and dreamlessly.

The River Cottage

When my father Morton Travis died (finally), my brother Sebastian flew in for the two of us to work out how to divvy everything up. Quite a bit of the family money had gone to cover medical expenses, first for Mum, and then for Dad, both of whom had lingered for months before finally succumbing to cancer. They had both been heavy smokers – so much so that the house had to be fumigated afterwards.

I met Seba at the airport and we drove to the house. He was jetlagged, so he soon went off to bed. He told me that he wanted to get everything settled quickly, as he was to go to some meetings in Calgary on the way home. I wasn't happy with that, but didn't say anything; it was best to just go along with what my brother wanted – he hadn't been remotely interested in helping when Mum and Dad were sick.

Anyway, it turned out to be pretty easy. Neither of us wanted to live in the family home – there were too many uncomfortable memories of disagreements and illnesses hanging about in it. Seba just wanted it sold, and his share of the proceeds. I wanted the river-cottage, an old barn of a place down by the river over a hundred yards away from the house. I also needed enough money to make it livable.

I contacted a lawyer and a real estate agent I knew through EXPM – Excelsior Property Managers Inc., the property management company I worked for, and we signed all the necessary papers just before Seba flew off to his meetings.

About fifty years ago, Dad had acquired a three-acre parcel of river frontage from a company called CedarHills which owned a stretch of riparian land originally planned for a fancy riverside housing development which just never happened. There had been some logging done to clear part of the land, but that was all. CedarHills has sold off a couple of other chunks, but still owns the rest, including the section next to our parcel.

Dad first built a small building down by the river, part barn, part living accommodation, which he and Mum lived in until we children started to arrive. Then he had the big house built, and the first house came to be called the River Cottage. By now, it either needed to be pulled down, or extensively repaired and renovated. It was the sort of challenge I needed.

The paperwork involved a subdivision of the property so that I could have separate title to the River Cottage plus about one acre. The easement for the long driveway from River Lane to the cottage required a sign-off from CedarHills. The whole thing took a few months. Then we sold the family home for close to what Seba and I wanted – or more accurately, what I *needed*. A little over a year after Dad's death, the estate was wound up, and the distributions made.

My divorce was also finalized during that year. Eunice didn't want anything more to do with me, the family home, or the Travis family assets, such as they were, and the lawyer made sure she couldn't claim any part of my share by having her sign a thing called a quitclaim deed.

I used to have arguments with Eunice about excess. About once a month there would be a clean-out of the fridge, where half-empty (or still half-full, depending on how you looked at it) containers would get chucked. Garden watering and irrigation taps were left running, doors stood open, the heating always seemed to be on in the winter, and the air conditioning in the summer. I would close my eyes when the utility bills arrived.

And then there were endless gas guzzling trips in her fancy car to stores in the city – evidently the local shops weren't good enough. When Eunice left, she didn't even take a whole pile of her stuff, so I took it to the Sally Ann.

She called me a tightwad. I just think I'm thrifty, but there you go. Maybe if we'd had children things might have been different.

Before I moved into the River Cottage, I wanted to make it comfortable, but I also became really interested in making my home environmentally friendly. So I did a pile of things, or I should say I had a pile of things done; I'm no handyman!

The well dated back to when Dad first built the place. I had it tested, and was told there was a good water supply, and that the water was fine, but I had a water purifier/filtration system installed anyway. A new pump with a pressure tank was installed in the pump house over the well, and its roof's rotten old cedar shakes were replaced with asphalt shingles. I was comforted by the salesman's assurance that, as long as I had the pump serviced every couple of years, I would probably never have to touch it, "except, possibly, if the power goes out".

The old septic field needed an upgrade, including a septic field pump, to meet the present required standards. It turned out to cost way more than I expected. I got a bit of a break because the purchasers of the big house also needed work done on its own septic field, so we got them both done at the same time.

I spent quite a bit of time researching heat pumps – *another pump!* – and ended up paying a lot of money for one using geothermal heat, plus all the things needed to make it really efficient, including an underfloor heating system on the ground floor, big radiators and making the building airtight (or as close as I could get to it). Thank goodness there was no basement or crawl space. I had on-demand water heaters installed in the kitchen and in the two bathrooms, and in the passageway next to the downstairs one I installed a new washer and dryer.

By the time the renovations to the River Cottage were finished, it had a wide entrance area which became a sort of mudroom; the open-area living room had the original wood-burning fireplace; and I added a fan for better heat circulation (I was glad I did, but more of that later). At the far end stood the big old dining table salvaged from the big house. French doors opened out onto the patio where there was a view of the river, and the kitchen had open access to the dining area. A door one side of the open area led to the main floor bedroom and bathroom. I didn't think I'd ever have a need for that second bedroom, unless my brother came to visit – *unlikely* –but there was room for it, and I was persuaded that, down the road, it would be difficult to sell a one-bedroom house. I made the bed up. *The bedding might as well go on the bed instead of taking up storage space, which I don't have much of.*

The stairs against the far side wall went up to what had been an open upper floor, sort of like a hayloft. I had it converted into a big bedroom for me, which also doubled as my office – well, a sort of office, with a desk, chair and filing cabinet. The bedroom, with the big bed Eunice and I used to sleep in – that didn't concern me, I realized – had its own bathroom, so the house insurance guy grandly called it 'ensuite'.

One luxury, I guess some would call it, was a state-of-the-art sound system, so that I could listen to my music – I'm a classical music aficionado – in what they call surround-sound, anywhere in the house. I really love the Mahler symphonies with their huge waves of sound, but for evening comfort there's nothing like Bach.

Outside, I added a small stand-alone garage – really just a big shed, to house my car, but kept the carport attached to the side of the house, to be used as a storage area and a place to stack firewood. I had to get the municipal planning department's approval for the garage, which took a while.

I also invested in a gasoline-powered home-standby generator. After all, I was out here in the woods, and if the power went out it might be a while before they got around to me. I had it installed in the old carport, so that I wouldn't have to go far. It's a top of the line portable one, powerful enough to run what I really need if the power goes out, but not including the heat pump; after all, I did have the wood-burning fireplace, and the generator would run the fan to circulate the heat. I could have installed a ridiculously expensive generator which would have run more stuff, like the oven, and the washer and dryer and so on, but enough was enough. They showed me how to switch over from hydro to the generator, and how to start it up, and left an instruction manual for me to look at when I got around to it *–I put it somewhere, I know.*

Finally, I researched solar panels and solar shingles, and became a sort of expert in photovoltaic and thermal panels and shingles. In the end, I had one side of the roof – the south side facing the river – covered with solar shingles, which looked nicer than panels, with it all hooked into the house system. It was all an awful lot of money, but I was told that, if I lived long enough (!) I would actually save money.

And, best of all, I invested in an electric bicycle! I kept the car, of course, for trips out of town (not an electric one, I admit), and housed it in the big old garden shed. But I was determined to use the bike for everything local. I thought that battery charging would be a challenge, but soon found that unlocking the battery and bringing it in to the house to plug in and charge became just part of the schedule. In good weather I found it took about twenty minutes to cycle up River Lane to the main road and into town to my office. As I am nervous about cycling if the weather is really awful, I can walk up River Lane to the main road and catch the bus into town, which, I discovered, didn't take much longer.

My brother told me in his Christmas letter he thought I was crazy, frittering away my share of our inheritance on a bunch of 'unproven gadgets'. I never asked him what he did with his share – he probably put it all in Government Bonds.

The first night I was finally free of workmen and installers was on a weekend, Saturday, March 21, the first day of spring, and Bach's birthday! I celebrated with his Mass in B minor, all ninety minutes of it, and afterwards fell asleep to the insistently mournful call of a great horned owl, somewhere out there in the woods.

I was all settled, convinced that I would enjoy my newly remodeled home, and also my life, newly remodeled.

In late September, the weather began to change, and we had a couple of cold and rainy spells. My heating and solar systems had a good test-out, and I was feeling pretty happy about the renovations. I made myself cycle into town even when the weather threatened to be miserable. But, if it was already raining when I was ready to leave, I would walk to the main road, and bus into town. One day I was really glad I had not biked, as, when I was trudging home along River Lane at about 5:30, it was really pissing down. I was thinking about how dark it would be when coming home after the clocks change. *I'll need a flashlight or headlamp.*

I was a couple of minutes from my driveway when I saw a flash of blue through the trees where the remains of a bumpy old logging road led down to the river. I peered down through the rain. *What is it?* I didn't want to traipse through the woods in the pouring rain, so I headed on home. But I did think about it that evening. *Perhaps it's a blue tarpaulin. Is some homeless guy sleeping down there?* Although I was getting used to living all on my own in the woods, I was nervous; I don't understand, or don't have a good feeling about homeless people. *I need to make sure everything is locked before I go to work tomorrow.*

The next morning, a Friday, the skies had cleared, so I got the bike out, and left early. I stopped at the logging trail, and saw that there were tire marks leading off the road into the wet dirt and down the old track. Some of the stuff grown up down the middle had been flattened, with some leaves and twigs broken off. *So maybe there's a car or a truck or something down there.*

I was just about to cycle on when I saw a tall man wearing a hoodie walking up the trail towards me. He raised a hand, and I tensely watched him approach as I sat straddled on my bike. Then he pushed back the hoodie and smiled at me – a broad grin lit up a clean-shaven face with a full head of blond hair. I was confused; this didn't look like a guy sleeping rough.

"Hi," he called out.

"Hello."

"I'm walking to the bus – do you live around here?"

"Yeah," I said cautiously. "What are you doing down there?" I gestured down the trail.

"Well, I've got an old VW van down there, and – "

"How did you manage that – how did you know about the trail?" I knew I sounded truculent and suspicious.

He watched me as I swung off the bike. Then it seemed he decided to explain. "I used to work for CedarHills, the company that owns the land along the river, so I knew there was an old logging road here" – he waved an arm at it – "and so I thought I might stay down there for a while."

"You know it's private land."

"Yes, they know about me being there. I was parked for a while on a road closer to town, but the neighbours complained, so I – well, so here I am." He grinned at me.

"Well, I live in a *house*" – I stressed the word – "back there." I pointed towards it.

"Oh, so you must be the son, maybe, of Mr. Travis – I was involved with the conveyance a couple of years back when I was still with the company."

I felt he was trying to be friendly, but I found myself irritated by the fact that he seemed to know stuff about me, while I had no clue about him.

Suddenly he held out his hand. "So, my name is Miller – Davidson Miller; everyone calls me Dave."

Feeling trapped into revealing who I was, I reluctantly shook his hand, saying, "Brenton Travis".

"Yes, my goodness, I remember your name from the paperwork at CedarHills."

Whether he really did, or was just trying to cozy up to me, I couldn't tell.

"Well, I must be on my way," I said, swinging a leg over the bike. But the guy didn't seem to take the hint, saying, "How do you find you're doing with an electric bike?"

"Fine – I'm very happy with it." I pushed off. "See you."

As I cycled into town, I felt myself annoyed with the guy's pushiness, but also with my churlishness. Yes, I had moved into the River Cottage to be alone, but that didn't mean I had to be rude to people who were just being civil. But then again, I thought, what was he doing squatting on the CedarHills land right next door to me? I guess I can't do much about it – it's not like he's on *my* land. Or maybe I could talk to the CedarHills folks. He said they know about him.

I quickly shelved the whole thing because, when I arrived at the office, there was a full-fledged 'situation' going on about a tenant in one of our buildings who had been arrested during the night in a drug bust.

But I realized, as I was pedaling home late that afternoon, that the glimpse of blue and my interaction with – what was his name? – Dave – *Davidson* – *what a fancy first name for a, what, a homeless guy*, had been niggling in the back of my mind all day. And he had introduced himself by his surname, before telling me his first name, like a business man would do – *'My name is Miller – Davidson Miller.'* That's not how a homeless guy is meant to speak. But what do I know. How old do I think he is? Maybe forty, something like ten years younger than me. Looks in good shape – better than me.

Then, what do you know! – as I was cycling down River Lane towards home, there he was just ahead of me, walking, tall, carrying a bag of what looked like groceries, and with his hoodie up. It had to be him. Obviously I couldn't just go right by him, so I called out, "Hi," just as I was coming up to him. He jumped a bit, and pulled his hoodie back as he turned to look.

I pulled up beside him, nearly at the logging road. "Sorry, I startled you."

"Yeah, I don't hear much with this thing," he gestured at his hoodie. Then I saw a hearing aid behind his right ear. He was smiling at me. "Say, why don't you come down and see where I am – I guess you're a bit nervous about me being there."

Again I had this weird feeling that he seemed to know just how I felt. *What the hell.*

"Sure. Can I go down there on this thing?" I pointed down at my bike.

"Well, I got the old bus to do it," he laughed.

So, with Dave leading the way, I cautiously wobbled down the logging trail, head down, watching for ruts and roots. *Am I going to be able to get back up the hill on the bike?*

"Here we are." He sounded almost proud about it. I stopped and looked up to see an old, faded grey VW van pointed down towards the river. The front wheels were up on blocks to counteract the slope, and, on the side, a blue awning stretched out over a rickety looking table on which sat a small barbecue. Beside it was one of those canvas director's chairs, with an attached side table. That was it.

I looked at him. "Home, sweet home," he said.

"Nice," I said, not knowing what to say, really. "It's a nice view of the river."

Dave grinned; "A water-view treasure, as the realtors might say. So, would you like a beer? I can break out the deck chairs."

"Thanks, but I need to get home." *I'm a wine man myself.*

He looked a bit crestfallen, and I was near to changing my mind when he said, "OK, see you around."

That evening, over habitant soup from a can, I decided I had to find a way to interact with this guy. I needed to step outside my crankiness with him, and, at the same time, satisfy my curiosity. Although tomorrow would be Saturday, because I seem to be the company problem-solver, I needed to go into the office to deal with the aftermath of the drug bust debacle; but I planned to get back by no later than mid-afternoon. *I'll go down there on my way home.*

It was a fine fall afternoon as I turned my bike down the trail towards the half hidden VW van. I dismounted and knocked on the door. Silence. Was he sleeping? I knocked harder. No response. I fished out a receipt from my wallet and wrote on the back; *Hi, Dave – Saturday 3 pm. I came by but you were away or asleep. If you can, why don't you come to the house around 7 this evening for a drink. Brenton.*

I wedged it through the crack in the door by the handle, and hoped he would see it there. I felt pretty good about doing it. While in town I had bought a bottle of Australian red wine and also some beer – *I don't know much about beer, so I hope he likes what I've got. Come to think of it, the receipt I used for the message was the liquor store receipt, so if he doesn't come, it may be because he looked, and doesn't like that brand.*

I *am* a worrywart.

So, surprise surprise, just after seven, I heard a quiet knock on the door, and there he was, smiling, and holding out a bottle of red wine.

"Hi, Brenton. Thanks for the invite." I gestured for him to come in. "I saw from the back of your message that you bought my favourite type of beer, so I figured I should bring a bottle of Okanagan wine from my stash."

A stash of Okanagan wine! What kind of homeless guy is this? And how come he knows my taste in wine?

It was a cool evening, so we sat inside, me sipping red wine, he quaffing his beer. I saw with relief that his clothes were pretty clean. I rootled around and found a big bag of chips for us to share. After the usual chit chat about what a nice house, and the lovely view of the river, etc., I sat back.

"So, Dave, you don't come across as the typical homeless man, or at least what I've always assumed about them. And you sure don't look like one. So I hope you don't mind, but how is it that you're living in an old VW bus in the trees?"

It sounded rehearsed.

He smiled at me. "Funny you should ask, as I was going to explain anyway."

It was a riveting story, or at least I found it to be so. Davidson, or *Dave*, as I had come to think of him, became so open about the bad as well as the good, that I began to wonder whether it was all true, and what he hoped to gain from telling me.

"Actually, I'm what I like to call a professional handyman." He grinned and raised a hand. "And before you go off thinking I'm one of those guys who says he knows how to fix something and you then find he's learning on the job – *your* job, that's not me. During high school I found I loved being able to build stuff and fix things. So I spent some years taking courses and getting certified in electrical and plumbing, I learned about appliances, I apprenticed to learn about painting, drywall, flooring and roofing – I took courses and got qualifications in a whole raft of things, all financed by my dad. And I amassed an impressive shedful of fancy tools." He smiled, and said, "I had very doting parents, but I did build them a super kitchen, and it all worked, so there."

He was sounding pretty slick, like he'd made this speech before. I wondered where it was going.

"After trying to run my own handyman business for a while, I realized that I'm good at doing the stuff, but not good at the business side of things – preparing proper estimates, keeping track of expenses, making appropriate arrangements for payment, and, worst of all, sorting out when and how to subcontract part of a job. So, I finally recognized that I need to work for someone other than myself, so that I get to do the stuff I do well and enjoy, while someone else does the paperwork."

He looked across at me. "That's how I got to work for CedarHills."

I looked surprised.

"Well, I expect you know that, in addition to this riverfront property"– he waved out the window – "they own the biggest Shopping Centre in town, and, while I worked for them, they acquired another one – actually more of a strip mall than a flat-out Shopping Centre, but they liked to call it that. Both have a high turnover of tenants, which means there's always renovation, upkeep and maintenance work to be done.

"Anyway, they figured, or I persuaded them, that the most efficient way to deal with repairs, equipment maintenance and modifications is to have someone in-house to do those things, rather than contracting everything out. I had the responsibility for attending to tenants' improvements done on the Landlord's ticket, and also arranged with the tenants to do things that were the tenant's responsibility, and the *tenant* paid. Generally I did it all myself, sometimes with another worker to help when needed. And I did some pretty fancy stuff, like a security system for a jewellery store, custom built box shelving, a dog washing and grooming facility for a high-end pet store, and a decorative fountain and waterfall with fancy underwater lighting. But I also did the run-of-the-mill stuff – washrooms, storage areas, display cabinets, and so on.

"Things were good. I bought a little apartment and a fancy car, which came with a girl, or maybe it was that when I got a girlfriend I needed a fancy car. It was sort of a package deal – I needed the car to drive the girl around, and I needed the girl when driving the car around. A couple of summers ago we tooled across to the Okanagan with the top down."

I wondered when he would stop. But then he did – briefly. He waved his beer can at me, and I got the message. So I went and got him another. Dave glanced at me.

"Thanks." He took a long drink. Then he started up again. "This is the bit you won't like. Things – *I*, actually – started to go off the rails. I was a happy guy, good at my job, and popular. My girlfriend and I liked going to the casino in town, where we could eat and drink and play the slots. Then I got introduced to the tables, and, well" – he glanced at me and sighed, "I guess it's the typical story of doing well at the start and then getting in over my head. I got to figuring I just needed one big win to get out of the hole – an ever deepening hole" – he looked down. "But it never happened."

Dave took a long swig, wiped his mouth, and tried to sound brave. "So, I lost my girl, traded the car in for a beater, and ended up owing a loan shark a bundle of money. You can probably guess where that led me." Dave paused and looked at me.

"I began to steal from my employer. It wasn't difficult – in fact it was too easy. I thought I could get away with it forever, if you know what I mean."

He shifted uncomfortably in his chair. "What I was doing was double-dipping. I would do work for a tenant and bill him for it, while at the same time sending invoices for the work to the accounts office at CedarHills classifying it as tenant's improvements for the landlord's account. They trusted me so much that they didn't question it. It worked for nearly a year, and I got away with nearly thirty thousand dollars before I got caught at it. It wasn't difficult to catch me, because I didn't have a clue how to cover my tracks. They were sort of stunned as to why I was doing it, so I told them about my gambling debt, which was really embarrassing."

He put his beer down and cleared his throat.

"They told me if I paid it back and signed up with Gamblers Anonymous they wouldn't get the police involved. I went and talked to my Dad and asked for help, but he told Mum, and they were furious, and pretty well told me to get lost." He sighed.

"So I sold my car and my bachelor pad and a bunch of my fancy tools, which gave me enough to get the loan shark off my back. I'm paying CedarHills back in monthly instalments, and have a way to go yet. I bought the VW off my brother – actually he sort of gave it to me but with the deal that I pay him if and when I can. I've got a job doing maintenance work at Paragon, you know, the other big Shopping Centre in town." I nodded. "CedarHills gave them a reference that said I was good at my job but needed supervision with the money side. I guess they were happy to see me gone. And, hey, I *am* going to Gamblers Anonymous meetings, well, sort of, when I can."

"So, that's why I'm where I am."

I glanced at Dave uncomfortably. "Quite a story. You tell it as if you've described it all before."

"You have to explain everything at GA – Gamblers Anonymous. That's part of the deal."

"So, how did you know my name when we first met the other day? You said you knew about me and my family from working at CedarHills, but – "

Dave waved a hand. "I know, I said I was involved in the land deal, but not really. I happened to be in the office the day all the stuff was getting signed, and they got me to be the witness to their signatures. I saw your name, and it sort of stuck with me – I once had a drinking buddy called Travis."

He sat quietly for a moment, then put the beer can down and stood up, looking weary. "Thanks for hearing me out."

As I got up, I said, "Another thing I'm curious about; you look so neat and clean. How do you deal with things like washing and – ah, toilets and stuff?"

Dave laughed – *my goodness, what a warm laugh* – "Questions often thought but seldom asked! Actually I have an oversized propane tank in the back of the bus which, if I'm careful, will keep me in hot water for a while, so I can boil the river water for things like shaving and even drinking. I haven't died yet! And one of the things I learned way back is how to construct a pit-toilet in the woods. You won't even be able to find it if you come down to see me, or," he chuckled, "even smell it! The other thing is that the administration office at Paragon has showers in their washrooms – they're pretty basic, but they're better than nothing."

As he was leaving, I awkwardly reached out and put my hand on Dave's shoulder. "That was pretty admirable, facing up to it all."

"Well, it was either that or jail."

Over the next few days, I saw Dave in the distance a couple of times, and we waved cheerily at each other. It seems he went to work earlier than I did, and often wasn't back when I went by on my way home. I guess I was impressed by that.

I don't know what made me do it – I guess I was looking for company – but on Friday the weather was pretty dreary again, and it was dark walking home. After some supper, I went out and, using my newly acquired headlamp for the first time, stumbled my way down to Dave's VW. I could see the light from his oil lamp through the side window, so I knocked, calling out, "Hi, Dave."

He opened the door and grinned down at me.

"Hi. I was thinking, the weather looks as if it will be pretty crummy for a few days, so if you aren't doing anything else Sunday morning, how about coming over for breakfast about eight. And," I chuckled, "you could have a shower in a nice bathroom for once."

Dave laughed his warm laugh, and said, "You're on, mate. I'll bring some bacon."

I started away, when Dave called out; "See that thing over there?" He pointed toward the edge of the awning. "That's my new toy – it's a propane gas fire pit! Pretty nifty!"

He came for breakfast and a shower, and I felt good about it when he said how lucky he was to have me as a neighbour.

It started to become a regular habit for Dave to come over for a Sunday breakfast-and-shower. He always brought bacon or sausages. We both had an interest in national and world affairs. I usually bought the Saturday edition of the Globe and Mail when I did my weekend shopping, so we would share the paper and our views over breakfast, and mull together over the notoriously difficult Saturday Cryptic Crossword. I would have some music going. Once, just after a blast of Mahler, Dave asked me to turn it down a bit. He pointed to his hearing aid. "It makes it buzz," he said, with a grimace. I was careful about my choice of music after that. After a while, Dave would have a luxurious shower, and leave around eleven.

An event the last weekend in November was a game-changer. On Saturday afternoon, I was down near the river on my property, doing some fall clean-up, when I heard some talking coming from Dave's place, and his hearty laugh. I figured, *what the hell*, and, leaving my wheelbarrow, walked down the river bank until I could see him sitting under the awning with a slight, hooded figure, both of them hunched over the little fireplace. Dave looked up, saw me, and gave a cheery wave. "Come on up!"

As I approached, Dave said, "Meet Joanie." The figure pulled back its hoodie, and I looked down at a tiny, strangely monkey-faced girl-woman with an untidy mess of black hair, who stared back at me impassively, her inky-pupiled eyes deep under shaggy brows, her thick lips tightly closed. Then she muttered "Hullo" in an oddly dark voice. I was confused and dumbstruck. Who is this strange person, and why is she here?

Then I realized Dave was talking. "Joanie is one of the cleaners at Paragon. She had a bust-up with her guy, and had nowhere to go, so I said she could stay here. She doesn't take up much room," he laughed.

We both looked at her. *She can't weigh more than ninety pounds.*

"Well, uh – good – good to meet you, Joanie. Well, I'd better be going." I started back, then called out, "See you tomorrow for breakfast, Dave?"

"Yes. Say, would it be OK if Joanie came too?"

"Oh – of course. I'll see you both around eight tomorrow." I walked back along the river.

"I'll bring bacon," I heard Dave shout.

Breakfast the next morning was different. It felt more formal. Joanie was dressed in a tracksuit which made her look like a teenager. She moved comfortably – almost sinuously. Her presence in the house was strangely alluring.

She hardly spoke at first, but when she finally did, it was an almost guttural sound. Instead of Dave and me chit-chatting about the latest political events, I think we both tried to make Joanie feel at home, so we talked about working at Paragon. Joanie finally joined in. In her strange deep voice, she explained that she was one of the cleaners for the public spaces – "the washrooms, seating areas – stuff like that, but not the Food Court – they have their own staff for that."

"She's the best," Dave smiled. "Being tiny, she can squeeze into all the corners."

"Oh shaddup," Joanie muttered, but she looked sort of pleased.

Breakfast over, Dave looked at his watch – I later wondered if this had all been planned – and said, "I have to go to work this morning – they've got a blocked drain, and I need to put my plumbing expertise to work. So I'll skip the shower. I can get one there after work. You can take my place, Joanie," he grinned.

So Joanie helped with the dishes. She was silent, but I was intensely aware of her standing down there at my side. I looked down at her and realized with a rush that her eyes weren't black – they were a sort of haunting deep grey.

As I was giving her a towel for her shower, she turned, smiled skittishly at me, and began to unzip her tracksuit.

"So, d'ya want it to be hand-beaten or blown off?" She added, in a low whisper, "I'm good at both."

I stared at her, shocked. "Why on earth are you asking me that?"

"I've got nothing else to pay for breakfast."

"Joanie, It's my pleasure to give you breakfast; you don't owe me anything for it."

"So I get breakfast and a shower, and you get the pleasure of providing them?"

"That's about it."

"OK, so I'll have a shower, and *then* we'll fuck."

And so that's what she did. And then that's what *we* did.

She was all arms and legs and lithe and hairy, with hard dark nipples. She swarmed all over my pale body like a questing monkey, nibbling and scratching. It was amazing.

After it was all over, and as we were getting dressed – *well, there's a use for the downstairs bedroom!* – I said, "What about Dave?"

"Whaddya mean, what about him?"

"Well, will he mind, if he finds out?"

"Oh, he'll know, but don't worry. It's all part of the deal."

She was right; Dave did know, or I figured out that he did. And she was right a second time; he didn't mind, as far as I could make out.

So that's how I got introduced to transactional sex.

That evening, there was a whale of a wind and rain storm. Early on, I figured with amusement that it was nature berating me for my misbehavior with Joanie, but when I started to hear branches crashing down, things became serious. Suddenly the lights flickered, came back on, dimmed, and then went right out. *So here I go with my generator! I never did look for that manual.* I stumbled around, looking for my headlamp, found it in the mudroom, and went out to the carport where the generator was installed, hoping I could remember what I had been shown for starting it. Just then, there was a fierce gust of wind and a squall of rain. Then I heard a loud crash from the other side of the house. *Shit!* Following the path lit by my headlamp, I went round, huddled against the rain. I shone my light ahead, and gasped when I saw, through the downpour, a massive fir branch cascaded over my newly re-roofed pump house. I stood there, stunned, and then heard a shout in the night. Turning, I saw a light wavering through the wildly swaying trees, and then saw someone coming up the bank from the river. It was Dave, and then I saw, right beside him, Joanie, clutching on to him, staggering as gusts of wind were nearly blowing her off her feet.

"We've got a tree down on the van, and I've lost the awning." Dave called. Then he saw the branch on the pump house. "Uh-oh!" he grunted.

"Come and help me see if we can get the generator going, and we'll all get inside before we get soaked to the skin," I shouted into the wind. We got round to the lee side of the house and into the carport. Dave went straight to the generator. He shone his flashlight around for a moment, and I heard him mutter, "Let's see, now."

"I have the manual somewhere," I said.

"That's OK," Dave responded. He turned a couple of switches, inserted a plug, and pressed a button. The generator roared to life. Dave swiveled around and, with a wide grin, gave me a thumbs up. I looked through the window to see the welcoming sight of lights in the house.

"Now let's have a quick look at the pump house, to make sure all's well." Dave was taking charge. He saw my power saw leaning against the wall in the corner. "We'll probably need that tomorrow."

We got Joanie into the house "so you won't blow away," chuckled Dave. "Don't run any water until we've checked things out," he called to her. Hunched against the howling wind and stinging rain, we went round to the pump house. Dave bent down and crawled under the branch. He somehow pushed the door open and scrambled in on his knees while I lit his way with my headlamp. Again, Dave looked at the pump for a minute, then called out, "The pressure tank needs to be primed." I had no idea what he was talking about. I could see him working at a valve in there. Then he pressed a switch and the pump started to hum.

"All's well, here," Dave grinned at me through the door; "Get it? All's *Well*, here".

Good god, I thought, here we are, in the middle of a storm, and he's making puns!

"Let's get inside and warm up," I spluttered.

We hustled back to the house, flung ourselves into the mudroom, and gasping, got out of our soaking raingear. Joanie had found the linen cupboard and brought towels, grinning at us as, shivering, we toweled off. I went and found sweaters for Dave and me, and we went to huddle by the fire. I was grateful for the fan blowing warm air out into the room.

As the three of us sat drinking "hot toddy" Dave called it, which was really just scotch I had located at the back of the kitchen cupboard – a gift from a grateful client – with some hot water and a squeeze of lemon, I told Dave I couldn't have managed it all without him.

"I love dealing with stuff like this. However, the tree on the old bus is another matter. I'll have to deal with that tomorrow."

"Well, for starters, you'll both stay here, of course."

So, with a fleeting recollection of Joanie sprawling over me on the bed just a few hours before, I got the downstairs bedroom and bathroom ready for the two of them, and we all settled down for what was left of the night. At least the wind had died down, and the rain had subsided to a drizzle. Sometime in the early dawn the power came back on – I was awakened by the bedside light coming on. Next, I heard Dave go stomping out to the carport. I left him to deal with the generator – *he knows what he's doing; he doesn't need me, but I sure need him!*

Then I heard the heat pump kick in. *Thank goodness for Dave.*

Monday morning came far too early for me and, I suspected, Dave and Joanie, who greeted me blearily. We all had to go to work, so I got the car out and gave Dave a house key in case they got home before me. I drove them to the bus stop – "We'll get breakfast in town," they said. Then I drove to my office, stopping to pick up a muffin and coffee at Tim Horton's on the way. Everyone was talking about the storm and the power-outage.

It was late and dark by the time I got home. Dave and Joanie must have got back by mid-afternoon, as Dave had already dragged the branch off the pump house, and was cutting it up with my power saw. He and Joanie had found the blown-away tarpaulin, and had used it to drape over the damaged pump house roof. "I'll have a proper look at the roof next weekend. It doesn't look too bad – just a couple of shingles to fix, I think."

"What about your old bus?"

"It is badly dented – "

"Caved in, I would call it," snorted Joanie.

"– and I've still got to get the tree off it. I've taken pictures of it. I don't have insurance, but I never did transfer ownership from my brother to me, and he's probably got coverage. I phoned and told him about it. He took it quite well, actually," Dave grinned. "He probably would prefer to have the money rather than getting that old clunker back."

Dave always seemed to be able to see the bright side of every event. I wish I could.

And Joanie had obviously put her skills to work, as the mudroom, left in a mess from the night before, had been tidied up and swept.

I was so happy to have their help that I took the three of us out for supper at the White Spot in town. Dave gave me his cellphone number "just in case you need my expert opinion on something when I'm not there," he laughed. He had quickly discovered how inept I was with all my new-fangled stuff.

Over the next few days, although things were hectic at the Paragon Mall, where Dave was in charge of some pretty astonishing Christmas decorations in cut-throat competition with other local malls, he was able to find a towing company that was prepared to haul the old VW bus out. After some chain-sawing and bushwhacking, it was safely removed. Also, Dave repaired the pump house roof, and helped me clear up the rest of the storm damage. He's a strong and healthy guy, as well as being insatiably cheerful.

As for Joanie, when she wasn't working her shifts, she took on cleaning my house, better than I ever had. I told her she didn't have to, but she said "I do it because I like to – for me, it's not a job." Dave and I called her "an obsessive housekeeper", and she said "Aw, shaddup."

For my part, I got into the regular pattern of fixing us all supper – breakfast was more of a grab and dash – and afterwards we sat and harangued or played Scrabble; we hardly ever watched TV. I put on some of my favourite evening music, but they weren't impressed. "I'm a jazz man, myself," said Dave, and Joanie mentioned some names I had never heard of, like Mariah Carey. But when we were listening (well, I was – they were putting up with it) to some Bach and Beethoven (which they *had* heard of) and I told them the performers were Yo-Yo Ma and Barenboim. They didn't know either of those names.

Getting everyone off to work became a bit of a problem, as Joanie's shift changed to the evenings, so if it was raining, Dave would borrow my car and drive to the main road to pick her up from the bus when she phoned, or would walk down to meet her if the night was fine. He took good care of her.

It was a funny liaison. Dave was very solicitous about Joanie, and I'm sure they had sex down there in the bedroom a few times – one night I heard a lot of muffled laughing – but he wasn't protective, and didn't act as if she was his girlfriend. Nor, come to think of it, did she treat him as her boyfriend. There was no *ownership* in the relationship. They were just friends who happened to be sharing the same bed, and each other, for the moment. And they were both equally casual with me.

Friendly, though. Looking back, I recall those few weeks as one of the happiest times in my life. We were thrust together by circumstance, and, without any effort, took great pleasure from the experience. It was, for me, a time out of time.

And yes, Joanie and I 'did it' once again, when Dave was working one Saturday. I was in the kitchen when she came to me, smirking and naked. "My turn," she muttered. I turned to grab her, and she ran, giggling, into the bedroom, where she splayed herself across the bed. I realized that this time it was my turn to pleasure her. She growled. I thought women were meant to moan, but she growled. *I couldn't remember Eunice making any noise at all.* After that, when I entered her, she locked me in with her skinny legs akimbo, and it was I who moaned.

I didn't feel any guilt towards Dave, and I don't think Joanie did either. It was, as I have said, sort of transactional – for being the housekeeper? – but also immensely satisfying.

It was the weekend before Christmas when the second game-changer – sort of the reverse of the first one – happened. It was actually a series of serendipitous events interacting.

First of all, Dave and Joanie told me over supper on the Friday evening that Paragon had announced that, after the Christmas-Boxing Week-New Year Sales rush, they would be closing the south side of the Paragon Centre for an eighteen-month teardown and rebuild. This would mean a reduction in staff. Neither of them seemed to be particularly worried about it, and mentioned quite casually that a termination bonus was being offered to those who chose to take it. Joanie muttered something about being released from being shackled to a millstone, and Dave grinned at her. It seemed to me that they weren't exactly happy at Paragon.

We played a game of Scrabble that evening, and Joanie and I got through a bottle of wine while Dave kept chugging beer. Nobody bothered to keep score, so I have no idea who won. It was all very relaxed.

The next morning was December 22nd, the Saturday before Christmas. I had nothing planned, but Dave and Joanie were working, as it was one of the Centre's biggest days of the year. So I left Dave and Joanie to fix their own breakfast, and muzzily heard them leave to walk to get the bus.

It wasn't even 8 am when I got the call from my boss at EXPM. He was, to put it mildly, pissed off. One of our prime clients was Harrowgate Apartments, a high-rise luxury apartment complex where the apartments were occupied by wealthy tenants who prefer to lease rather than own, for all sorts of reasons. Most of them had principal residences somewhere else in the world. They expected top-notch service. To look after the building, EXPM had installed as resident managers a husband-and-wife team, the Crowthers. Martin Crowther, a retired Major, and his second wife, Tamara, were a high-decibel couple, but they were efficient and respectful, which was what was needed. They had a suite on the ground floor next to the office and lobby. The building's owner, Jim Harrowgate, lived in the Penthouse. Jim was a needy client, and you jump when he calls. And he had called. It was about the Crowthers, or, more accurately, their absence, that Jim had called.

In a nutshell, as relayed to me by my boss, during the night there had been a marital dispute which had spilled out from the Crowther suite into the lobby, wrecking the Christmas decorations so lovingly installed by the building's 'Functions Group', and smashing the mirror by the front door, placed so that one could check one's appearance before venturing out. The police had been called by a second floor tenant. It was unclear whether Tamara was walking out on Martin, or whether Martin was throwing her out. In the end it didn't matter.

Worse than that, neither of the Crowthers was there anymore. Major Crowther was in jail on charges of assault causing grievous bodily harm, assaulting a police officer and resisting arrest. Tamara was in hospital with serious but non-life-threatening injuries. And as far as Jim Harrowgate was concerned, they were never to return, he having summarily fired them, though technically, not being their employer, he had no right to do so. He was particularly pissed about having been phoned by the police at five in the morning – Jim's number was the first number on the office notice board to call in the event of emergency.

To cap everything, as far as Jim Harrowgate was concerned, the Harrowgate Apartments' traditional Christmas function 'The Night Before the Night Before' was due to take place in the Entertainment Suite on Sunday evening, December 23, and the organizers, the Crowthers, were not exactly available.

For some reason, my boss's tone of voice made it sound as if he thought it was all my fault. In any event, he certainly thought the solution was all my responsibility.

First, I needed coffee.

Then it came to me.

I found Dave's cellphone number and called him.

"Hi. Is this a good time to talk?"

"Lemmee call you back in five."

Actually, it was more like ten minutes.

"Sorry – just repairing Santa's sleigh after it got attacked by a four-year old with a hammer."

"I hope you disciplined the kid."

Dave laughed. "Actually he and his hammer helped me fix the damage. So, what's up, doc?"

"Do you know the Harrowgate Apartments?"

"That ritzy place downtown? Yeah, I went to a party there once. Met the owner who acted like we should all bow and scrape."

"Well, how would you like to be the manager there?"

"What are you on about, mate?"

"The manager is in jail, his wife is in hospital, the annual Christmas party is due to start in the Entertainment Suite in – let's see – about thirty hours from now, and the place needs to be readied. I know you and Joanie are good at what you do, and that you both may be on the lookout for a change."

There was a long pause. Then, "Can you come down here to the Mall at noon? I can get Joanie in here, and you can tell us about it."

So, at noon (by which time I had heard from my boss and from Jim Harrowgate, both of them asking how I was going to deal with the situation), I met Dave and Joanie in the food court at the Paragon Mall. I told them what had happened, that I was in a bind, that in addition to the regular pay, I would arrange for them to get what we grandly referred to as a 'signing bonus', and that I would personally recommend them to both my boss and Jim Harrowgate so as to get around the usual job checks and references; we didn't have time for those. "So, don't let me down, guys."

"That guy Jim is a bit of a tartar, by all accounts," Dave muttered at Joanie. "He likes to be in control, and wants to be seen as being in command."

"I've dealt with those types before," Joanie grinned. "I'll have him sorted in no time."

Dave and I looked her, then at each other, and laughed. We both knew she was perfectly capable of dealing with Jim.

"Okay, you're on," Dave said. "When do we start?"

"Can you just walk out of here?"

"Just watch us," Dave grunted, as they both stood up.

I was so relieved, I hugged Dave, then leaned down and hugged Joanie.

They went and got their personal stuff, left resignation notes at the office, and joined me in the parking lot. I drove them back to the River Cottage, where they packed up incredibly quickly. I phoned my boss to tell him the problem was solved. He sounded a bit panicked about the fact that he didn't know these people. I told him that as he had made it my problem, he had to trust me to solve it. I said that Dave was a wizard at equipment maintenance, and Joanie was obsessive about keeping places clean. I was a bit astounded at how positive I sounded.

Then I called Jim Harrowgate and told him I would be bringing Dave and Joanie Miller to meet him and move in to the manager's suite. I didn't know Joanie's last name, so pretended they were married. *He'll find out, sooner or later, but by then they'll be settled in.*

I drove Dave and Joanie down to Harrowgate Apartments. I dialed Jim's number, and he came down to let us in. He looked a bit perplexed when he saw Joanie, with her monkey face and scrawny build, but Dave greeted him cheerfully, said they had met before, and generally took control. If Jim thought he was going to conduct an interview, he just never got a chance. Dave asked who the caterers were for the party the next evening. When he found that Jim didn't know, Dave said, "Well, at the last party I was at here" (he said it as if he regularly came to parties there), "the caterers were Gastronomy for Gatherings – I'll call them." I watched, spellbound, as Dave found their number, called them, ascertained that he was right, and made the necessary arrangements for Sunday evening.

While he was doing that, Joanie looked around the manager's suite for keys to the cupboards. She found them and did a quick survey of the cleaning equipment, clucking and shaking her head, but then announced that it was all very satisfactory. They completely took control, and Jim went away happy. The "Millers" were settled in by four in the afternoon, which meant the whole mess had been solved in eight hours.

Exhausted, I drove home and went in to my once-again empty house. Privacy and solitary living was what I had planned for when I first inherited it, but I now realized it would be some time before I became readjusted to the calm and quiet. I figured I would miss the two of them. I hoped for the call of the great horned owl, but there was nothing.

Sunday, March 21, 2010

I've decided to keep a diary! Well, sort of, in that I'm going to try writing something here every Sunday. I've tried before, without much success.

Anyway, this is the first day of spring, and also Bach's birthday! – I have Bach's Well-Tempered Clavier going in the background. So, it's a good day to start, as I've been here exactly a year. Also, it's a Sunday, and Sundays have become sort of special for me. Sunday breakfasts with Dave, and then with Dave and Joanie, were a pleasure. And it was a Sunday when I got sort of seduced the first time by Joanie. That Sunday was also the night of the storm, when Dave came to my rescue.

Since they moved into the Harrowgate Apartments, I haven't seen much of Dave and Joanie. I did get invited to a Valentine's Day Party there. Jim asked me as a sort of thank-you for finding Dave and Joanie for him. I didn't stay long, but long enough to see Jim looking at Joanie in a bemused way. She and Dave were in charge of refreshments, and she was dressed as a sort of weird provocative cupid. Dave saw me looking at her and Jim, and winked. So, as she had said she would, she had Jim corralled.

And Dave and Joanie spent the better part of a day here a couple of weeks ago. Dave showed me how to do maintenance on the pumps – I still can't believe I have three of them – and the generator, and wrote down a to-do list for emergencies, like when the power goes out. While I was getting lunch ready, Dave went out with Joanie to check the pump house, and reported back that "all was Well", and this time we laughed at the pun. After lunch, Dave said it was a good thing to run the generator occasionally, and went off to do that. "And, as the weather's good, I think I'll go over to where the bus was and fill in the old pit toilet, and make sure we cleaned everything up. We left in such a hurry." While he was gone, Joanie did her obsessive housekeeper thing with the mudroom, and then asked me, with her lopsided grin, if I wanted anything else. I said no.

I said no because, when they arrived, it seemed to me that there was something different happening. I couldn't quite place it at first, but when I'd looked out the window at them coming back from the pump house before lunch, I saw that they were holding hands. That's different.

I can't work out whether I miss those few weeks, or whether I'm relieved that they're over, and that I'm pleased to be back to what I intended this to be – a remodeled life in a remodeled home.

Anyway, they're coming over for supper this evening; Dave tells me he has paid off CedarHills, and has bought an electric car! I won't ask how he found the money to do that. So they're coming in his car, and I'm looking forward to seeing them. He says he and Joanie have something to show me. I bet it's a ring.

p.s. They've gone now, and, yes, I was right about the ring. I'm happy for them. They are an odd couple, to be sure, but perhaps that's what works for them. So, here's the thing; somehow I have a feeling of release, so that I can get on with stuff – my life – as planned. People talk of closure, which I've never really understood. But I do see myself as, not so much at the end of my first year in the River Cottage, but at the start of the rest of my time here. I feel that maybe I'm now better equipped to do that. As I write this, I have just heard the great horned owl way out there, solemnly concurring.

Ripple Effect

Zero hour

It was 9:00 am on the first Monday in December on Vancouver Island. Far too early in the week and the day for anything serious to happen at the College. Joel Proteous, aged nineteen and wearing a hoodie, walked into the Atrium of the Cohen Presentation Centre with his father's old hunting rifle, and opened fire. He shot and killed Blair Trainor, who was standing in line to pick up his transcripts. Then the gun jammed and Joel dropped it. He ran out through the wide open doors into the winter sunlight.

Joel didn't know Blair, and Blair didn't know Joel. Blair was an undistinguished student who wasn't going to make any difference in the world.

That's what made it all the more senseless.

One minute after

As Joel was running across the grass towards the staff parking lot, a bull of a man appeared at the top of the stone steps, framed by the cavernous open double doors of the Atrium. He yelled, "Stop that man!" His booming shout shattered the morning slumber. Two security men standing at the College gates, one smoking, jerked around and, startled, saw a hooded figure zigzagging across the lawn. They struggled to pull their pistols out of their holsters. They had never done this before. They started running towards the sprinting man. He reached the first line of cars in the lot and ducked down behind a van. The security men stopped, uncertain. For a soundless instant no-one moved. Suddenly a scream echoed out from the Atrium, releasing the frozen moment.

The man in the doorway lumbered down the steps and, gargantuan in the slanting morning sun, strode across the grass. He reached the crouching boy just as he straightened up, sweeping his hoodie back from his face. Joel looked up at the man towering over him.

"Hi, Dad," he said, shakily.

Forty-nine year old Professor Winthrop Proteous, head of the Faculty of Commerce and Business Administration, did something he had never done before. He enfolded his son within his massive arms and cried, his sobs ringing out across the sunlit campus against the blare of the first sirens approaching the gates. The security guards, uncertain, stood waiting.

Then the police arrived and took over.

Two minutes after

The first peripheral casualty to suffer collateral damage was the College Chaplain. Happening to walk through a side door into the Atrium a minute after Blair Trainor was shot, Ted Manter was shocked to see a grotesquely crumpled body sprawled on the flagstone floor and a rifle lying starkly nearby. There was a girl, unkempt hair flopping down over her face, bent over the body. He hurried to her side and crouched on one knee beside the body. Blood was welling out from underneath the torso. Ted had no experience with such things, but this person was clearly dead. He had no idea what to do, or what he was meant to do. As he knelt there beside the now sobbing girl, he felt his faith, already challenged by the assaults of college life, dribble inexorably away through a hole somewhere deep within. After a while, he got up and went away.

Ninety minutes after

That day, Blair's parents, Joe and Marylynne, had gone to the Mainland by the first ferry, and had driven to Port Coquitlam to visit with their daughter, Caytlin, Blair's older sister, and her young husband Barry. They had just arrived at the rental apartment. It was 10:30 in the morning. Barry had arranged to take the day off. Caytlin had just told her parents that she was pregnant, and Marylynne and Joe were ecstatic. Marylynne was hugging her daughter for a second time, and Joe was pumping Barry's hand and thumping him on the back when the phone rang. It was the Coquitlam RCMP, asking if Blair's parents were there.

"Yes, why?"

"We've had a call from the Vancouver Island RCMP; they've been trying to contact them. Are they there now?"

"Yes, why?"

"We are on our way."

Joe and Marylynne looked at each other. Had the house been broken into?

Five minutes later an RCMP van pulled up and Barry pressed the button to let two officers, a man and a woman, into the lobby. They came up and introduced themselves. Then they all sat in the tiny living-dining room, the police at the table for two in the window. They told Marylynne and Joe, and Caytlin and Barry, that Blair was dead "in a shooting incident at the College."

Caytlin watched as her mother disintegrated in Joe's arms.

An hour later, the RCMP having provided contact information before they drove away, Joe and Marylynne left for the ferry terminal to return to the Island. They were so preoccupied that they ran out of gas just before the causeway to the ferry terminal. After getting towed to the nearest gas station and getting back in line, they only just caught the 7 pm ferry. They arrived home late and exhausted.

The next day, Caytlin miscarried.

Also ninety minutes after

Chelsea Fanning had been in her Vancouver office since eight that morning. She liked getting an early start before the others, and this morning she had a personal matter to deal with, involving a phone call to head office. Her divorce from Winthrop Proteous was finally through the decree nisi stage, and it was now only a matter of weeks before the decree absolute. Her change of name back to Fanning was completed and she had a new passport. She had moved to Vancouver and had established herself in her Vancouver office, but the financial and 'place on the ladder' arrangements with her newly merged accounting firm still needed the authorizing signature of the Managing Partner in Toronto. He finally called her back after lunch, Toronto time, to tell her it was done. Chelsea pumped a fist in the air, and then, as she was putting the phone down, her assistant Danny poked his head through the door.

"The radio has something about a shooting at your old stomping ground, the College."

Then her phone rang and, as she picked it up, Chelsea looked at her watch. Ten-thirty.

"She could hardly understand the hoarse groan. "Chelsea – it's me – Winthrop."

Chelsea got up, clutching the phone. "What's wrong?"

"It's Joel – he – he – "

"Winthrop, I can't hear you properly."

"Somebody got shot – "

"What – Joel got shot?"

"No – you need to come."

Chelsea yelled, "Winthrop, tell me what happened – is Joel alright? Is he shot?"

"No – he – I – they think he shot someone."

"Where is he?"

"I'm at the police station, and they have him here, but they're talking about – Oh, Jesus, I don't know – taking him to the hospital."

"Winthrop, I'm coming."

She slammed the phone down and yelled "Danny", then turned and saw him standing at the door.

"I need to go – find out when the next harbour-to-harbour flight leaves, and – oh God, find out where the hell the police station is near the College."

On the seaplane for the twenty minute flight, Chelsea remembered the letter Joel had written to the two of them, pleading with them not to live apart. She could recall some of it word for word. "I hate the idea of going back and forth; I will feel like a double agent, reporting to each about the other."

Three hours after

Winthrop's sister Natalie, affectionately known as 'Natty' at the bus station, was a driver for the community bus in a little coastal town up-Island. She had just heard about the College shooting on the radio while on her noon break. No names were given. She was thinking of calling Winthrop, when Jinx, the receptionist in the office handed her a scribbled note. *Your brother called. He's at the police station with Joel. He will call again when he can. Don't call back.* Natty looked at Jinx.

"He sounded really stressed. I guess it's about the shooting."

"Yeah. Well, I have to go. I'm not allowed to take calls on route, so if he calls again it'll have to wait till I get back."

Just as she was pulling out, Jinx came running across to the bus window.

Natty leaned down – she didn't want the passengers to hear, though there were only two, and she knew them both.

"He says they say he was the shooter."

"Who was?"

"His son."
"Jesus!"
"He says call him on his cell when you can."
"Oh, God!"
"Natty, are you OK to drive?"
"Yeah." Natalie put the bus in gear and drove out. Her brain was churning about what she should do. She dropped off both the passengers and picked one up. It wasn't a busy route this time of day. She was trying to figure out if she could go down the next day. She drove right by a stop where young Billy Goreham was waiting, all dressed up in clean jeans and a North Face long-sleeved T shirt, waiting to catch the bus to go to a job interview at the town's hardware store. He missed the interview and his name was crossed off the list. He really needed the job.

That afternoon

Winthrop's afternoon disappeared in a haze of phone calls, Chelsea arriving, and trips between the police station and the hospital. At some point during all the chaos, a law professor friend at the Law School got him linked in with a local criminal lawyer – "the best there is for this type of thing". Winthrop wondered bleakly what 'this type of thing' was. The lawyer emailed him that he had found that Joel would stay in the hospital for at least two days for observation. On release, he would most likely be charged with murder, after which there would be a bail hearing, where he would have 'no chance' of being released. The judge would probably order that a psychiatric evaluation be undertaken. Joel would then be moved to The Victoria Youth Custody Centre. The email concluded with: "I would like to meet with you as soon as possible to review the situation and plan a way forward. I will also seek to meet with your son as soon as permissible. On no account are you or any member of your family to engage in any way with the press, who will likely be persistent. We will also need to discuss a retainer. I send my condolences for this dreadful situation."

Two years before

For Joel's seventeenth birthday, his father got him a hunting license, and took him deer hunting. Winthrop, for whom hunting was a cherished annual breakout, approached the event as a rite of passage for his son, while for Joel it was agonizing. He didn't want to do this, but it was beyond him to stand up to his father.

At the camp, before leaving in early dawn, Winthrop showed Joel his trusty Remington, and how to oil and clean it. He explained that good rifle preparation was essential. "Otherwise it tends to jam."

Their guide, as usual, found them a great opportunity – a 4-point mule deer, standing upwind from them in the shade of some trees. Winthrop handed his gun to Joel and whispered, "It's yours for the taking, son."

Joel awkwardly raised the gun. The movement of the barrel seemed to alert the deer. It raised its head, appeared to look directly at Joel, and then turned. As the deer moved, Joel swung, fired, and missed. The deer bounded. Winthrop made to grab the gun, but the deer was gone.

Back at home that night, Winthrop lay beside his wife in their conjugal bed and vented.

"Here's the thing – it seems to me that it's almost as if he deliberately missed it."

"Winthrop, what is it about you; you sound as if you see this whole thing as some sort of trial you've created to challenge Joel to prove out something – what, his manhood?"

"No, it isn't that. Well, maybe."

Crouched at his listening post by his parent's bedroom, Joel saw the slim sliver of light under the door go out, and padded silently back to his room.

Eighteen months before

The 'College Tragedy', as the Press came to refer to it, came at the end of what the Porteous family had already recognized as their 'Annus Horribilis'. Actually issues had started to surface even earlier. While Joel was still in Secondary School, his elder brother Nicolas, 'Nick' to everyone except his father, got into serious trouble with the city police about drugs. They weren't interested anymore about illegal drug use, but drug trafficking, even to a small degree, was relentlessly targeted. Nicolas claimed vociferously that he was just sharing stuff he got with his friends, and what if they gave him a gratuity or two. But the authorities weren't having any of it. Nicolas went off to the Vancouver Island Regional Correctional Centre for 6 months.

While their son languished at the Centre, Winthrop re-established contact with a long-lost Australian cousin, and Winthrop's wife, Chelsea, connected with her accounting firm's associated company in Melbourne. The result was that, when Nick emerged from a not particularly onerous incarceration, he found a plane ticket and letters of introduction ready for him. He laughed about being dragooned out of town 'like a modern-day Remittance Man'. But, if truth be known, Nick was delighted to get away from what he saw to be his manipulative parents. While he virtually rejoiced in his parents' excommunication of him from the family, Joel agonized over it. As it happened, he had no part to play in the process, as he was away on a school trip when his brother left.

"Don't I have something to say about this sort of thing?" he plaintively said to his mother on the phone.

"Now, Joel, don't be like that. It's for his own good."

A year before

Adding to the strain the Nicolas debacle brought, both Winthrop and Chelsea became simultaneously involved in stressful developments at work. The College became embroiled in a 'scandal', or so the press described it, where some faculty members appeared to have taken payments for accepting manipulated exam results to enable kids of wealthy alumni to qualify for entry to the College. As a highly respected College representative, Winthrop headed up the investigation. The press put a searchlight on the issue and there was strenuous pressure applied for a quick determination. For a couple of weeks, Winthrop was seldom to be found at home. When he was there, as often as not he was on his home phone to others involved in the issue, as he had the feeling that his office phone was not secure.

One evening, at the height of the situation, Joel tapped on his father's half open study door – not something he often did.

"Hi, son. I'm just in the middle of something here. What is it?"

"Well, I just thought we could talk about – you know, my plans for next year, and stuff."

"Yeah, right. Ah, Joel, I'm really tied up in this College faculty thing right now – sorry, not right now Joel; let's try some time tomorrow."

The next morning, at the breakfast table, Joel said "How about after supper this evening?" And Winthrop said, "Sure." But that evening Winthrop got up after supper and headed for the door. Joel said, "Dad?" And his dad said, "Oh, sorry, not right now, Joel; I've got to go."

Joel muttered, "I'm beginning to think that's my name."

"What is?"

"Not right now, Joel"

"Oh, come on, son. I've got this crisis on my hands. I promise you we'll sit down about it before the weekend."

But they never did.

Also a year before

Contemporaneously, Chelsea had been politely but firmly coerced onto a committee her firm formed to negotiate a merger with a national accounting firm. As the youngest partner on the team, she felt an obligation to represent the needs and aspirations of the young partners and associates, and found herself spending many evening hours participating in spirited discussions, often lubricated by fine wines.

She also had a personal stake in the proposed merger as it would mean that, if she played her cards right, she could escape her stultifying situation in Victoria, both professionally and personally. She made it clear to those on the national accounting firm's team, with some of whom she shared those fine wines, that a condition of the merger, as far as she was concerned, was a move by her to the Vancouver office. She could, she explained, commute by helijet from Victoria. She also was prepared to rent a small apartment in Vancouver where she could stay during the week. Chelsea didn't divulge that there was a much simpler possibility, which was that she might leave her husband and live permanently in Vancouver. In any event, the plans she laid out were enthusiastically accepted by those on the other side of the table.

This in itself led to Chelsea's one and only marital indiscretion. She immediately bitterly regretted it, as she realized that, for years, it would colour her interactions with the individual involved, as well as with those who came to know about it, or at least suspect it, the rumour mill in the firm being somewhat sieve-like. A big auburn haired woman with big appetites, Chelsea's sexual relationship with Winthrop, a mountain of a man, had always been tempestuously gratifying, while not necessarily emotionally fulfilling. She compensated for some of the vacancy created by this flaw with hard work and a voracious drive for achievement. Her fine dress sense did not entirely conceal from her associates the existence of importunate breasts, and thighs that could, as one indiscreet colleague described wryly, "snap a man's neck, given the opportunity".

The object of Chelsea's momentary lapse into infidelity was a visiting member of the national accounting firm's negotiating team. He was also everything that Winthrop was not. He was slimly tall and lithe, a dapper dresser, and, above all, he was funny, which could never be said of Winthrop. His attitude with Chelsea was, if anything, a touch condescending rather than domineering, as was Winthrop's wont. It was this attitude which put Chelsea on her mettle. She rose to the challenge and surprised herself and her prey by leading him at three in the afternoon, after an animated group lunch meeting at one of Victoria's finer restaurants, to a room in the hotel next door.

Chelsea arrived home at seven that evening. She had not been there for supper three days in a row, and here she was, late, feeling a bit disarrayed, and not exactly pleased with herself. After all, she didn't have to do it to seal the deal. It actually came to her as she was driving home, that this was a good thing, because if she had bedded the man to ensure her move, it would have changed a nice romp in bed from being gratuitous to transactional, and then she would have been permanently in thrall to him. By the time she got home, she had already categorized the event as a one-night – or, she thought wryly, a one-*afternoon* stand.

It was a relief to find the front door locked and the house empty. She began throwing things together for a light supper, wondering if she had time for a shower before Winthrop or Joel arrived – she wondered if she smelled of sex – when the front door banged.

"Who's that?"

"Joel. Remember me?"

"Oh, Joel, don't be silly. You know I've got a lot on my plate right now. Don't try to make me feel guilty about missing supper last night."

"And the night before, and the night before that."

"Well, you're a better cook than I'll ever be, so what's your problem?"

Joel looked at her quizzically.

"What?"

Just then Winthrop stormed in to the house, frothing about 'those damned dinosaurs of professors', hardly noticing his wife turning away from him. Joel wheeled around and walked up the stairs to his room.

Also a year before

As to Winthrop's affair, it was, as with all things for him, more calculated – controlled, some might say – than Chelsea's. One of the lecturers at the College, Claudia Dibello, reflected her Italian ancestry with olive skin, luxurious black hair and black eyebrows, but there it stopped. She didn't much like pasta, and wasn't particularly demonstrative. In fact, she was an intense and committed researcher and lecturer in linguistic anthropology. Their introduction was as banal as it could be – spilled soup at the Faculty Club cafeteria (by her on his trousers), followed by apologies (both ways, by her for his bespattered trousers, by him for his intemperate language), and an invitation (by him to her) to join his group by the window (turned down by her).

Not a man accustomed to be thwarted, Winthrop stopped by her table on the way out and, handing her his card, asked if he might have hers, which she reluctantly gave him. A subsequent phone call, a quiet drink in a secluded bar downtown, and a walk in the park culminating in a searching kiss, was what it took for him to achieve recompense, in a conveniently available downtown apartment provided by a colleague, for her initial rejection. She quickly came to recognize it as a dead-end affair. It was all over in three weeks.

Except that, for Claudia, it was not all over. Three weeks later, she ascertained that she was pregnant. She agonized over whether to keep the baby, but, in the end, decided she didn't want a child with that man's genes. So, without informing Winthrop, she terminated her pregnancy. She felt she could never forgive herself, or Winthrop, about it all.

Nor, actually, was it all over for Winthrop. His brief but unfortunately public rendezvous in the park had been noticed by an unscrupulous college senior who was an iphone enthusiast. He provided Chelsea, for adequate compensation, with information sufficient for her to structure a convenient exit from a marriage already dead, at least from the neck up, and unraveled beyond repair.

Her divorce papers were uncontested.

One day after

The news of the shooting spread wildly through the College, but Claudia Dibello, who was with a linguistics research team on Haida Gwaii, only heard, when she returned the next day, that Winthrop's son had shot someone. For a year, she had deliberately avoided the Commerce building where Winthrop worked. She just didn't know what she might say to him, or he to her, if they were to meet. Feeling strangely fragile, she walked over to the Commerce Building. Winthrop wasn't there, a staff person told her. "You've heard –"

"Yes, I just wanted to leave him a note." She handed the woman a sealed envelope. "Please see that he gets this." The woman nodded as she reached to pick up her ringing phone. Somehow the note never reached Winthrop. It would have told him that, even from the most unlikely sources, there are people who hold his grief in their hearts.

And in the Vancouver office of the national accounting firm, upon hearing that Chelsea had rushed off to Victoria, the soft-spoken partner, who had brokered the deal that included Chelsea's move to the Vancouver office, arranged for flowers to be delivered to Chelsea's new Vancouver home with a note of support on behalf of the firm. The envelope was pinned to the wrapper. The flowers lay, untended, on the doorstep for days. When Chelsea finally returned from Victoria, she threw the withered flowers out. She never saw the note.

Also one day after

Nicolas Porteous, Winthrop and Chelsea's first born, and Joel's older brother, struggled out of sleep, wincing at the phone's sharp ring. He waited for the answering machine to click in, rolling over to squint at the clock. 7:30 am. Christ. No-one calls at this time. He was in a long-stay hostel in Melbourne, with a hellova hangover and lying next to a woman he hardly knew. Suddenly there was his father's voice.

"Nicolas, it's Dad."

Dad? Dad never calls. How did he get this number – it must be that stupid cousin up in Brisbane.

There's been an – an incident at the College." *An incident? What the hell is that?* "Somebody got shot – shot dead." Nick could hear his dad breathing deeply. "Joel is involved, and is going to be charged. I wanted to let you know before the press find you. Call me when you can."

The answering machine clicked off just as Nick was reaching across the woman – *what's her name?* – to grab the receiver.

"What's up?" what's-her-name mumbled.

"I dunno – that was my dad calling from BC. Let's see – it's yesterday afternoon there. He said something about some guy shot dead and my bro being charged, and the press. I'd better call him back. But I gotta pee first."

While he was in the bathroom the phone rang again, and the woman stupidly picked it up.

"Yes?"

"Yes, he's here." Nick was frantically chopping a hand at her, but she handed the phone to him. "Yes?"

"Mister Porteous, this is Brady Manning of the Herald Sun – "

Nick slammed the phone down, cursing.

"What's your problem, mate?" the woman whined. "You just don't answer if you don't want to talk to them."

"You stupid cow – now they know where I am."

"What's your problem?" she repeated.

"If you must know, I'm not exactly welcome in this country – they don't like my – my lifestyle."

As if on cue, the phone rang again and when the answering machine clicked in, it was the hostel's front desk man, sounding frosty. "Nick, there's a press guy here wants to 'ave a word. You better come on down. He ain't goin' nowhere 'til he sees you."

Nicolas dressed quickly, stuffed some clothes and things in a carry-all and, without a word to the woman, walked out the door, down the hall to the emergency exit and down the fire escape. Neither the hostel nor what's-her-name ever saw him again.

Three days after

Barry had watched in frustration as his sweetheart consoled her mother and then grieved herself over her brother's meaningless death. His exasperation festered into rage a day later at the loss of their unborn and innocent child.

He watched the lurid press coverage railing about 'US style mass murders' – "If the gun hadn't jammed, how many more would this troubled boy, taught by his father to love guns, have massacred?" He read even worse diatribes on Facebook and Twitter.

On the Thursday after the 'incident' Barry saw in the press that Joel had been released from hospital where he had been under observation, had been charged with murder, and that there would be a bail hearing at the Victoria courthouse the next day. Barry called the RCMP officer who had left his contact information and found that the bail hearing would be at 10 am.

Early in the morning, Barry kissed his mournful wife and said he had to go to work or he'd lose his job. But he didn't go to work. He drove to the ferry terminal, parked his car, walked on to the 7 am ferry, and caught the bus into Victoria. He walked into the courthouse at 9:30 am.

He was carrying a switchblade. He had it tucked into the inside pocket of his parka.

In his last year at Secondary School, he had gone with the school band on a concert tour in northern BC, the Yukon and Alaska. It was a crazy time. After the concert in Fairbanks, Barry bought the switchblade as a bravado dare. He had never told anyone other than the school friend who dared him. Caytlin didn't know. It was just a prank. Until now.

Barry had never been in trouble with the law, and had never been inside a court house. He found a notice board, and saw that "R vs Porteous – Bail hearing" would be at 10 am in Court Room 3. He saw some people across the lobby and walked over. It didn't register for a moment, but then he realized he was looking at the arch of a walk-through metal detector like the ones they have at airports, and a security guard in some sort of uniform standing behind a long table beside the metal detector. Finally it registered with him that, to go down the hallway to the court rooms, he would have to go through the machine. *Maybe this contraption won't pick up the knife.*

Well, it did. As Barry stepped through the arch, a buzzer sounded, and a red light started flashing. The uniformed man at the table motioned for him to come to the table, and said, "Take off your jacket and empty your pockets please, sir."

Barry took off his parka and laid it on the table. The security guard felt in the pockets and found the switchblade. He called another guard over, an older man, who looked, and said to Barry, "Come with me, sir."

In a small side room, Barry tried to maintain that the knife just happened to be in his pocket. He said he was going to the bail hearing because he had read about it in the paper, and wanted to see Joel in person and hear what he had to say about what he did. He heard himself sounding false. The older guard looked at him. "Sir, they do bail hearings by video conference. The prisoner won't be in the court room. And most likely a lawyer will speak for him."

Barry stared at him, stunned. He felt foolish.

"Sir, it's a criminal offence to possess an article like this. With your permission I'm going to confiscate this."

Barry mumbled, "Can I go now?"

"Yes, sir. And we'll be keeping this." The guard picked up the knife and put it in a plastic bag.

As Barry stumbled out of the Court House, he realized he had no idea what he would have done with the knife even if Joel had been there.

Four days after

The lawyer sat down with Winthrop and Chelsea the afternoon after the bail hearing. Winthrop was in a chair by the lawyer's desk; Chelsea sat by the door. She was staying in a downtown hotel. The lawyer told them the bail hearing had gone as he had expected, and that Joel was on his way to the Youth Custody Centre. The court had also ordered a psychiatric evaluation.

"I had a few minutes with your son," he said. "He told me he doesn't want to see either of you at the moment. In my experience, that will change, but perhaps not for a while. I tried to get at the fundamental question of 'Why', but without success, I'm afraid." He paused, then went on. "I'm no expert in psychiatry, but I do have to tell you that what I think we have here is a very lonely young man. He told me he didn't think you – either of you – would recognize him if he walked into the room."

Five days after

The day after the meeting with the lawyer, the psychiatrist appointed pursuant to the court order that an evaluation be done, met with Chelsea 'just for background information.'

Asked whether there was anything she could tell him about Joel's relationship with his parents or with one or the other of them which might have a bearing on why Joel had done what he did, Chelsea said, for the record, "Well, I can't think that any of it was my fault. You should talk to Winthrop. After all, it was his gun."

A week after

On the Monday following the College Tragedy, Winthrop Porteous purloined a pistol and some bullets from the armoury of the College Shooting Club, walked into the forest behind the College Campus, sat down, put the gun in his mouth and pulled the trigger.

He left no note.

He had no need to do so.

A Guy With A Dog

That Sunday, after he had taken Wendy home from church, Grant drove out to talk to his older brother at his trailer half hidden by brambles and nettles in the far corner of the municipal campground. It was part of a little assemblage of dilapidated accommodation for what the manager called 'rounders', who lived in the campground year-round, some of whom had been there for some years. They, who preferred to call themselves 'Permies', were a tight-knit bunch of misfits who looked after themselves and each other just fine, thank-you very much.

Grant parked his Lexus, looking out of place beside Danny's trailer, and went to bang on the door, glancing at the build-up of moss on the roof.

I don't know why I'm doing this again, he thought. *It always ends up a disaster. It's not as if he's ever done anything for me.*

The day before, at breakfast, Grant had taken a deep breath and looked over the top of the newspaper.

"Wendy, I've been thinking – "

"Uh oh."

"Well, now that Brian's moved out we have a totally empty suite downstairs and –"

"And you want to ask that bum of a brother of yours if he would like to try civilization again for a while."

Impatiently Grant swished the paper. "I don't want to argue about it. I would just like us to think about it."

Silence. Then;

"There would have to be some limits – some rules." Warming to the point, Wendy said, "I mean you would have to lock the liquor up, and he can't have his music blaring at all hours – that's what got him kicked out of that motel."

"Well, not everybody likes classical – "

"Not *anybody* likes music *anytime* at the sound level of a *jetplane* taking off." A pause. "Would he pay us rent?"

"I don't know – I haven't got that far. I'm just trying to find out if you would let me put it to Danny."

A sigh. "Well, I suppose so – he will have to clear it with his parole officer."

"I know," impatiently, "I've thought of that."

So here he was, banging on Danny's grimy door. He winced at the sound of an orchestra belting out something wild, and banged harder. Then the door scraped open and Danny, framed by the full blast of the music and dangling earphones, yelled, "Come in!" Grant was immediately assaulted by Pluto, Danny's over-friendly three-year-old yellow dog of indeterminate ancestry. Grant dodged by the dog, and Danny lunged across the room and turned the music down, then looked at Grant and, with a reluctant shrug, switched off the CD player. "Mahler in ecstasy," he grinned.

Grant, dapper in his Sunday sweater and slacks, looked at big, sloppy Danny, with his wild grey hair and soiled cardigan, and again wondered why he was doing this.

Daniel offered Grant some of the meal he and Pluto were sharing together. Grant shuddered and declined. Then, perching on the edge of a grey looking sofa, he made the offer.

"Why are you doing this? What's the motivation?"

"Come on Danny, don't be like that – you can't stay in this rathole over winter, and we have the basement suite empty now, so – "

"I bet Wendy doesn't want me there."

"Well, she wants a few – understandings to – "

"Rules you mean".

"Nothing more than your parole officer would want to see."

"Him" – scornfully.

So that is how it came about that, a couple of weeks later, Danny Merchant vacated his trailer, though he arranged to pay a storage fee to keep it in the campground, and moved into the basement suite of the home of Grant and Wendy Merchant in the upscale subdivision called The Orchard. "Just for a while, mind you, so we can see if it works for all of us."

There couldn't be a bigger difference between two brothers than between Grant and Daniel. The younger Grant, driven by ambition and fueled by success, was, at forty-five, the senior partner in the biggest independent accounting firm in town, staying resolutely disconnected from the national and multi-national mega-firms. He had made a provident marriage, and remained securely betrothed to Wendy Squires of the Squires family. He had recently been elected to the Town Council, and was the proud father of Brian who, at the age of eighteen, was off to college and showing awesome potential as a hockey player.

Danny on the other hand was a dreamer, an untidy intellectual, and a supporter of causes, usually for inexplicable, or at least unexplained, reasons. He had never married, had been arrested far too many times, and jailed more than once for causing a disturbance, blocking the road, public mischief and/or public drunkenness. He also had an insatiable appetite for, and broad knowledge of, 19th and early 20th century 'classical' – or, as he put it, 'serious' music. And he made a spotty living writing about it. One of his more constant, though declining, sources of revenue was royalties from a compendious tome with incredible lithographs and prints entitled *Keyboard Instruments; One Thousand Years In Development*. It was a seminal work when first published twenty years ago, and was still bringing Danny a little revenue.

The frustrated local police and judiciary now had Danny in almost perpetual bondage to a parole officer, George, with whom he had established a guarded friendship. After checking with George, Danny was allowed to move out of the trailer to the Merchant's basement suite recently vacated by Brian.

And he brought his best friend, his dog Pluto. He entered into an arrangement with George with respect to curfew; as long as he was walking Pluto in The Orchard, his presence on the streets after dark was acceptable.

Danny also brought with him his sole means of transportation, a wobbly, rusty bike, together with his impressive CD collection and his less impressive kitchen gear. As conditions of residence, he promised to use headphones when listening to anything loud, promised to use the fan when cooking, promised not to sing or hum too loudly or too incessantly (as was his wont), promised to pick up after the dog, and agreed with Grant and Beverly to stay off the booze – at least in public. "After all, that's my deal with George."

"Yeah, well, that's a deal you take pretty lightly."

Danny looked a bit huffy, but didn't respond directly. "Come on, Pluto. Let's check out the smells in the neighbourhood."

The neighbourhood was, indeed, to Pluto's liking, with tree-lined streets, an assortment of other dogs to meet, and one or two cats to harass. Danny was soon noticed by the neighbours, with his scruffy graying hair, his disreputable dog-walking coat, his shamble of a walk and, of course, Pluto.

"Hey, Grant, have you seen that guy around with a dog – I don't recognize him." Merv Warren lived across the street and a couple of houses along. He was the self-appointed local watchman of the night, as well as the chair of the local Neighbourhood Watch. He knew everyone, and knew when they went away and when they would be back.

"Yeah, he's my brother Danny – he's moved into the basement suite now that Brian's off to college."

"Oh – I thought he was – sort of – under some sort of supervision."

Prying, Grant thought. "Yes, we got it arranged with the authorities that he could live here."

"Oh. Well, in that case I guess it'll be OK. People have been asking."

Grant felt like punching him.

At first, Danny hardly noticed the baleful looks of the people he passed as he and Pluto walked around the blocks – he was usually thinking about music, and would smile at everyone.

It was only a couple of weeks after Danny's arrival that there was some excitement the next street over. The clocks had just changed, so by six it was dark for Pluto's post-supper walk in misty rain. Danny was wearing his dog-walker gear, and Pluto was hitched to a piece of rope, his lead having gone missing in the move.

They both heard the sirens; then there were people running. As they turned the corner they saw the fire truck, lights flashing, at a house half way down the next block. Danny hauled Pluto to his side, went to stand at the back of the small crowd, and watched as the firefighters efficiently doused the smoky remains of a little shed in the house's side yard. There was not much conversation – a man and woman in the yard were talking to one of the firefighters, but everyone else was standing, hands in pockets, glumly watching. A small man, shoulders hunched in the cold, suddenly was aware of Pluto beside him, panting and with his tongue out. He turned and looked at Danny. "This your dog?"

Danny held up his end of the rope-lead as if an answer was not necessary, and started to speak, when the man turned away, muttering "Gawkers." A couple just in front of Danny turned and looked at him, the man a rangy fellow, and the woman aggressively blonde under an umbrella.

"Haven't seen you before," said the big framed woman.

Danny, grinned, his grey hair untidily plastered by the fine rain, and said "No, I just" – but the man took his wife by the arm, said "Come on," and walked away.

The next morning Danny and Pluto went by the burned-out shed which smelled of soggy, burned wood. A car backed out of a driveway further up the street, and the big woman who had accosted him the previous evening stared at him as she drove by. Pluto watched the car with some inquisitiveness. Danny pulled on the lead and chuckled; "Come on, Pluto, that's just Big Blonde Bertha checking us out."

Danny told Grant that evening about the fire, and found he had already heard about it. "You don't have very friendly neighbours."

"Well, they're a bit upset about the fire."

Three mornings later, earlier than usual, Danny was trudging along in the fog of dawn, with Pluto dragging behind. Danny's hangover from listening to too much Scriabin, which had led to drinking too much cheap firewater, was matched only by Pluto's reluctance to be walked in early morning mist. Danny was doing this, not so much as self-punishment, but because he had an appointment that morning with a magazine editor who wanted a series on 'Why Music Moves Us So'. Danny was desperate enough for the job that he had risen early to clear his head before his planned bike trip into town to catch the bus to the city an hour down the highway. Pluto would be left to guard the basement for a few hours.

Danny was still investigating the streets in The Orchard, and found himself on a road without a sidewalk he couldn't remember having walked along before; maybe the fog was confusing him

The smell of burned wet wood came to him and Pluto simultaneously. The dog suddenly tugged at the rope, eager to investigate, and Danny lost his grip. Pluto bounded across the road, ignoring the yellow 'Caution Do Not Cross" tape stretching between two trees which Danny could dimly see through the mist.

The dog buried his nose into a pile of smelly ash and soggy wood stacked in an upended two wheel hand cart parked just off the road in the front yard of a small house. The cart's wooden sides were charred black.

"Get out of there, Pluto," Danny hissed as he ran across toward the pile. Then he heard, like an echo, someone near the house yell, "Hey, you get out of there!" Pluto ignored both commands, so Danny grabbed the end of the rope and hauled Pluto out onto the road. As he did so, he caught a whiff of gasoline.

"Whadja think yer doin?" yelled the man; "can't you see that's a crime scene?"

"Crime scene – what crime scene?" called Danny.

"Cantcher see the yellow tape?"

"Sorry – the dog got away from me. What happened?"

The man came out onto the road, his hair tousled, his face ruddy and unshaven. He peered at Danny, with his mess of lank grey hair and frayed coat.

"Haven't seen you around here before. Lots of odd people around all of a sudden. Shouldn't be surprised if you aren't one of the bunch who torched my cart earlier this morning."

"I don't know what you're talking about."

Suddenly Danny became aware of two men on the road, walking through the fog towards him. Pluto stiffened, watching them.

One of them said, "Get out of here." And the other said, "I'm calling the police."

Danny breathed, "Come on, Pluto," and turned to go back the way he had come.

Then he heard, "We don't want jail birds around here," and the sound of someone punching numbers into his phone.

Danny was so distraught when he got to his room that he forgot about his appointment with the magazine editor until it was too late to make the trip to get there. He fell miserably on to his bed, Pluto watching him anxiously.

That evening, Danny did something he wasn't encouraged to do, but he felt he needed to try to deal with the situation. So he wandered upstairs, finding Grant and Wendy sitting in front of the TV with supper trays.

"Oh, sorry, I – uh – "

"No that's fine, Danny," said Grant, glancing at his wife, who was staring at Danny's torn sweater. "What's up?"

"Well, I keep on bumping into neighbours of yours who seem to think I have something to do with the fires there've been around here in the last few days."

"Yeah, well, they're an odd lot, and I heard that there have been a couple of others on the other side of the hill as well, so they're all a bit uptight."

"You can say that again. But why me? I don't even know the way over the hill, and, anyway, I'm not allowed out of The Orchard."

"Well, you know how it is, you aren't known around here, so I guess you're a convenient suspect."

No, I don't 'know how it is, thought Danny. He wasn't used to such judgmentalism where he came from.

"Look, there's a Neighbourhood Watch meeting at Merv's next week. Why don't you come along and meet some of them socially?"

Wendy looked at her husband with a shocked expression, and Danny saw that.

"No, I don't think so, but perhaps if the fire thing comes up, you might tell them I don't know anything about them."

It was only a couple of days later when Pluto plunged his cold nose into Danny's sleeping face at two in the morning and Danny groggily heard sirens. He sat up to see flashing lights through the curtains and heard the roar of a big truck passing the house. Pluto was already by the door to the garden, his wagging tail whapping the hall table. Then Danny smelled smoke. He got dressed very quickly.

They reached the road just as, with a thumping roar, something blew up and Pluto turned into Danny, trying to get between his legs. Flames shot skyward and Danny saw the motorhome in the driveway of the house at the end of the block engulfed in fire, caught in the pulsing glare of the fire truck's flashing lights. The heat hit him just as he saw people running, and he put his hand on Pluto's back. "Steady, boy."

As they stood in the road a crowd materialized out of the dark, everybody watching the firefighters silhouetted in the glare. The police and the fire chief arrived, and there was a lot of pushing as they set up a barricade across the road. Danny could feel Pluto pressed against his leg. There were a lot of people, and then Danny saw his brother and Wendy coming towards the crowd. He turned to go to them when he felt a hand on his shoulder.

"You again." Danny turned his head to look at the man, but didn't recognize him. Then, right in front of him was the blonde woman. "What are you doing here?" A man was beside her saying, "You sure seem to be on the scene each time, don't you." Suddenly there was Grant. "Hold on, Merv, I don't like the suggestion." Then there was some shoving, and Danny slipped and let go of the lead and Pluto started barking. A police officer at the barricade shone a flashlight at them, and Danny got Pluto under control and walked away, his legs shaking.

The next morning, a Saturday, Grant came down and knocked on Danny's door around ten. Danny looked disheveled, but Pluto was happy to see him, and milled around him as Grant edged into the room.

"Am I too early – I could come back later."

"For what?"

"Well, we need to talk – some of the neighbours gave me an earful last night, and I just need to hear from you what's going on."

Danny scratched his hair. "About what?"

"Can we sit down?"

Danny swept some magazines off the couch, and Grant perched on the edge, looking tense.

"Lemme get the dog his food first," Danny muttered, and shambled into the kitchen, Pluto eagerly pushing ahead of him.

With the sound of Pluto crunching gratefully in the kitchen, Danny came back and slumped heavily into his chair by the desk.

"So, what's up?"

"Well, the story is that since you moved in, there have been some fires in the neighbourhood, and each time you have been seen there."

"Yeah, with half the people who live around here as well."

"Yeah, Danny. Here's the thing. They all know each other, but they don't know you, and they are putting two and two together and–"

"Making a whole load of shit," exploded Danny.

At that moment they both heard the front door bell ring, and the clicking of Wendy's heels as she walked to the door. Pluto padded to the basement door, his tail waving.

Grant said, "It might be some of the neighbours – they said they wanted to talk to both of us this morning."

"Good god! What is this – some sort of vigilante brigade?"

They heard someone coming down the stairs, then a knock. Pluto stood at the door, ears up. Danny sat, unmoving, so Grant went and opened the door. There was a uniformed policeman, asking if he could come in. Pluto sniffed warily at his crotch. He ruffled Pluto behind an ear, introduced himself as Constable Lambert, and asked again if he might come in. Danny looked at him with astonishment, and muttered something about kidnapping school kids to do a man's job. The policeman said again, "Is it alright if I come in?" and Danny grunted "OK".

Grant introduced himself as the owner of the house, and then said, "and this is my brother Danny."

Standing by the door, Constable Lambert explained that he was investigating a series of fires in the area.

Pluto lay down with a sigh.

"Two doesn't make a series," Danny said belligerently.

"Well, sir, there have been several in the town in the last couple of weeks, with three of them in this immediate vicinity and a couple more over the hill." He sounded a bit pedantic, as if he was reading from a script.

"What's that to do with me?" Danny almost bellowed. Pluto's head shot up, and Grant said, "Calm down, Danny."

"I've been told that on each occasion there has been a guy with a dog there; 'hanging around' was the phrase used."

"Yeah, with all the other neighbours 'hanging around' too!" Danny growled.

"Well, sir, they all know each other, but they say they don't know this man, and that" – he glanced at his notebook – "they only see him around when there's a fire."

Grant cut in. "Wait a minute – that's nonsense. They do know Danny; I've explained to a couple of them that Danny's my brother, and that he's staying here."

"And I walk Pluto *every* evening," Danny spat, "and they can see me doing that if they care to look. And I *don't* walk Pluto over the hill. George – my parole officer, has told me to stay in this area. And, anyway, I just don't light fires – I doubt if I even know how to get one going, or keep it going, at least."

"Well, I do have to say that I checked with your parole officer –"

"Oh, you did, did you?" Danny growled menacingly.

"– and he said lighting fires was definitely not something he figured you would do."

"Well, bully for him!"

Grant butted in. "Hold on, Danny. Constable – Lambert is it?" – the policeman nodded – "is just dealing with a complaint."

"Yeah, well I may have a complaint about him talking to my parole officer."

"Sir, if you can't be more helpful, I may have to talk to him about not allowing you to walk your dog after hours."

"For god's sake!" Danny exploded, and stood up.

Grant grabbed him by the arm. "Danny, for goodness' sake calm down." Danny shook his brother's hand off and went to look out the window.

The policeman stood up. "Well, this hasn't been very helpful, but I'm suggesting that everybody be extra vigilant about suspicious activities."

"Like walking a dog?" Danny couldn't stay quiet.

"OK. I'm on my way," said the policeman, obviously exasperated.

Grant took Constable Lambert upstairs, and Danny heard him leaving a couple of minutes later. Grant didn't come back down. Danny put on his headphones, and turned on a Wagner CD.

The Neighbourhood Watch meeting was, Grant decided afterwards, one of the most difficult evenings he and Wendy had experienced. It was at Merv Warren's home, and his wife Doreen, famous for her scrumptious appetizers, outdid herself. Nor was there any shortage of wine and liquor. Merv had brought their son in from the college to work as a barman.

Often these gatherings are not well attended, but this evening it seemed that someone had been beating the drum. Of the thirty homes on the Neighbourhood Watch list for this end of The Orchard, only five were not represented. Merv and Doreen finally got everyone seated in the Games Room, some on window ledges, and some on the floor.

"So, we have an arsonist in our midst," Merv led off. Grant snorted at the bias, but Buck from the next street over glared at him, so he sat back to listen.

After a description of the three incidents in the vicinity and two others over the hill, Wes, who had built his home back when the area was still a big orchard, looked over at Grant. Grant figured Wes, as the senior guy in the area, had been primed by Merv.

"Grant, we haven't had this sort of thing until now. And your brother and that dog of his seem to be on the scene each time."

"That's not true. Danny wasn't where the stuff happened over the hill – in fact his parole officer has told him he can't walk the dog in the evenings outside The Orchard."

As soon as he said it, Grant realized it was a mistake. "So his parole officer just wants him to set fires here!" came a voice from the back. "We pay just as much taxes as those guys over the hill!"

Merv sat still, letting the discussion go from bad to worse. One of the women said to Wendy, "You should be ashamed, allowing a convict into our neighbourhood!"

"Convict!" spluttered Grant. "My brother is about as far from being a convict as anyone here." He realized he was sounding defensive and inadequate. He leaned back, deflated.

The upshot was that Merv voiced the mood of the meeting when he said, "Grant, for his own good, I think you and Wendy should reconsider having your brother stay with you."

To make things more difficult, Grant had the feeling that Wendy agreed with that, though she loyally stood up for her husband as they were leaving, saying to Doreen, "I think our husbands should get together over lunch some day. Merv needs to hear Grant's side of the situation."

Walking home, they turned into their driveway, and saw Danny sitting on the front steps of the house, shivering in the cold, with Pluto by his side.

"I just thought I'd wait here to find out what happened."

"Not good, Danny," Grant admitted. "Everybody seems to have it in for you. Perhaps you need to lay low for a while."

"Well, if you think I'm going to stop taking Pluto for his nightly walk, you've got another think coming."

With that, Danny, Pluto in tow, stalked off into the night.

The very next day, a Monday, the whole issue should have disintegrated into nothing.

Constable Lambert phoned Grant at his office to tell him that two young men just out of High School had been arrested for the fires over the hill, and were to be charged with arson. All the fires had striking similarities, which led the police to assume they were all set by the same person or persons, except, maybe, the early morning fire, which might have been set by a copy-cat. They also reasoned that the culprits probably used a car, as the incidents were quite widely spaced out, and the arsonists seemed to get away quickly. This put Danny outside of their focus. The kids had been caught red handed, or, as the constable put it, "smell handed", as they were apprehended in a car leaving a small roadside fire with hands redolent with the smell of fire-starter. They were being urged to come clean, as their "modus operandi" (constable Lambert used the phrase with some pride) linked all the occurrences, including those in The Orchard. They were evidently driven to set the fires out of bravado to impress a couple of girls.

"Incredible what testosterone can be blamed for," said the constable.

Grant phoned Wendy to tell her. She said she hadn't heard a sound from the basement, not even the shower running, or Danny's incessant humming. She said she thought that Danny might still be in bed.

That evening, when Grant got home, he called down the basement stairs and asked Danny to come up. "I have some good news."

Danny came up and sat down in the living room, looking drained. *He's been drinking*, thought Grant. *I was going to offer him something, but no.*

"So, that policeman who was here the other day called me to tell me they've arrested two young punks for the fires, including the ones in The Orchard. So, you're vindicated!"

"That's good." Danny sounded deflated.

"Aren't you pleased?"

"Well, you know, it's not whether I did or didn't do it – I know the answer to that. It's more about how the people who live around here behave – it's more about their moral values as far as I'm concerned."

"Wait a second, Danny. They didn't know you, and – you look–uh–"

"Come on, say it – 'different from them', or just plain 'different', so therefore I'm a prime target."

"Danny, I'm sure that, when they hear about what the police have to say, their attitudes will change. Actually Merv already knows, because Constable Lambert told me he had called him and told him, as he was the one who made the initial complaint."

"And Blonde Bertha?"

"I'm sure she and her husband know by now – they play mah-jongg with Merv and Doreen every Monday afternoon."

"You know, Grant," Danny chuckled scornfully, as he looked at Wendy, "you are sometimes even more naïve than I am, and that's saying something."

Grant and Wendy stared balefully at Danny.

Danny struggled to his feet. "I'm taking Pluto for his Parole Officer Sanctioned Walk."

Danny was, of course, right. When he got back to the house, he gave Pluto a bone, marched, uninvited, up to Grant and Wendy's living room, and stood, legs apart, in front of them.

"Here's, verbatim, what the ferocious foursome had to say. There I was, just walking my dog, when Merv and Doreen and Big Bertha and what's his name, came out onto the road from Merv's house; I swear they were lying in wait for me.

"'Hey, you,' Merv yells. I don't think he knows my name, even now, or doesn't want to stoop to use it. Then he says, basically, that they don't care what the police have to say, and, despite everything, they don't like me walking around 'their' streets at night, and that they would be 'keeping an eye' on me. I asked perfectly civilly

"– Grant muttered "I'll bet–" and Danny insisted – "No, I didn't shout, I merely asked politely who the fuck they thought they were, telling me I couldn't walk my dog at night as allowed by my parole officer. Well, you would have thought Big Bertha had never heard the word before, the way her skinny husband came at me yelling, 'Don't use that language in front of my wife!'"

Then, with a satisfied voice, Danny said, "And I'm afraid I told him that, being married to *him* and all, she probably didn't know what the word meant anyway."

Grant put his head in his hands and groaned, and Wendy said, "Danny, that's enough for tonight. We'll talk more about this in the morning."

Danny nodded, and got up to go downstairs. Then he turned, paused, and said, "So I'm pleased to tell you that, amongst us all, Pluto is the most accomplished critic. When it was all over, he squatted and pooped on Big Blonde Bertha's lawn, and I was so impressed with his acumen that I left it where it belonged, right there. And now, Pluto and I are going to have a drink and go to bed."

It was a matter of mutual understanding, and without debate, that Danny and Pluto would return to the municipal campground, and 'that right soon'. The plan was to move Danny and Pluto over the next weekend. The weather cooperated, as Saturday proved to be a lovely November day.

The first trip by the determined trio of Wendy, Grant and Danny was without Pluto, but with Danny's bike mounted on the back of the SUV. They took armloads of cleaning materials, buckets, mops, bleach, Windex, and moss removal spray. While Wendy started on the inside, Grant got on a ladder Danny borrowed from Farley, his next door buddie, and started on the moss-grown roof. As for Danny, he did the important stuff, like reconnecting with a couple of the other Permies, and, although it was only a couple of hundred yards, biking down to the office to shoot the breeze with the manager and arrange to move back in.

The clean-up took a couple of hours, during which – "Look what I found!" – Wendy found Pluto's collar and lead, stuffed down between the sofa cushions. Then they drove over to the pub for burgers and beer. Grant had intended that it would be just the three of them, but somehow Farley got invited along. He was a bit taciturn, but seemed to be really pleased that Danny was coming back, and even said he looked forward to being kept awake by "that jarry music you seem to like". He tried, but not very hard, to pay for his share of the lunch bill. It was actually Grant who picked up the whole tab.

For much of the time, Grant and Danny chatted away about family and friends, and laughed at old jokes and events. Wendy sat and watched them, quietly marveling at their camaraderie.

They were just beginning to think about returning to the campground for a final 'spit and polish' as Grant had called it, when Wendy suddenly said, "Why don't the three of you walk back to the campground, and I'll go to get Pluto and meet you there. So then, Danny, you and Pluto can move in this afternoon."

They looked at her. The plan had originally been for Danny and Pluto to do the actual move the next day, but Danny grunted, "Why not? The place is as ready as it will ever be. I've never seen it so spiffy."

"Don't worry," said Grant, "I'm sure you'll have it looking homey in no time."

Danny looked faintly guilty, and said, "Yeah, Farley and some of my other buddies were planning to come over tomorrow for a jar or two, so now maybe they can come over this evening instead."

"Or even as well as," chuckled Grant. "Well, as for making the place look welcoming, that should do it. Don't forget that your parole officer said he'd be by to check on you soon. Go easy with the booze."

"Ah, yes, George," said Danny. "He needs some training yet, but he's coming around."

My goodness, thought Wendy; *it's so refreshing to see these two so relaxed and happy with each other.*

"Are you sure you can manage Pluto, honey?" asked Grant.

"Yes – remember, I found his collar and lead."

So Wendy went home, tussled Pluto into the back seat of the SUV, and was back at the campground in time to see the three men walking down the trail from the pub, Danny gesticulating crazily as he finished some presumably outlandish story, and Grant roaring with laughter and punching Danny on the shoulder.

Wendy let Pluto out of the car, and the dog went into a frenzy, greeting Farley, and a couple of other men who suddenly appeared, as if they were all his oldest, greatest friends. And then these guys descended on Danny with hugs and laughs and high-fives that would have felled a lesser man.

An hour later Wendy and Grant were ready to leave. Grant gave Danny a hug, and even Wendy did the same.

On the way home, Wendy driving, she said, "It was so nice to see the two of you joking and joshing. It must have been like the old times together."

"Not really; we never got to communicate much when we were teenagers, and, after that, we went our separate ways."

"Well, it was good to see the two of you getting on so well anyway. Do you think it's because you're relieved at getting rid of him, and he's just as happy to be back where he's welcome?"

"Yeah, probably. Actually, I haven't had such fun in a long time. I feel almost jealous about how comfortable he is amongst his buddies – they're way less judgmental than our bunch."

"You can say that again," said Wendy.

As he slowed to turn into their driveway, Grant looked across and saw the curtains on Merv and Doreen's front windows twitching. He tapped Wendy on the shoulder and gestured over to Merv's house; "I detect that we're under surveillance."

"Well, at least *they* should be happy as well," Wendy muttered, and they looked at each other and grinned.

Wendy parked by their front door. As he and Wendy stood in their driveway, Grant softly murmured, "I wonder who got to pick up the poop."

Wendy snorted, and, grabbing his arm, led Grant into their home.

Later that evening, much later, with Wendy snuggled against him, Grant murmured, "You awake?"

"Uh-huh. Why?"

"Well, here's the thing. I've been thinking about how we just don't seem to be able to get along with these neighbours of ours. That brother of mine, together with Pluto – what did the policeman call them – 'a guy with a dog' – revealed how nasty and nosy they are. And then at the campground this afternoon, Pluto led the charge to show us how friendly and – I guess, – *accepting*, neighbours *can* be."

Wendy sighed. "I know, but what can we do about it?"

"Well, with Brian off to college, so that the basement suite is surplus to needs again" – Wendy sat up – "Not another lodger!"

"No, what I'm thinking is that we don't need a house this size anymore, with a self-contained basement. We could move closer into town, maybe into one of those new patio homes they've just built. I hear they are really nice."

Wendy sat up. "And to hell with the neighbours?"

"Yes, to hell with them."

"But how can we be sure we don't have awful neighbours again?"

"Well, we'll have to take a chance, I guess."

Wendy nestled back down next to her husband. "I guess the theory is that lightning never strikes twice." A long pause. Then, "Let's do it."

That weekend Wendy's brother-in-law Jordan, who was one of the town's more successful realtors, came over, and they discussed a listing. "With the fully equipped basement suite, this should sell well," he said, rubbing his hands.

Jordan named a price which surprised Grant and Wendy. "That much?"

"Well, it's an attractive neighbourhood with a reputation for everyone looking out for each other – "

"That's one way of describing it," Grant chuckled.

" – so that adds to the value."

Without another word, Grant and Wendy signed the listing.

The house sold in two weeks, by which time Grant and Wendy had signed up to buy a corner-lot patio home in the brand new development nearer to the centre of town.

A month later, Mr. and Mrs. Merchant drove away, waving goodbye to the watching neighbours.

Performance Evaluation

Some say that divorce is a competition between grief and relief. Ours was, my lawyer told me, a reasonably amicable one as divorces go. It was stressful for me, more, I think, than it was for Christine, who appeared to treat the whole process with vengeful calmness. The final decree was, ironically, within days of what would have been our silver wedding anniversary – a milestone usually, they say, celebrated as achieving a plateau after having struggled strenuously through the peaks and valleys of child-raising and nest-emptying. However, for us it was more a relief from the lawyer-and-accountant-driven process of suspicion and uneasy compromise, an exercise we found to be both unsatisfactory and confrontational. Nobody won, and, more depressingly, nobody wanted to win. Even our two achievement-driven children, now adults and in relationships themselves, stayed neutral, repeating too many times, "Whatever makes you happy."

Happy! I'm certainly not happy. Perhaps Christine is, with a new man in her life –a hot-shot tax expert. I'm not sure whether he's just a surrogate, though that makes me sound complicit in some sort of pre-arranged swap, which it definitely was not. He's got a fancy name – Sterling. He's better looking than me, from what I can tell from a distance, and he's probably got a bigger cock, though at our age that shouldn't count. And he's also definitely got a bigger bank account, which does. No contest. To flaunt it – the bank account, I mean, the last time I saw Christine, she was driving a bright red Fiat Spider with a vanity licence plate that said WAVE. That's a bit above her pay scale as a dental hygienist.

So, what to do? Start drinking heavily, or chase that woman in the lawyer's office who helped with the sale of the house and the other paperwork? She seemed to send "I'm available" messages. Or shall I become a curmudgeonly recluse? These are, from what I can see, three of the options open to recently divorced middle-aged men. I'm safely but boringly employed in a government office in a 'low-level management' position, so none of the three will jeopardise my pensionability, or, indeed, as far as I can tell, my continued employment. I know plenty of guys in the same block of government offices who are drunks or skirt chasers or grouchy or more than one of these, and still have their jobs.

I sighed, poured another scotch, and flipped the channels.

The next day, I was standing at the front desk of my lawyer's office paying off the last (I hope) of my bill – it's a mystery to me how lawyers' bills are calculated, but I was just glad to be shot of the whole thing. At least there are no underage kids to factor into the deal. Then the 'possibly available' woman came walking along the hallway – Perry something. Nearly as tall as I am, not much younger than me (though I'm notorious for mis-estimating women's ages), brunettish, and relaxed-looking, but stylish. Not that I made this assessment right there and then; I realized I'd been thinking about her, and, I suppose, setting her off against Christine (or setting Christine off against her?). Christine is short and snappy, blonde (still, but now with some help), certainly looks younger than me, and comes off best in a tee shirt and jeans.

She stopped at the counter. "Hi, Jeremy. All done and dusted?" (And an encouraging smile, too.)

"Yup. Glad to be shot of it all. I moved into the apartment last weekend. Say, thanks for your help."

"You're welcome. Glad to have been of assistance. These things are never easy."

She turned and started away.

"Say, Perry, I don't know your name – your last name."

"Oh" She pulled a card from her pocket. "Here, in case you ever need anything." She handed it to me, smiling.

'Need anything'? Is this an invitation? I glanced at the card. "Perry Wellington – thanks for this." I shook her cool hand. Blue-grey eyes. Christine's are – I don't remember.

It was a couple of days and a double scotch before I took a deep breath and phoned her.

"Perry, it's me – Jeremy."

"Hi, Jeremy." Her voice sounded warm. "What's up?"

"Well, I was wondering if we might have lunch tomorrow."

"Sure – is this a business call, or – " a little chuckle.

"No, I know you said if I need anything, to call, but this is just to ask you to lunch as a thank you."

So we had lunch that day, and got on pretty well. She's a good listener. That led to dinner on Friday at a special place a little out of downtown. I picked her up after work after having had a quick one at the lounge at the corner, and drove us there.

We shared a bottle of wine – actually, she had a glass, and I had the rest. I learned that Perry had been married, "but it didn't work out"; that she got the house when they parted (he got the summer cottage); that the house is a split level duplex, where she lives in the upper part and rents out the lower part – she only wants people who make long term commitments.

I got a warm feeling about her, and felt that she's very comfortable to be with, unlike Christine, who was – is – a dynamo, who was exhilarating to marry, but became exhausting to live with.

I told Perry a bit about myself; that I had been an up-and-coming young chef in the city, and was a part-time instructor at the foremost culinary arts school on the west coast – the youngest on faculty. I also told her about the food poisoning debacle at my restaurant, and how, although I was eventually absolved of any responsibility, I just lost my nerve, and started drinking a bit. With Christine nagging me about the responsibility of two young kids, I turned to my friend Landon, a restaurateur I had worked for, who, through his influential father, had connections in the Civil Service. Through Landon I got recommended for a quiet, no pressure, government job, where all I had to do was basically tick boxes.

"So, that's where I have been for the last fifteen years or so. I still stay in touch with Landon. He says I was one of the best chefs he's known, and would sort of sponsor me if I ever wanted back into the business. Now you know why I like going to good places to eat."

And Perry also learned that I was happy to be divorced but unhappy to be by myself.

As we left the restaurant I stumbled a bit at the door, and laughed. "See what you do to me, Perry, you've gone straight to my head. C'mon, I'll drive you home."

"No, Jeremy, I'm fine taking the bus – there's one that goes right by here. I think you've had a bit too much."

"Huh? I'm fine."

But she insisted.

I left things for a week. Actually, I had quite a busy few days, as there was some sort of foul-up at the office about a report that somehow didn't get done on time, so the ADM was a bit hung out to dry. Everyone was looking for who to blame, but I didn't think it was really my fault. By Friday, with the weekend coming up, I was needing some relaxation.

I called Perry to invite her out for dinner.

"Jeremy, (last week she was calling me 'Jer') it's nice of you to ask, but I don't want to be just company for you while you drink too much."

It hit me in the gut. "Oh, come on, Perry, I've been in some stress lately, not only with the divorce thing, but at work as well, so–"

"All the more reason why you need to take care of yourself."

"Well, thanks for the lecture."

I hung up, stormed out of my apartment, walked to the liquor store, bought a mickey, took it home and drank it. That'll show her, I thought.

It wasn't until Sunday evening that I felt able to call Perry.

"Hi, Perry. It's me, Jer. I just wanted to apologise for my rudeness the other evening." I could hear her breathing, but she didn't say anything. "You were right, and I'm sorry."

"That's OK, Jer. So, what are you going to do about it?"

"About what?"

"Your drinking, Jeremy." She sounded a bit tense.

"Well, I don't think it's – I don't think I have a problem. I mean, I know guys who drink more than I do, but, well, I sure like having dinner with you, so what if I cut it down when we're out together?"

"Jeremy that really isn't the point."

"Well, if it isn't, I don't know what is."

There was a pause. Then she sighed. "OK, Jeremy, let's try it. But I can't this week – my downstairs tenant left, and I'm advertising and interviewing for a new tenant."

"OK. Anyway I've got a bit of a fire going at work. How about I call you next Sunday?"

She agreed, and, as we hung up, I felt pretty happy.

So, the next Sunday, I phoned, and said, "Let's try that new place out at the club house at the golf course – I know the chef, and you don't have to be a member to eat there. I'll drive by and pick you up. And I promise just some wine."

She sounded cautious. "That's lovely, Jeremy, but don't come to pick me up – I'll drive out there."

"Nonsense; I'll pick you up in ten," and hung up.

As I pulled in to Perry's driveway a few minutes later, I stared in confusion at the little red car parked there. The vanity plate read WAVE.

Suddenly there was Perry, opening my passenger door and sliding in.

"What the hell is *that* doing here?"

"Oh, that's my new downstairs tenant's."

"It's Christine's."

"Yes; Christine is my new tenant."

I stared at her and turned the engine off. I was in turmoil. She looked defensive.

"Isn't there something you lawyers have, called conflict of interest – I mean, weren't you, or aren't you my lawyer?"

"Jeremy, I'm not a lawyer – you know that – I'm a para-legal. And anyway, that's all finished now. And having Christine as my tenant isn't a conflict. You know that too."

"Jesus! What about the fact that we're, or I *thought* we were, friends?"

"What does that mean? That I have to check with you about who I take as a tenant?"

I sat slumped in the car, suddenly worried that Christine would come out to her car.

"Does she know, you know, about us, like–"

"She knows we have supper together occasionally, and she's fine with that."

I exploded. "What does 'fine' mean – it was *she* who left *me* for money-bags, so I don't think she has any right to think 'fine' or anything else, for that matter." I was shouting. I swiveled towards her. "So, are we having supper or what?"

She put a hand on my arm, and I angrily brushed it away.

"Jer, I don't think supper is a good idea. Let's drive somewhere and just sit and talk for a while. "

I started the car, and drove towards the club house, then remembered there is a little pull-out where you could look out over the golf course. I pulled in and turned the key off.

"So what do you want to talk about?"

"Jeremy, don't be like that." Then she said, tentatively, "I had a long talk with Christine the other evening, before I accepted her as my tenant."

"Huh? Well, what I want to know is, how come she's a tenant at all! How come she's not living with money-bags in his fancy house on the hill?"

"That's what we – or part of – what we talked about. I wanted to be sure her move into my house wasn't just temporary."

"And it wasn't?" I asked incredulously. I was feeling completely disoriented.

Perry sighed, and laid a hand on my arm again. This time I didn't brush it off.

"Jeremy, I want to explain this to you, because you're going to hear about it anyway, so I think it's best that you hear it from me first."

I could feel apprehension bubbling up.

"Christine told me, and I believe her, that she didn't leave you because she had fallen in love with Sterling. He was, as she described it, a convenient bolt hole at the time."

I began to splutter, but she pressed my arm. "Let me finish, Jeremy. She quite quickly realized that Sterling isn't as advertised. Frankly, she soon discovered he's what they call a trophy hunter."

"What's a 'trophy hunter', or do I not want to know?"

"Use your imagination, Jer; he's not into long term relationships. Christine found she was just another notch on his scabbard."

I felt a little surge of gloat. "So she got what she deserved."

"Well, I don't see that either of you came out of it very happy."

"Are you saying she wants to, sort of, try – try again with me?"

"That's not even remotely possible." She paused. "You won't like this – "

"Try me," I blurted.

"Well, Christine told me she didn't leave you because she had fallen in love with Sterling; she left you because she figured you had completely lost interest in her, and she certainly doesn't have any feelings of love – or even affection – for you anymore."

"So, what are you – some sort of marriage counsellor?"

"Jeremy," she said tautly, "I didn't ask to get into this, you know."

"Well, I don't have much affection for her either." I sounded aggressive.

Perry said softly, "Christine tells me it wasn't just lack of affection, it was more like lack of any attention to her."

I swiveled to look across at Perry. "This sounds like some sort of PE."

She looked at me; "PE? What's that?"

"That's what we call it at work; each of us in management has an annual Performance Evaluation meeting with our boss. Mine for this year is due any day now. What you and Christine did feels like it was a sort of PE about me, but in this case I wasn't even there." I realized I was sounding petulant.

Perry sighed. "Jeremy, I'm going through all this because Christine said she wants you to know why. She says she isn't just a stupid bitch, as you once called her."

"Well, she called me things too."

"Like what?"

"I don't know – stupid stuff."

We sat there in silence, looking out, unseeingly, at the golf course.

I felt a very dark thought developing. I had the crazy idea that losing Christine in a competition with another guy is one thing, like at least you lost a battle, and have some scars to show for it. But her leaving because she just couldn't stand living with me anymore is something completely different – it's much worse. No battle scars to flaunt.

I drummed my fingers on the steering wheel.

"A notch on his whatever sounds painful," I grunted.

"I meant metaphorically."

"So Sterling turned out not to be sterling silver." Stupid joke. Perry sighed. She was not amused.

"Anyway, what you're telling me is that she left not because she fell in love with another guy, but because she couldn't stand being with me anymore."

"Well, she was getting messages that you felt the same."

"What on earth do you mean by that?"

"Well, for example, do you even remember when her birthday is?"

"Oh, that – that was just a mix-up, and anyway I bought her some flowers."

"A week late." Perry turned, and faced me full on.

"Jer, she doesn't really care about any of that anymore. She is resolved to get on with life, and put everything – including you and Sterling – behind her."

Perry took a deep breath and plunged in.

"So, here's the thing. I think that's what Christine wants you to try and do. And I do, too. You both made mistakes, and Christine has faced up to the fact that running off with Sterling was a mistake. So she thinks, as do I, that you need to face up to the fact that mistakes were made, and instead of wallowing in misery and" – then bravely, – "and drink, you pull yourself together and get on with life – maybe even get a new job. You don't sound very enthusiastic about your present one."

"So, at my time of life I'm to go out into the job market, like Christine went man-hunting? See where it got her!"

"Well, as far as I can tell, she's pretty happy with the change, even if it took an unexpected turn. And maybe that's what you need – a change."

I glared at her. "Is that meant to make me feel better?"

She sat quietly waiting for me to stop fuming.

"You know," I murmured, "I've parked in this pull-out before. Christine and I parked here in my rusty little Ford, my God, twenty five years ago. This is where I first kissed her – where we first kissed. It was – *electric*."

"And now the fuse is blown, Jeremy, and the lights have gone out."

I sat there miserably. Glancing across at her, I muttered, "I suppose it was – *is*, what they call a mid-life crisis – for both of us, actually."

Carefully, Perry said, "I think you're getting it now, Jeremy. The next thing is to work out how to handle it. That's what Christine is doing."

I started the car up, and drove Perry home. As she got out, I didn't even look at the little red car. Half way to the house, Perry stopped, hesitated, and then, fishing something out of her pocket, came back to my side of the car. I put the window down, and she handed me a business card. "You're a good man, Jer; you need to think about this."

I looked at the card. It had the contact information about Alcoholics Anonymous.

I almost threw the card out onto the driveway. Instead, I tucked it in my pocket and drove home, seething.

Monday morning at work, I was feeling pretty fragile. Charlie, my boss came by and told me it was time for my annual PE, and asked me (told me, really,) to meet him in his office the next day at two. "Sure thing, Charlie." He's pretty easy-going.

I've been moved around the Division a few times, but for the last while – a few years now, actually – I've been in the same branch, and Charlie has been my immediate boss. The top guys and Charlie set operational goals for people like me and my little group. They're meant to be done in consultation with me at each annual Review and Evaluation, but I don't ever remember there being much of a discussion at those meetings. It's all so meaningless. I just do what I'm told.

To tell the truth, recently, I guess I haven't always done what I'm told. I've missed a couple of deadlines, which got a bunch of people a bit pissed off. But Charlie seemed OK about it. And who cares anyway.

I walked home via the liquor store, and was sitting in front of the TV on my second shot of whiskey when the phone rang. It was Charlie.

"Hi, boss. What's up?" He never phones me at home. I muted the TV.

"Jeremy, I'm glad I caught you at home." (Where else would I be?) "About your Performance Evaluation tomorrow, we've changed the time and place. It'll be at nine tomorrow morning instead of in the afternoon, and it'll be in Building C with me and the Division Director in the meeting room on the third floor. OK?"

"Wow! OK – what's his name?"

"Boy, you haven't being paying much attention, have you. *Her* name is Denise Plummer – Ms. Plummer. She also has responsibility for HR."

"Oh, sorry. OK, I'll be there." I pressed OFF and put the phone down.

Suddenly, I was sweating. I felt bad.

Really bad.

Then, out of the blue, it came to me.

If Christine was unhappy, well then, so was – so *am* I. If she had the guts to up and leave, not just once, but twice – first me, then Sterling, to seek a new start, why can't I.

That would show her, and Perry too, for that matter. And me, I suppose.

I got up and walked with my empty glass into the kitchen to find the bottle of scotch. There, beside it on the counter with my car keys, was the AA card. I hesitated for a second, and then I tipped the bottle and poured its contents down the drain. As it gurgled down, the initial sensation of 'what a waste' turned to a thrill of – I don't know – liberation?

I stood at the window, staring at nothing. Then, I thought, *carpe diem*.

I flipped my phone open, found Charlie's number, and called him.

I had hardly let him say "Hi, Jeremy," or given myself time to reconsider when I told him I wouldn't be attending the PE meeting the next morning, and that I would be providing him with my resignation immediately. I hung up before he could respond.

Then I called my old buddy Landon. "Hi, Landon, remember me, Jeremy?"

"Hey, Jer, long time no hear. When are you going to get tired of the humdrum?"

"Well, it's funny you should ask."

Landon and I had a good talk, and we arranged to get together at the weekend. He said he had a proposition for me.

As we were about to hang up, he said, "Say, Jer, hope you have the old booze habit under control."

"No problem, my friend. See you on Saturday."

I sat staring at the muted TV screen for a long time. Then I got up and went into the kitchen. I picked up the AA card, and saw that there was a local 24/7 number. I dialled it, and almost immediately a strong voice said "Hello, this is Jim. How can I assist?"

"Jim, my name is Jeremy, and I need help."

"That's what we're here for, Jeremy."

Hallelujah!

Blind Man's Bluff?

John 9, 1 – 34

Incident Report

From the Daily Duty Scribe to the Temple Security Council (TSC) of the Sanhedrin.

I am providing the TSC of the Sanhedrin with this Incident Report in conformity with the Temple Rules, which require me to record and report on any events that come to my attention which may bear upon the safety and security of the Temple and of its Authorities. The details of this matter were reported to me by yesterday's main gate Senior Duty Guard, Elazar. He, not himself being able to write, required me to record his observations and understanding of the incident.

Background. *Elazar advises that a blind-from-birth man, Celidonius, is well known to the main gate guards, as his father has, for many years, brought him, every Sabbath, to his accustomed place by the side of the gate. The Sabbath is a good day for beggars, as it is then that generosity to them is publicly recognized. A place by the main gate is coveted because of the crowds passing through it to the Temple.*

(It is to be noted that the man's family secured this desirable spot through an especially generous decision by the Temple Administration, after receiving a special contribution to the Temple Maintenance Fund from the father. The Temple Administration took this step in recognition of the family's straightened circumstances, despite the sinfulness demonstrated by the deformity of the son from birth.)

The man begs throughout the day, and then is led home by his father. He has had no sight whatsoever since birth, and is not known to importune aggressively. Elazar understands, from enquiries he made after the incident, that Celidonius and his parents are generally regarded as being of good behaviour. The man was in his accustomed place yesterday morning.

Lead-up to the Incident as observed. Yesterday morning, a Nazarene, a recent arriver in the city, known as Jesus, approached the main gate with some of his followers. It is understood that this man is already well-known to the Temple Authorities, and the duty guards have been instructed that he is a troublemaker to be closely watched. Elazar heard one of Jesus' followers explain to Jesus that he knows Celidonius' family. Then, apparently to show off his grasp of established theology, he asked Jesus to expound on the sinfulness of the man and his family, as illustrated by the man's blindness from birth. Elazar described Jesus' answer as an example of his self-aggrandisement, as he claimed the man's blindness was so that he, Jesus, could show off his healing powers.

The Impugned Incident. Thereupon, in clear violation of the fundamental injunction that no work, including any activity whereby a man exercises dominion over another, shall be performed on the Sabbath, and in full sight of the Duty Guard Elazar (and, it was later ascertained, an on-duty Ceremonial Guard, Gideon), Jesus purported to cure the man's blindness. He made a mud patty from dust on the ground and his own spittle, smeared it onto the man's eyes, and sent him off to the Pool of Siloam to wash the dirt off. Being familiar with the path down the steps to the pool, Celidonius made his way, unaided, to the pool. Neither Elazar nor Gideon followed him, not wishing to leave their posts. Nor did Jesus or any of his followers go with the man; in fact they immediately left the area.

A few minutes later a man emerged, running up the steps, and shouting, "I can see!" That man spoke animatedly with several people by the gate, and then, apparently, left, shouting that he wanted to go home but didn't know where to find it, or how to get there.

Despite vigorous efforts by the duty guards and the ceremonial guards, the impostor has not been found or apprehended, and the present whereabouts of Jesus and his followers is also unknown.

Conclusions drawn. It is the considered opinion of Elazar, having closely observed this charade, and supported by the independent view of Gideon, that the man who ran up the steps was not Celidonius, but another man who was garbed similarly to Celidonius, so as to lead those in the area to believe he was the blind-from-birth man. Elazar described the man as taller and more upright than Celidonius, and considerably more fluent and animated than he had ever seen Celidonius to be. The whole incident was a fraudulent and elaborate hoax, designed to enhance the spurious reputation of the man known as Jesus as some sort of miracle worker. Jesus' injunction to go down to the pool to wash off the mud which Jesus himself had daubed on the man's face, was a ruse to provide the opportunity for the charlatan to take the place of the blind man, who presumably was in on the plot.

Recommendations. It is respectfully recommended that the following actions be considered, and, if accepted, implemented by the TSC in the name of and under the authority of the Sanhedrin:

i. that the TSC summon the parents of the blind-from-birth man to establish that the man with sight is an imposter, and not their son, but that no further action be taken with respect to the parents, so that they may continue to be beholden to the Temple Administration;

ii. that the TSC recommend to the Temple High Priest that Celodinius, having knowingly participated in a scandalous hoax on the Sabbath, be expelled from the Temple for such *period of time that the TSC deems appropriate, after having interrogated him;*

iii. that both the Duty Guards and the Ceremonial Guards be instructed to immediately seek, find and apprehend the Nazarene known as Jesus, and such of his followers as may be discovered with him, for interrogation and suitable consequences;

iv. that Elazar be appropriately rewarded for his vigilance.

Signed and certified by the Daily Duty Scribe for the 13th Sabbath of the year.

Caiaphas, the High Priest rolled up the parchment, and sat with the scroll in his hand. He glanced at a dish of figs on the draped table by his side, then reached out and rang the golden bell hanging by his couch. He rootled around in the dish for a plump fig, then settled back with a sigh. He heard the swish of the drapes, and the Temple Administrator stepped into the chamber, bowed low, and murmured, "Good morning, most noble High Priest."

"Ah, Yehuda, thank you for coming to me at such short notice."

The Administrator raised an eyebrow, taking from the use of his given name that this was to be an informal discussion. Their relationship went back a long way.

"What can I do for you, Excellency?"

The High Priest sighed again. "This Jesus business."

Aha, Yehuda thought; *am I surprised?*

Waving the parchment at him, Caiaphas said, "I've read the Duty Guard's report to the Security Council – they sent it on to me; thank you for seeing to that. Also, I've received some disturbing reports about further developments since then. So I think I need to get directly from you what's been going on, rather than hearing things second hand, like this report. So," he gestured at a chair, "sit down and tell me."

Somewhat astonished at being invited to sit in the presence of the High Priest, the Administrator sat, and began.

"Sire, I felt it necessary to act on the report immediately. So, yesterday morning, being the day following the Sabbath day when the incident occurred, I had the duty guards apprehend the fellow claiming to be the blind-from-birth man."

Yehuda waved an arm. "It wasn't difficult, as he was running around the plaza outside the main gate shouting and clapping people on the back, and asking where he could find this Jesus fellow. Elazar told me that some of the regulars who hang around there told the guards they recognized him as the blind-from-birth man, while others said that was nonsense. They put him in the guard house, where he made quite a ruckus, I'm told, explaining to anyone who would listen how he came to be able to see. Elazar said it looked like bit of a pantomime performance to him.

"Fortunately, the regular meeting of the Security Council was about to start, so I had the guards bring the man in. It was quite a scene, Sire, as he wouldn't stop raving on and on about how it all happened. I'm afraid he said some quite blasphemous things, Sire."

"Like what?"

"Well, he said he didn't care whether or not it happened on the Sabbath, and kept on praising Jesus, even calling him a prophet. Some of the Council said the man was a raving lunatic, and that the whole thing was a waste of their time, but others wanted to get to the bottom of whether the man was or wasn't the blind-from-birth man, and, of course, if he was, how he came to be able to see."

The High Priest looked at the Administrator with a little smile. "So, what did the Council decide to do?"

"Sire, they followed up on the Duty Guard's recommendation, and instructed me to bring the blind-from-birth man's parents in. Actually, the guards easily found them, as they were right outside the guard house, asking about their son. The guards brought them to the meeting chamber right away. Then they brought the man in from the guard house. I can tell you, Sire, it was pretty wild, as the man started laughing and crying and trying to hug the parents, and shouting out about how Jesus had got him to see. He went on and on about how Jesus had done it, and then the parents started to cry. I've never seen anything like it before in a meeting chamber!"

Caiaphas chuckled. "Well, there doesn't seem to be much doubt that he is their son. So, what happened?"

"Sire, they had the guards take him out of the room, and then Senior Councilor Levi asked the man and the woman if the young man was their son, and they both said he was. He then asked them whether he was born blind, and, if so, how he could now see. I have to say, Sire, that, at this point, both the parents began to look very nervous, and, as I watched, the mother reached over and touched her husband's arm, as if to say—"

"Be careful," the High Priest suggested.

"Yes, Sire. Then they both blurted out that, my goodness, you have him here, why don't you ask him, he's a grown man, he was there, we weren't, and so on. They were very agitated."

"Did Senior Councilor Levi ask them if they knew Jesus?"

The Administrator looked cautiously at the High Priest. "Why, yes, he did, actually. And they both said vehemently that they didn't know the man or anything about him."

"Well, they would, wouldn't they," the High Priest muttered dryly.

"Anyway, Sire, the Council then had the man brought back in, and told him to calm down, which he did for a while. Then one of the Council said something like "You know this Jesus breaks the laws of Moses, and is a sinner," which set the fellow off again, yelling that he didn't care, as all he knows is that he didn't see before and now he does. Another councilor asked him to go over again how it all happened.

"I suppose that councilor didn't like the answer he'd already been given."

"That's what I think, too, Sire, because, if you think it through, the result could be an extremely uncomfortable one."

The High Priest nodded. "You have that right, Yehuda."

"So," Yehuda continued, "he started ranting about how he had already told them, and that if they wanted to ask Jesus how he did it, perhaps they should become one of his followers and watch how he does it."

"I can imagine how that got them *really* upset," said the High Priest.

"Sire, some of them began to behave almost as badly as the man himself, with everyone yelling, some shouting that Jesus was a sinner and a nobody from nowhere, and accusing the man of being a Jesus follower, not a Moses follower, so that he too was a sinner."

"It's odd how riled everyone gets over this Jesus fellow," Caiaphas said softly. He looked at the Administrator, then added quietly, "I can tell you that I even got a message from the Governor this morning about this fracas. He asked me to look into it, which is one of the reasons for my asking you to come this morning."

"Governor Pontius Pilate asked about this?" The Administrator was startled.

"Yes, well, evidently his wife has been having some sort of dreams about the whole Jesus situation."

The High Priest looked uncomfortably across the table, fished out another fig, and said, "Anyway, tell me how things went after that."

"Well, Sire, the most extraordinary thing happened next. The man stopped shouting and crying, and, totally calmly, lectured them as they sat stunned. He told them that if they were so high and mighty, how come they don't know about this Jesus, who he is and where he comes from, and how come they don't know about this man who opened his eyes, even when he was blind from birth. It was, he said, God's work, so that means Jesus is a godly man and can't be a sinner. If he wasn't a godly man, he couldn't have done what he did." Yehuda paused, then looked at the High Priest. "His logic was too much for them."

"Almost as if they didn't want to hear it," the High Priest said quietly. "So, what did they do?"

"Well, the lecture did it. Until then there were some councilors questioning whether the man should be punished at all for having something happen to him which he basically had no control over. But then they seemed to lose touch with the issue that had brought him in front of them, and just decided that he was a sinner regardless, so he should be punished. They bellowed at him, upbraiding him for daring to lecture them, and asserted that he was irredeemably steeped in sin from his birth, so that he was unsalvageable. They unanimously decreed him to be a sinner and recommended that you expel him from the Temple for the rest of his life. I expect Senior Councilor Levi will be here soon to deliver the news personally."

"So, they were so blinded by their rage that none of them bothered to think through how it came to be that he, blind from birth, could now see?"

"No, Sire."

Suddenly, with a violent gesture, the High Priest swept the bowl of figs off the table, and they scattered crazily across the floor. The Administrator sat transfixed.

"You know, Yehuda, I have to say that having to work with the Sanhedrin with all its internal rivalries is a trial in itself." He kicked a fig away.

"But one of the biggest complexities about my job is to try to maintain a balance between things that need to be done in the interests of the peace and orderly governance of this place – this Holy Temple – and those things that we are required by the law and tradition to do to for the glory of the God of our Fathers. This Council has blindly – I would say *capriciously* – determined to destroy a man's life by refusing to stay with the simple question, which was whether the blind-from-birth man is the same man as he who stood before them and shouted for joy that he could see. Either he is, or he isn't. But they didn't like where the answer to that issue was going to take them. So, in a rage, they ignore the answer to that simple question, and turn to the laws and traditions, and use them as a rationale to condemn him. They, and, frankly, all of us, are being held hostage by our laws and our traditions."

Caiaphas sat for a long time – so long that the Administrator wondered if he should leave. Then the High Priest roused, and said, "Well, I have the reputation of leaving recommendations to others, and then doing what they recommend. What is it the Sanhedrin members say of me behind my back – 'He doesn't do much, but he does it very well'. So, I will carry out their Security Council's recommendation. Is the man still in the custody of the guards?"

"No, Sire – they felt they had no authority to hold him until you make a decision."

"So where is he?"

"Well, I heard this morning, as I was coming here, that he was once again down by his old place at the main gate, telling everyone about what is now being described as a miracle. The man is incorrigible."

"Yes, I've noticed that tendency among those touched by Jesus."

The Administrator glanced quizzically at the High Priest.

"He's got something, Yehuda, you have to admit." He looked over at the Administrator. "He's the real enigma in all this, this Jesus. Have we any idea where he is?"

"No, Sire. He is reported to have several places in the city which might be called safe houses, where he is able to stay in seclusion. He is, as you say, an enigma, and an elusive one. On my way here, I heard some scuttlebutt about Jesus being at the main gate this morning, and that Celidonius had some sort of conversation with him, and then knelt before him, which, of course, would be a sin in itself, but it's not substantiated."

"Ah, Yehuda, ever the cautious one. But, you know, we have to find a way to keep track of this elusive enigma, as you call him. Somehow we need to find a way to infiltrate his inner group."

Suddenly the High Priest stood, and the Administrator, rising, watched him as he recloaked himself with the cape of authority. The informal chat was over.

"Thank you for your help and advice. I expect Senior Councilor Levi will be waiting to see me with the expulsion recommendation." The High Priest paused, then, "By the way, I think that, far from commending him, it might be wise for you to reprimand the Duty Guard – Elazar, is it?" Yehuda nodded – "for his completely misleading analysis of the situation, which led to a lot of confusion, and also his failure to keep track of the whereabouts of material participants in the incident."

He had resumed his public persona. He picked up the parchment scroll.

"Perhaps a week's pay?"

"As you wish, most noble High Priest," the Administrator murmured. He bowed low and turned to go to the exit, then paused.

"Your Excellency, if I might – "

The High Priest stared at him imperiously.

"Well?"

"Your comment a few minutes ago, Sire; I think I might know of a way whereby one might be able to put in place a process whereby inside information about the Nazarene man and his followers might be achieved."

The High Priest inclined his head.

"Sire, it recently came to my attention that one of Jesus' followers, actually the one with responsibility for safekeeping the group's funds, such as they are, recently attended an inn in the city which, I'm afraid, is frequented by people of doubtful reputation. I am given to understand that there was unseemly drinking and carousing, and – other goings on, and that he used some of the funds in his care to gamble – er – unsuccessfully, I'm led to believe. His status with his brethren is, to be blunt, in jeopardy unless he is able to cover for the missing funds." The Administrator raised his head and looked straight at the High Priest.

"Interesting. It sounds as if this fellow might be eager to be helped out of his predicament. Tell me, from whom did you obtain this precious information?"

"From Elazar, Your Excellency."

"Aah," softly. Perhaps your friend Elazar has already redeemed himself."

"Thank you, most noble High Priest."

"By the way, has Elazar shared with you the name of this man so in need of assistance?"

"It's Judas, Your Excellency; Judas Iscariot."

The Scribe

It was the eighteenth summer of Cody's life – a summer he had been looking forward to for months. Some of his school friends, including his sort of girlfriend Tara, had been talking about taking a gap year before they started college with another round of classes and tests and learning and all that stuff. But Cody didn't think he could put up with any more of the rituals of education. He was pretty hopeless at math, bored by science, and didn't see himself becoming some sort of computer whiz. But he had found he was interested in history, and really enjoyed English. He had done some of what he liked to call 'scribbling', and one of his teachers had been quite encouraging about his writing. But his dad had been scornful about it. "That won't put food on the table."

And Cody didn't look like a geeky writer. He was pushing six feet and two hundred pounds, and he could throw a mean fastball, his blond hair flopping with the exertion. He was generally liked, and there was a vague air of disorganized innocence about him which girls found either endearing or aggravating.

At any rate, he hadn't thought of what was coming up as being a gap year, but more like a summer of relief before he got thrown into what his dad used to call 'the real world'. Dad had always made that statement as if somehow school wasn't an authentic part of life, and also that school was a piece of cake compared with what he described as 'the grind of life'. His dad hadn't been very encouraging about growing up.

But then, just over a year ago, in the spring of 2019, Cody's dad had disappeared – just walked out of his and his mum's life after twenty years of marriage, so why bother about what he had to say about anything anyway. All he had left behind were a shelf-load of tools in the garage, some girlie magazines in a bottom drawer, an aging and unlicensed second-hand car, a mortgage, and his cranky dad, Grandpa Billy, who had sometimes been referred to by Cody's dad as 'Billy the Goat'.

The mortgage meant that, even after the divorce settlement, Cody's mum, Nancy, had to go back to doing housekeeping for rich folks. But she stayed independent of the organized firms, getting work by word-of-mouth and an ad in the local weekly paper, so she could pretty well plan her week to suit herself. It wasn't much, but it was enough.

As for Grandpa Billy, he had just been moved into a care home with what they called a terminal heart condition. They had, they said, done all that could be done. Cody knew that when his mum talked about 'they', she didn't just mean doctors; she meant specialists.

Cody told his mother he couldn't sort out if she was furious or relieved about Dad walking out. Neither, she said, could she.

Cody had been looking forward to another summer working at his Uncle Larry's fancy fishing lodge up the coast. His mum had persuaded her brother to take him on last summer, mainly, he figured out later, to get him out of the house while she dealt with the detritus of her marriage. "Anything for you, Fancy Nancy," Uncle Larry had quipped.

Cody had loved working there, preparing and stocking the boats for the daily fishing trips by people staying at the lodge, cleaning them up and restocking after they returned, and sometimes bussing in the restaurant, where he got occasional tips.

So he had figured he would spend another summer up there, and then think about the future.

But then a bunch of things happened to ruin all that.

First, Uncle Larry phoned early in March to say that there had been a fire in the boathouse, and it had caused a lot of damage. He'd lost one of the boats, and he was negotiating with the insurance gestapo. But, thank goodness, the Lodge itself was unharmed. Uncle Larry said on the phone that he was going to get everything sorted out, and that for sure Cody could still come up for the summer job.

"What about this Covid thing?" Cody's mum asked.

"Don't worry about that, Nancy – we're isolated."

But Uncle Larry hadn't figured on what happened next. The March 17th announcement of a province-wide Covid lockdown resulted in a bunch of safety protocols and what he later called a tidal wave of cancellations. In mid-April Uncle Larry phoned to say he was closing the Lodge down for the summer. He sounded very angry. "The Covid police have made it impossible."

So, after a Covid-destroyed Grad; and after Tara told him her family was moving north because her engineer father had gotten a job on the Site C Dam, and that, yes, she was going with them but hoped that they would keep in touch; and after he found that none of the food places in town were hiring summer staff – some of them weren't even opening – Cody found himself at home with nothing to do other than to cut the lawn for some old folks in the neighbourhood. He wondered who would be the next person to walk out of his life.

It was a rainy Saturday morning in June when his mum was getting ready to go on the bus to visit Grandpa Billy in the care home, that Cody said, "Why do you have to do this, Mum? He was such a grouch when he was here for Christmas, and anyway he's not even *your* Dad."

"Cody, he's family."

"No, he's not."

"Look, when I married your father, one of the things that came with him, for better or for worse, was his father, your Grandpa Billy. That's the way things work. Now that he's in the care home, and your dad's not here, I go to see him twice weekly, because if I don't, nobody will."

"What if Dad turns up there?"

"Fat chance of that happening."

Later that month, on a Tuesday morning, Nancy was packing her mask and sanitizer along with her other equipment to go to one of her housekeeping jobs. She turned to Cody lolling around in the kitchen.

"Cody, I'm going to visit Grandpa Billy this evening, unless you'd like to go instead."

"Mum!"

"Well, unless you have something else in mind, it would help me out, and he might enjoy seeing a different face."

"Mum, he's so grumpy, and he doesn't like me I don't think. He hardly talked to me when he was here at Christmas."

"Cody, maybe now is the time for you to find out how to deal—"

And anyway," Cody interrupted triumphantly, "they don't allow people in because of Covid, do they!"

"They allow him one family visitor at a time. You have to sign in when you go in the front door and go straight to his room. And I've given them your name, so they have you down as a visitor for him," she said, sounding a bit smug.

"Mum, you rat!"

"I'm not forcing you. Think about it and we'll talk about it when I get back this afternoon."

"I don't know how to talk to him! Can't we both go?"

"As I said, they only allow one visitor at a time." She pulled her gloves on and walked out.

That evening, as they were having supper, Cody asked his mum for change so that he could take the bus to go to the care home. Mum had told him they have supper at six over there, so that Grandpa Billy would be finished by the time he got there.

"What will I talk to him about? I don't know anything about him." He was still fighting to get out of it.

"Well, tell him that! Say you don't know anything about him, and maybe ask him to tell you what he was doing when he was your age."

Then Cody remembered when one of his teachers had gotten the class to write a short piece about their first memories. That had been a blast. Cody had written about when he was, he thought, three or four, and a wasp had gotten into a jam jar on the supper table, and Mum had trapped it by putting the lid on, and the wasp had banged against the lid, buzzing frantically. He remembered asking his mother what she was going to do with it. "Kill it," she had said. Cody remembered both being terrified by the angry buzzing of the wasp, and at the same time horrified by his mother's apparent cruelty.

"Perhaps I could ask him what his first memory is."

"There you go."

As he was rushing out the door, Cody's mum gave him a small box wrapped in blue paper. "They're chocolates. He may be a bit sour, but he has a sweet tooth."

"Thanks, Mum."

"Have you got your mask?"

"Yup."

The door to the care home, euphemistically called the Bluebell Residences, was locked, and there was a Covid sign on the window with detailed instructions. Cody hesitated, then sighed, and rang the bell. An efficient masked woman came to the door and, after a brief cross-examination about his name, his health, and where he had been recently, she let him in. He went through the hand sanitizing and signing in requirements – he saw his mother's signature on the previous page – and was directed to room 111 down the hall on the ground floor. "You must keep your mask on."

Cody knocked, and, after a moment of silence, pressed the latch and went in.

"Hi, Grandpa." His grandfather, skinny, sparsely grey-haired, bespectacled and red-faced, was sitting in a chair by the window, glaring at him over a book. He was maskless and breathing noisily. Cody stood by the door.

The old man put his book down on the little side table, along with his glasses. "What are you doing here." It wasn't a question, it was an irritable statement.

"I'm Cody, Grandpa."

"I didn't ask *who* you are. I said what are you doing here."

"My mum asked if I would come and see you. If you don't want me to come in, I'll leave." Cody stared over his mask at him.

"No, no; she told me you might come, but I didn't know if you really would. Now you're here, come on in." His voice was raspy.

Cody closed the door and walked over to the window. The old man gestured at a chair beside the side-table. "You can sit there."

As Cody sat, he said, "Mum gave me these to give you." He held out the little box.

"Huh. Put them here." He gestured at the space by the book, and muttered, "Tell your mum thank you."

They stared at each other. His grandfather was wearing a collarless shirt open at the neck revealing a tuft of grey chest hair, jeans which were faded at the knees, and a pair of slippers which Cody figured were old and comfortable. Cody had dressed up a bit for the visit, with a long-sleeved T-shirt and cargo pants. He hadn't had a haircut in weeks because of Covid, so his long blond hair flopped messily around.

"You can take that thing off your face."

"They told me at the front desk that I should keep it on."

"Well, I say take it off so that I can see what you look like."

Cody took his mask off and laid it on the little table.

"Do you want something? I've got pop in the fridge over there." He waved, and Cody turned to see a tiny kitchenette which looked totally unused. "No, I'm fine, thanks."

"I don't think I've seen you since your dad left over a year ago, so I don't know what you're up to."

Cody wondered for a moment if he should remind his grandfather that he had come to the house last Christmas, but then said, "Well, I've finished school –"

"Yes, your mother told me that," testily. "What are you going to do now? Got a girl friend?"

Cody sat rigidly, feeling himself riling up. "I don't know."

"Don't know what you're going to do or don't know if you have a girlfriend," Billy croaked caustically.

"Both actually."

Billy stared at the boy, then put his head back, opened his mouth to reveal aging teeth and barked a sharp laugh.

"You'll do, Cody; you'll do." He grinned at him and Cody grinned back. This might work after all, he thought.

"Actually, Grandpa, you say you don't know what I'm doing, but, ya know, I know hardly anything about you."

"What's to know? I'm a dying old man."

"I mean, like, well," plunging in, "we once did this thing at school where each of us had to write down about what our very first memory was, and I wonder what yours is." He rushed the last bit.

Grandpa Billy stared at his grandson for a long moment. "Well, you sure are something else. Get yourself some pop while I think about it." Cody found a can of Sprite in the fridge and sat back down next to his grandfather.

The story Grandpa Billy told Cody fascinated him, not just because of its content, but also because, as the old man told Cody what he remembered, he watched his grandfather become more animated as he went along.

"When I was four, so that would have been 1949, we moved from the Okanagan to Victoria because, I found out later, my dad had found a government job which was more his style than fruit farming. We were a family of four, my mum, my dad, my brother Franklin, who was ten years older than me, and myself. We drove down to the coast and I'm told we went from Vancouver Harbour to Victoria Harbour on the Princess Marguerite. I think it was an overnight trip, though I have no recollection of any of that."

Billy coughed and shifted uneasily, then glanced over at Cody. "My first memory is of early in the morning. I was standing on the deck holding my dad's hand, watching us come into Victoria Harbour, when a plane came in sight alongside us, skimming over the water. I remember being scared for the plane – all the planes I had seen before were high in the sky, and here it was so low. Then it hit the surface, and a huge plume of water sprayed out behind it like a rooster's fantail, and the plane's engine roared, then stopped. I saw the plane settle back, and I thought it was going to drown. I yelled at my father, 'Is it deaded?' And my brother laughed. Then I think I started to cry, and my brother said, 'It's a seaplane, silly,' and he went on laughing."

Billy sat, breathing more quietly.

Cody looked at his grandfather, who said, "That's it."

"Golly," Cody breathed. He wished he had brought a notebook to write it down.

"I haven't thought about that memory for years, but I can see it now, clear as can be."

"So can I," Cody replied, smiling at his grandfather as he drained his pop.

"So, tit for tat, do you have a story for me?"

So Cody told Grandpa Billy his story about the wasp in the jam jar, and his grandfather laughed.

"D'ya wanna chocolate?"

"Sure."

Their mouths full, they grinned at each other like a couple of cookie jar rifling kids.

"So, how did it go?" his mother asked when he got home.

"Good; it was good."

She raised her eyebrows, but said nothing.

That evening, before he went to bed, Cody opened his computer and typed out the story of his grandfather's first memory. He figured he had remembered it well. I must take a notebook next time, he thought.

The next Tuesday, over breakfast, Cody said, "I'll go to Grandpa Billy's this evening if you like."

Well that's a change, thought Nancy, looking at her son over her coffee cup. "Okay, I'd appreciate that. And I think he will too. When I visited him last Saturday he said he'd enjoyed the chat."

That evening, Cody went into Grandpa Billy's room after the usual Covid rigmarole, and said hi.

"So you're back. I thought maybe you were a one-time show-up."

"No, it was good – I had a good time."

"Did ya bring any chocolates?"

"I sure did," Cody said, groping around in his backpack. He pulled out a little package of chocolates as well as a notebook and a sheet of paper.

"Grandpa, I wrote out your story – the one about the seaplane you told me. Can I read it to you to see if I got it right?"

Grandpa Billy looked sort of pleased. "Okay."

So Cody read him the story, and Grandpa said gruffly, "That's pretty well it, Sonny."

Cody couldn't remember his grandfather ever calling him that, or, for that matter, anything that made him feel warm like that did.

"Why don't you get a pop, and get one for me too."

"Okay."

Cody and the old man took sips, looking at each other.

"Grandpa, maybe you could tell me about another memory. I brought a notebook this time to scribble down stuff, so as to be sure I get it all."

"What is this – a budding reporter? I can't think of one."

"What about something about your brother Franklin – wasn't he a lot older than you?"

"Frankie died in 1956."

Cody stared at Grandpa Billy. "Oh."

"Yeah. He was just twenty-one." Grandpa grunted and shifted in his chair. "He had joined the army as soon as he could, aged eighteen. That was always what he had wanted to do. In 1955 he was sent to Korea. Although the Korean War was officially over, the Canadians were part of the ongoing peacekeeping force there. In February 1956 there was some sort of mechanical incident at the airfield where he was stationed, and he was accidentally killed. They never really told my mum and dad what actually happened."

"Gosh. How awful."

"Yeah. And that wasn't all of it. None of us knew about it at the time, least of all me – I was just ten, going on eleven – but he had gotten a Korean girl pregnant, and that summer she had a baby girl. That was the first my parents heard about it. I think they sent money to get it all dealt with. For some reason we found out that the baby was born on June thirtieth. So she would be sixty-four today, Tuesday, June thirtieth. And I don't even know her name."

Billy sat looking out of the window, and Cody watched him. Then; "Grandpa, can I write about that?"

"Yes, if you like." He waved a hand dismissively. "I never did get along with Frankie, anyway," as if to brush the whole business away. But Cody could see that the old man's eyes were glistening.

Their Tuesday evening get-togethers became a regular thing as summer came along. And Nancy kept going to see Billy on Saturdays. Usually Cody would take a written version of the previous week's memory, and seldom did Grandpa Billy suggest any changes. When he told Cody stories, they usually seemed to be true recollections, sometimes funny, sometimes sad; but other times they were more like confessions.

He told how, when he was seven, his dad and his brother took him fishing for the first time, and how he caught a small salmon and his dad helped him reel it in. It flopped about in the prow and Billy ran to the other end of the boat. Then Frankie banged it on the head and killed it. When Billy cried, Frankie said, "What did you want to do? Keep it as a pet?"

And he told about how, as a young man, he was keen on golf, and how, very early one summer morning he went out onto the course without paying the green fee, to practice. He was all by himself on the fifteenth hole which was a par three hole, and to his astonishment he did a hole-in-one. Because he wasn't meant to be on the course, he felt he couldn't tell the people at the Clubhouse, and because no-one saw it, his buddies thought he was making it up.

Another story he told was about when he and Granny Fran and their son Barry – "your father" – were on a camping trip.

"I was taking Barry to the nearby town. He was about ten. He wanted to buy a roll of film for his camera, and I was going to the liquor store. We were taking the bus, leaving the campervan in the campground, as Fran was inside having a snooze. So we were standing at this rural bus stop in the middle of nowhere. There was, of all things, a nun standing there, also waiting for the bus. At least, I guess she was a nun – she was dressed like one. Immediately across the road, in a field, there were two dogs by the fence. All of a sudden, this dog starts – you know, *humping* the other dog. I have never been so embarrassed, what with a nun on one side of me and my ten-year old son on the other. Nobody said anything, and then, thank goodness, the bus arrived. It was the most extraordinary situation. Barry and I never talked about it – I'm not even sure he actually understood all of what was going on. And maybe the nun didn't either! In fact I've never told anyone about it until now."

Cody glanced at his grandfather, and then they both exploded in laughter, and a nurse came in saying, "What are you two up to now?" which made them laugh all the more.

Another Tuesday, Cody said, "So tell me something about when you were the same age as me now."

"What are you? Eighteen?"

"I will be this September."

"Well, when I was a bit older than that – nineteen, going on twenty, I had a good friend, Clyde. Actually, Clyde was best man at my wedding a few years later, when I married your Grannie Fran. Clyde had an old convertible his dad had helped him buy. We used to drive around the town with Frances and Betty. Betty was quite a looker. One day the four of us were going to a dance at the Community Centre, and Clyde and I flipped a coin to decide which of us got first choice of which girl to ask to go as his date. Clyde won the toss, and chose Betty, so I was left with Frances, who I married three years later. The morning of my wedding, Clyde told me he wished he had lost the toss so that he wouldn't have had to choose, and that he wouldn't have minded if I'd chosen Betty so that then he could have gone with Fran. I told him that if I'd won, it could have gone either way."

Billy drank from his pop can. Then, softly, "I never did tell Fran about that."

"But – you loved Grannie Fran?" Cody felt himself blushing – he felt he was being sort of intrusive. But Grandpa Billy didn't seem to notice.

"You bet I did. It just took a while before I realized that she was the best thing that ever happened to me. When she died from cancer five years ago, I was sort of relieved, because it meant I wouldn't have to tell her about my heart thing which they had just figured out. I wasn't good at telling her those sorts of things when she was so sick herself."

He sat, staring out the window. Then, softly, "And Barry – your dad, wasn't particularly supportive during it all." He enunciated the word delicately – 'par-tic-ul-ar-ly'– to emphasize his anger about it. "Though your mum was," he added, glancing at Cody. Cody wondered if Grandpa Billy was just saying that to be polite, but then thought, that's not how he is – what he says is what he means.

"So, time you went off home. I'm feeling tired."

"Sure, Gramps."

"*Gramps!*" Where did that come from?"

"I dunno – I sort of think of you as Gramps. Anyway, you have a name for me – 'Sonny'."

Cody looked at his Grandfather and saw that he was smiling.

"Okay, Sonny, we have our special names for each other."

As Cody got up to leave, he said, "Perhaps next week you can tell me something about your job. You still haven't told me anything about that."

"There's not much exciting to tell about it, but I'll think up something."

But when Tuesday came around, Grandpa Billy said he didn't feel like talking about his job.

"But I'll tell you about how I met Premier Wacky Bennett one day. I was fifteen, and had gone to my father's office because he'd left what he called his second briefcase at home, and it had an important file in it – he later told me he shouldn't have taken it out of the office. He had phoned home, and my mother said I could skip school to take it. It was a half-day anyway. When I got to the front entrance of his building, Dad was there, and took the briefcase, and said, "C'mon, we'll go down to the cafeteria." When we got there, I recognized Premier Bennett, who was standing with my dad's boss, and Ray Williston, the Minister in charge of Lands and Forests, the Department my dad was in. Dad told me later they'd visited the cafeteria as part of what they called a 'Boost Morale Project'. Anyway, Dad's boss introduced my father to them, saying something about how reliable he was, and Wacky Bennett looked at me and said "And are you also reliable, young man?" Everyone laughed, and I was red-faced, but Dad told them I was his son, and the Premier said, "Any son of yours can have a job here, eh, Ray?"

Cody said that was a great story.

"Yeah, and do you know, I think it was that more than anything – even more than the fact that my dad worked for the government – that got me thinking about going into the civil service, though" – he chuckled – "God knows why they called it *civil;* some of what I had to deal with wasn't civil at all. Of course, they now call it *public* service."

As he was leaving, Cody said, "Perhaps next week we can talk more about your job," and Billy muttered "We'll see." Cody wondered why he didn't seem to want to do that.

Cody wasn't getting anywhere with his effort to get Grandpa Billy to tell stories about his job life, so he asked him if there were things to tell from more recent years – "like, you know, things that happened after my dad left home to get married, and after you retired, so that you and Grannie Fran were sort of on your own." Billy said he'd think about it.

But the next time they were together, he said, "You know, Sonny, Fran and I had some happy years together before she died. We called them our 'just us years'. And I have all sorts of good memories of them. But they're not *my* stories; they are *our* stories, Fran's and mine. For me to tell you about those memories wouldn't be right without her say so, and she isn't here to do that."

"Anyway, from what I can see, you're doing a good job with all the other things I've told you about. Now get outa here before I fall asleep."

So that was it.

When Cody arrived at the care home the first Tuesday of fall weather, the efficient woman at the front desk told him that his grandfather wasn't feeling well, and was in bed, but had insisted on letting Cody go in to see him – "just for a short time, mind."

"Is it Covid?"

"No, no, nothing like that – it's just that his heart condition isn't getting any better. But go ahead. He enjoys your visits – he told me they're the highlight of his dull old week, along with when your mother comes to see him."

Cody went down the hall feeling anxious, but happy at the same time about what she had told him. Grandpa was sitting up in bed, looking drawn and sort of breathless.

"Hi, Gramps! How'ra feeling?"

"The better for seeing you, Sonny."

"They told me not to tire you too much. Are you up for a story?"

"Well, I've been thinking about how to tell you this. I haven't told the whole thing to anyone before, but I think it's time I did. So, sit you down."

Feeling a bit apprehensive, Cody sat, and pulled out his little notebook. "Is it okay that I make notes, or is this sort of confidential?"

"No, go ahead. It's time I got this off my chest."

Billy sat for a moment, looking weary. He coughed, and shook his head as if to send whatever was irritating him away.

"I don't think you know much about what I did for a living, so I'll do some background stuff first. I spent a few years following my father in the Department of Lands and Forests. I was involved in all the stuff about issuing Forest Licenses, and became known, I guess, as 'reliable', as Wacky Bennett said. Being reliable is pretty well all that's expected of a public servant," he said caustically.

"Anyway, the Department of Mines was looking for someone to take a vacancy in the section involved in issuing licenses to mining companies. I had the right background, so when I applied I got the job. I stayed over twenty years in that branch, until I retired. Soon after I joined, I became part of a team that reported directly to the Chief Inspector of Mines."

Billy looked at his grandson. "Am I boring you? You aren't writing any of this down."

"No, Gramps – you said it was background stuff, so – "

"So you're waiting for me to get to the story. Well, the team leader was a guy we called 'Phil the Fixer'. He was a big, jolly man who you could see enjoyed his job, especially wining and dining the VIPs who were seeking mining licenses and things like that."

He stopped to take a long drink of water, and sat back. He was still for so long that Cody wondered if he had decided not to go on. Suddenly he looked at Cody.

"We had an application from one of the world class metal mining companies with a reputation for taking risks, but also for pulling off spectacular successes. Its CEO was a flamboyant Australian, and it was a darling of the stock market. I'm not going to tell you its name, as you're writing all this stuff down, and I don't want to get myself – or you – in trouble. They had a big project for a copper mine in an area up north that involved lots of difficult issues, like water pollution dangers and problems with First Nations rights. There was a meeting to resolve all outstanding issues – it was the same week that Barry – your dad – and your mum were getting married on the Saturday, and I was pretty strung out with all the pressures at home and at work. Also it was my first big meeting in my new job, so I was anxious to do my thing – you know, 'reliably'." He did a little mirthless giggle.

"Everyone was at the meeting, including the Australian guy, the CEO of the Canadian subsidiary, the Chief Inspector of Mines, who makes the final call on these things, and Phil the Fixer and his team, including me. Everything went swimmingly until we came to what's called reclamation. A condition of a mining permit is the posting of security to deal with what's called 'Reclamation and Closure' to cover the cost of restoration after the mine is closed. When we got to that item on the agenda, everyone looked at me. I said everything was in order subject to basically doubling the amount of the security proposed to be posted.

"Things got hot and heavy when the Ozzie suggested some sort of 'pay as we go' solution, and I said that the guidelines didn't allow that, and Phil the Fixer said there must be a middle ground, and I said we've never accepted pay as you go, and the Ozzie said that's always the trouble with you number crunchers, and then" – Billy sighed deeply – "Phil left me high and dry by saying 'leave it with us'."

Billy shakily took another sip of water, and Cody worried about whether one of the staff would come and shoo him out.

"So the meeting broke up, and I walked out into the hall where the Chief Inspector was standing, red in the face, berating Phil for not having everything 'tickety-boo'. I just went on to my office, but I heard Phil saying something about taking everyone to lunch.

"I spent a lot of the afternoon going over the application and the permit requirements, and got a memo ready explaining why we needed adequate security and that what was presently on offer was insufficient. I was late leaving my office, and was just putting my coat on when the door opened and Phil the Fixer came in. I could smell the booze. He said we needed to talk, and he sat down, so I sat down across the desk from him. He said I had done a great job, but that he would look after the file from here on, and asked me to give it to him. I pointed to it – it was on my desk, with my memo. As he reached out to take it, he felt in his pocket and brought out an envelope which he laid on the desk, and then he pushed it across to me.

"I stared at him and put my hand out to push the envelope back to him. He put up his hand and said, 'I understand you have a wedding coming up in your family this weekend. Why don't you buy your daughter-in-law-to-be something nice.' With that, he picked up the file and walked out, and I picked up the envelope and went home."

There was a long pause. Then Cody mumbled, "What was in the envelope?"

"Five one hundred dollar bills."

At that moment, as if on cue, there was a knock on the door, and a nurse came in. "That's enough, you two."

Cody watched his grandfather struggling a bit with his breathing, then taking a long slow breath and laying back on the pillows.

"Thanks, Gramps."

"Yeah, Sonny, you go. I'll tell you the rest next time."

Cody told his mum that Grandpa Billy wasn't looking too good, and she said she hadn't thought so either when she last saw him.

"D'ya think maybe we should go together next time?"

"No, I think he enjoys his private times with each of us – he told me that last time."

"What do the two of you talk about? He tells me stuff about his life, but what do you guys talk about?"

"Oh, you know, this and that. We've always been close, right from when I took Barry on in marriage. Billy knew better than I did what I was in for, and always looked out for me. He wasn't surprised when Barry walked out – he was, he told me recently, more surprised it hadn't happened earlier. So we talk about Grannie Fran, and what I'm up to, and sometimes about you, and stuff like that." She grinned at him.

"Like what about me?"

"All good stuff, Cody."

"Well, if you're not going to tell me, I'll ask Grandpa next time."

"No you won't!" She punched his arm.

Cody felt a bit like he was being somehow excluded from something, but couldn't work out what or why.

Later that evening, his mother said, "You know, Cody, my relationship right now with Grandpa Billy, as he's on his way out, is very different from yours with him. Ours is about reflecting on the past together – a sort of mutual reminiscing if you like. But yours is about him revealing some pictures of his life to you – a one way street instead of our two-way street. He and I talk about things that we wouldn't tell you, and I expect he's telling you things he wouldn't want you to discuss with me. Both of them are important to your Grandad. So that's why I think we should go on doing these visits the way we do."

"He sure is – what – *mellower* – is that a word? – than before."

"Yeah; under all that gruff, he's always been a sweetheart." Cody watched his mum choke up a bit.

Tuesday rolled around, and Cody went to the care home concerned about how he would find his grandfather. He was sitting up in bed, and, if anything, he seemed better, though his face was quite pale, almost ashen.

"Hey, Sonny. Get yourself a pop and one for me. Did you bring chocolates?"

"Yup."

Cody was still settling in when the old man said, "So, I bet you want to know what happened next."

"Yeah, Gramps. Are you still okay with me making notes?"

"Sure. The worst is over, or the best is yet to come, so why the hell not." He wasn't making a lot of sense. Then he plunged in, as if there hadn't been a week since their last session.

"So I took Phil the Fixer's advice, and bought your mother a special, between her and me only, wedding present, which I gave her privately the day before the wedding. It's a First Nations dream-catcher pendant with what I thought was your mum's birthstone in it. She was born in May, so it's an emerald – I looked it up. She didn't wear it at her wedding, but she did put it on when she changed into her going away clothes to go on her honeymoon. But I never saw her wear it again. I didn't know why until she told me recently."

"Were you upset about that – her not wearing it?"

"Not upset, but pretty bewildered. I was already having very confusing thoughts about the whole thing – the five hundred dollars, and why Fixer Phil gave it to me, and then wondering whether it was in some way jinxed so that whatever it was used for would turn out badly. I know that sounds sort of silly, but that's how I felt."

"But, Gramps, wasn't it just flat-out a bribe to get you to go along with it?"

"No, it was more than that. Here's the thing. You see, when I didn't push that envelope back across to him, he didn't just buy my silence with regard to the copper project, which, by the way, was and still is a great success. What he did was buy my complicity in his behavior. For thirty pieces of silver, as the bible says. I bartered away my integrity for, as far as I could tell at the time, the rest of my career. And, Sonny, I'll tell you this; reliability isn't the only key to being a good public servant. Way more important is integrity. And that's what, in my own mind, I lost, and what he stole. I've always regretted not pushing that envelope back across the table."

He lay back. "Gimme some water, willya."

Cody helped him to sip some water. "Gee, Gramps, couldn't you have – "

Billy interrupted. "No, there was nothing I could do. Anyway, as things turned out, it wasn't all that bad. Phil the Fixer moved on a couple of years later, getting a position with the staff of the Treasury Board, based, they said" – Billy did quote marks with his fingers – "'on his sterling reputation for getting things done.' So I was able to spend the rest of my years in the Department of Mines trying to forget about that episode, and working to sort of redeem myself to myself."

He paused. "But now I can't get it out of my head because you, my fine friend, kept asking for stories about my job."

"Gee, Gramps, I didn't mean – "

Billy waved a hand; "No, no, in the end I needed to tell someone. 'Better out than in', one of my college profs used to say."

Billy gave a little chuckle. "So the present I bought for your mother seemed to be tainted. I bought it in a hurry, and I gave it to her sort of surreptitiously, so I think she was a bit suspicious of the whole thing. I didn't know at the time, but she recently told me that she doesn't much like green jewelry. She says it doesn't go with her complexion. And also she says her birthstone isn't emerald. It *is* the birthstone for May if you go by the month, but she says you should go by the zodiac, and that the right astrological stone for May fifteen is sapphire. So she wore it on her honeymoon, but then put it away, and never wore it again."

He glared at Cody. "So there was five hundred ill-gotten dollars gone to waste."

"I wonder what the fixer Phil guy got for doing what he did."

"A few years later someone else on his team, who might also have been in on the whole thing, mentioned five thousand dollars. So I was a ten percent cost to him."

They got the call at five the next evening that Billy was on the way out, and that perhaps they should come right away. They didn't take the bus; they ordered a taxi. The woman at the desk said that, under the circumstances, the one visitor rule didn't apply. Wearing masks, Nancy and her son went down to Room 111. Billy was hooked up to an oxygen tank and was wearing an oxygen mask. He seemed to be sleeping. Cody went to sit by the bed, but then saw there was only one chair there. He had never been there together with his mother before. He brought another chair from by the window, and he and his mother sat, one on each side of the sleeping old man. He saw his mother take Billy's hand, so he reached out and took the other one. This seemed to rouse Billy, and he opened his eyes. He saw Cody, and the boy felt a little hand squeeze. Billy turned to look at Nancy. He made a petulant little sound, and Nancy rose, took the oxygen mask off and sat down. Billy smiled at her.

"My favourite daughter," he whispered.

"Daughter-in-law" she corrected him.

"That too. My favourite daughter-in-law."

"Your *only* daughter-in-law," she smiled.

"That also."

He turned his head to look at Cody, who felt his grandfather press his hand.

"And Sonny, my scribe. My trusty scribe."

Cody grinned at him and said, "Yeah, Gramps."

Cody watched as his grandfather closed his eyes. He felt the hand ease its grip on his, and then saw the eyes close in sleep. Nancy put the oxygen mask back on, adjusted it and sat back. He was breathing quietly when they left.

Later that evening, Cody's grandfather died in his sleep.

There was the usual stuff to deal with, one of which was for Nancy to contact Barry to tell him his father had died. Because of Covid, Nancy told him there could be no funeral or memorial service, which Barry sounded relieved about.

The next Tuesday, Cody was feeling pretty miserable, and also at a loss, there being no visit to the care home to look forward to. He had spent part of the days after his grandfather's death sorting out his notes of their talks, and had talked to someone at Island Blue about what it would cost to maybe get it put into some sort of booklet together with some pictures, and making a couple of dozen copies 'for family and friends'. But he didn't have the money, and so was sort of stuck. He sat watching his mother, who was staring out of the window.

"Mum, Gramps told me he gave you a pendant when you got married, but thought you hardly ever wore it. Is that right?"

Nancy sighed. "Yep. I think he thought giving me something would sort of make up for the disappointment he figured I would have in my marriage. He gave me a dream-catcher birthstone pendant, but I didn't like the emerald, and anyway I had a bad feeling about it – somehow the whole thing about his gift felt wrong."

"Yeah, we talked about it, Gramps and me."

"What did he tell you?"

"Oh, I don't remember exactly." Cody felt himself reddening. He got up. "I'm getting a glass of water; do you want anything?" She shook her head.

As he walked back from the kitchen, he asked, "So what happened to it – the pendant?"

"When your father left last year, I took all the jewelry I could find that had anything to do with him to an estate jewelers in town – my engagement ring, my wedding ring, another thing, a clasp he gave me, and the pendant. Although it wasn't Barry that gave it to me, I associated it with him. I didn't want any of it around. They sold everything pretty quickly – in a few months, except for the pendant, and they sent me the money for the other stuff. I never heard whether they sold it. I guess I should try and find out."

A week later, Cody walked down to the mail box, and came back with a couple of envelopes for his mum. One was a belated sympathy card, and the other looked more official.

"Well, waddya know," Nancy chortled, as she read what was in it, and a cheque fluttered out of the envelope to the floor. "This is from the jewelers. Remember we were talking about that pendant. Well, they finally sold it, and here's the money!"

"How much for?"

She picked the cheque up. "Two hundred and fifty dollars! That means they sold it for five hundred smackeroos!"

"That's what it cost originally! Why don't you get more?"

"The deal is that the jewelers get to keep half. And anyway, how do you know what it cost?"

"Oh, I think Gramps mentioned it," Cody mumbled awkwardly.

Nancy looked at her son. "Huh. It seems you know more about this than you want to say. Anyway, that could go to pay for your printing job at Island Blue."

She pushed the cheque across the table towards Cody. Cody had the oddest feeling, almost as if he'd seen that done before.

He leaned over the table, stretched out his hand to the cheque, and pushed it back. "I don't want it, Mum."

Nancy stared at her son. Then she picked up the cheque and tore it in half and then again into quarters and then again and again until it was in tiny shreds.

"Neither do I," she said.

As a sort of celebration, Nancy took her son out to supper at the White Spot.

Over supper, they talked.

"So your Gramps told you lots of secret stuff it seems."

"Well, most of it was stories about growing up and his job."

"Like what?"

"How he met the Premier, and how he had a boss they called Phil the Fixer, and other things. Some of them were fun stories, but, I don't know, lots of them seemed to be sort of personal things he told me about because he figured he had to get a load off his mind before he – you know – couldn't."

"Sort of like confession in church."

"What's that all about?"

"Well, in some churches you can confess to a priest about things that you've done or thought, and that you feel bad about, and the priest forgives you on behalf of God."

"Oh. So what if you tell him about a crime, like you murdered someone–"

"Good heavens! Did Grandpa say – "

"No, no! Nothing like that. I'm just wondering what happens when the priest gets told about a crime, and he goes to the police and – "

"Well, he doesn't. What he's been told as part of a confession is totally private between the two of them. And God, I guess."

"Oh."

That evening, after his mother had gone to bed, Cody sat down in front of his computer and pulled up the stories he had organized to take to Island Blue for printing. It came to thirty pages, single spaced. He read through the whole thing, and made a few corrections where he saw wrong punctuation and where the computer told him some word was mis-spelled. And he tidied it up so that it was neatly set out in paragraphs with the first line indented.

Then he highlighted the whole of the thirty page booklet-to-be, and pressed 'delete'. The little icon came up, asking him, *are you sure you want to delete?*

Danny pressed the confirm button, and it all disappeared. Then he opened the recycle bin and emptied it.

He had in his mind a little conversation.

There you go, Gramps.

Thanks, Sonny. Good job.

Hummingbird

Before Marnie let me move in with her, I knew she'd had another live-in partner. For a while I had been able to spend weekends away from home, house-sitting for a woman who used to go off to see her man. It was, for a time, an adequate solution to escape to her house in the trees, but I eventually realized that getting away at weekends didn't solve my problem. It wasn't exactly your typical 'pressured work-week resolved by weekend release' type of situation.

So, finally, I really moved out and away from home, and went to live with Marnie, even though I knew about HB, who, Marnie told me, was no longer around anymore. Somehow, though, HB seemed in a way to be still a part of Marnie's surroundings.

Marnie and I share a cramped basement place, much to my mother's dismay; my father wants to ignore the whole thing. I think they both think I'm some sort of freak. There are two little windows at grass level – at least, grass is mostly all you can see out of them. It's going to get pretty hot in there, Marnie tells me, when summer comes along, with no breezes to cool things down because of the high brick wall between us and the next door place. I told her I wouldn't care; anything would be better than feeling stifled.

Marnie is good to me – what do I know, she's the first woman lover I've ever had. To be honest she's the first lover of any sort

I've ever had. But when she looks after me, Marnie makes me feel whole. I don't know whether she learned from HB, or is just good at it.

HB is what Marnie calls her, though her name is actually Hannah Brown. Really, if my family name was Brown, I certainly wouldn't call my daughter Hannah. It sounds so – so dowdy, if you know what I mean, though Marnie tells me HB was far from dowdy – 'scrappy' she once described her. Anyhow, what I would do is hunt through one of those books of names you find on the same shelves in second hand bookstores where there are treatises on parenting. I would probably pick out something like Bethsheba. Bethsheba Brown is a name to contend with. At any rate, Marnie calls her HB, so I suppose it doesn't really matter what her real name is.

Marnie has a way of initialing, or shortening, everyone's name. She calls her mother 'PJ' – I don't even know why, and me she calls 'Bo', though my actual name is Belinda. She always has. She teases me that it's something to do with me being a bit like a lamb, though I don't understand what she means by that. No-one else calls me Bo. It's sort of like a branding. It's not that I don't like it – in fact, Marnie having a 'special' name for me makes me feel picked out, or chosen, which, I suppose, is probably why Marnie does it. She's a bit of a manipulator.

Marnie – I wonder if that's sort of a nickname too, like a short version of Marion or Marina, though everyone calls her that, which is the difference – is laconic. She speaks in a laconic way. She looks laconic as well, with that drawn-down-eyes mask of a face that drives me wild. Her body is curt and blunt, while mine is all statements. I've never known if I should be proud of that, or discomfited. Marnie walks around our tiny place in the buff, without discomfort. I envy her that. She even loves me laconically. "OK, kiddo," or sometimes (which I strive for), "That's it, Bo," she'll say laconically, after a fierce frenzy, which leaves me dizzy.

One evening, as summer approached, and as we lay in the sultry dark, side by side, Marnie told me the real reason why she calls Hannah Brown "HB". It isn't short for Hannah Brown. She had taken a long-distance call earlier in the day. Lying beside me that evening, I would have said she was more than laconic. In fact, I would have said she was being aloof, if it wasn't for her hand resting lightly on my tummy.

"You're thinking about HB," I said.

"Just a little," she said. I knew from that 'Just a little' rather than 'Yes', or 'Uh-huh' that she was thinking about HB a lot.

Then Marnie told me about how HB would thrum when she was happy, like when a cat purrs, or other people hum or whistle when they're cheerful. HB would, she told me, thrum like a hummingbird. I was confused, wondering if Marnie meant that HB drummed her fingers like a hummingbird beats its wings. But Marnie explained that it was a throat and tongue thing – a delicate manifestation of ecstatic happiness. So Marnie calls her HB for 'Humming–Bird'. She told me that in some cultures, such as the Haida, the hummingbird is seen as a messenger from the spirit world, and in others it is a symbol of happiness and joy.

And then Marnie told me how much she had loved HB, and how HB was dying of cancer.

Marnie and I came out to the house in the trees this weekend, and we will be staying here for a while, as the woman who owns it has gone away with her man, and wants me to stay here as a house-and-pet sitter. She knows about Marnie, and is fine with the fact that she will be here with me. She can help with walking the dog – a lovely, scruffy old lady. Dog walking can, I think, be therapeutic.

HB died last week. Marnie went to the Mainland for the funeral. She came back stone-faced.

Before she left to visit with her man, the house owner had festooned the front balcony of the house with a blaze of colourful flowers in hanging baskets and window-boxes – I suppose really they should be called 'balcony boxes' as they're on the balcony railings, not in the windows. The flowers – I don't know all their names, various types of Impatiens, I think – are a mix of vibrant oranges, pinks, and a whole range of reds. I didn't know, until Marnie told me this morning, that hummingbirds are insatiably attracted to brightly coloured flowers, especially red flowers.

As Marnie and I sat on the balcony in the evening sunset, the gently snoring dog splayed out in a cool corner, the riot of flowers in the balcony boxes attracted a hummingbird. Marnie, who knows about hummingbirds, told me it was called a Rufous, and that it was a female – you can tell by its green back and red-and-orange throat feathering, she told me. "She's a feisty one," she said.

We watched her hovering and darting about the balcony, and even around us as we rested there, pirouetting like a ballerina, the dog watching unperturbed. Then, with a delicious assault, the tiny creature plunged at the flowers with voracious display, hesitated, then dove in, burying her long beak and tongue to suck nectar from them, all the while thrumming her wings – all happiness and joy. As suddenly as she had arrived, she shot away.

Sitting by the balcony railing, I rested my hand on the top, and Marnie stretched out an arm, and laid her hand over mine, cool and sure. I turned my hand to clasp hers, protected within its strength.

Then something wonderful and extraordinary happened. The final rays of the sinking sun streamed flat through the surrounding trees, trying to blind us. We shifted aside, and I raised a hand to shield my eyes. Suddenly, careening in from those selfsame trees, the marauding hummingbird thrummed at us, then swerved, swooped, and stopped, suspended in mid-air, a tight-rope walker balanced on an invisible rope. Marnie and I sat transfixed, our hands clasped. Chipping and clicking, the tiny bird poised herself, it seemed, over us. Suddenly, as if to startle, she spiraled to the railing and, like the breath of a feather, brushed our entwined hands, bestowing, it seemed, a blessing, then zoomed away, thrumming into the gold blazed trees, this time for good.

I felt the strangest sense of endowment. I looked across at Marnie; she had closed her eyes. There was, on her calm face, a small smile of, perhaps, relief or, for all I know, release.

I arose and knelt, and, enfolding her in my arms, held her close.

I could do that now.